DANGEROUS

Poisonous Passions
Book Two

Mae Thorn

Text by Mae Thorn
Cover by Dar Albert

Dragonblade Publishing, Inc. is an imprint of Kathryn Le Veque Novels, Inc.
P.O. Box 23
Moreno Valley, CA 92556
ceo@dragonbladepublishing.com

Produced in the United States of America

First Edition May 2022
Trade Paperback Edition

ARE YOU SIGNED UP FOR DRAGONBLADE'S BLOG?

You'll get the latest news and information on exclusive giveaways, exclusive excerpts, coming releases, sales, free books, cover reveals and more.

Check out our complete list of authors, too!

No spam, no junk. That's a promise!

Sign Up Here

www.dragonbladepublishing.com

Dearest Reader;

Thank you for your support of a small press. At Dragonblade Publishing, we strive to bring you the highest quality Historical Romance from some of the best authors in the business. Without your support, there is no 'us', so we sincerely hope you adore these stories and find some new favorite authors along the way.

Happy Reading!

CEO, Dragonblade Publishing

Additional Dragonblade books by Author Mae Thorne

Poisonous Passions Series

Notorious (Book 1)

Dangerous (Book 2)

For my mother.

Chapter One

THE CHESTNUT COFFIN loomed before Abigail as if it kept vigil on her and not the other way around. She stared back as it was lowered into the ground, a victory of no small consequence. She stood motionless, without tears, while dirt was strewn onto the man who had been a source of bittersweet pain for the past month.

Abigail Riverton was not her usual smiling self; after all, it was a funeral. No triumph graced her posture, and no confidence accompanied her step. Though her back was straight with the firm determination to move forward, her suffocating wounds left a dull phantom weight.

She was vaguely aware of her brother, Samuel, leading her with a firm but comforting touch away from the cemetery. The sun shone with a blinding haze over the mourners. Even nature refused to give way to the few tears shed. And why should it? Nature would not be held accountable for the folly of youth.

Nigel Weston, the man, was no more. His body would surrender itself to the soil, while Abigail's blood would continue to flow through her veins, taking in the sun. Yet Nigel remained. As present as Samuel and as invasive as the glaring sun.

Her reputation, however, was buried along with his body.

Samuel helped her into the carriage as she directed her attention to her journey tomorrow. Her escape.

She leaned against the overheated window and contemplated her summer in Cornwall with Delia. The invitation from her dearest friend had come just in time to relieve her from her troubles with Nigel but too late to save her from his death. A death she had no business mourning. Yet she had attended with Samuel, who was an acquaintance of Nigel, in hope she could bury some of her pain. Instead, it dug up her memories and scattered them like soil across her thoughts.

She closed her eyes against the piercing sunlight, shutting out the city she had once cherished. New York harbored the whispers, the snubs, and the pitying glances from her family. Nobody but friends knew her in Cornwall. No reminders awaited her there. Cornwall stood at the end of the dark tunnel, waiting to whisk her away into the adventures from her novels.

The carriage halted outside of their house, bringing her out of her daze.

She let loose a long sigh and stepped down from the carriage. Her maid, Alma, was packing in preparation for the morning arrival of Mr. Hugh Travers, Delia's brother-in-law and Abigail's guide on the journey. His return home from military service coincided well with her visit. She intended to avoid him as much as the ship would allow.

The town was full of talk about the younger Travers brother. He used his easy charm and deviously handsome looks to lure widows and married women alike to warm his bed while his countrymen slaughtered hers. She had shared a number of dances with him before Delia had been swept off to England, and he'd insisted on treating her like a tedious little girl.

He embodied a villain in her novels, the man who misled the heroine into surrendering her virtue and later tossed her aside for the hero to piece back together. Yet she was drawn to him. Mr. Travers. The haughty rake who cared nothing for foolish bluestockings like her.

To say their journey together would be trying would be an understatement. Her mind was already occupied with her own poisonous thoughts, and she didn't need his devilish smile to addle her brain further. Delia must be unaware of their clashing personalities to have insisted on their shared journey, but Abigail had little choice. War occupied her family, and she knew nobody else to escort her and her maid.

The funeral had sent her back into herself, and the night passed in short bursts of recognition. She remembered little of what she ate for dinner. Alma helped her get ready for bed, but she only knew this because Alma always helped her to bed. Her mind was so driven to replay the last few months that she scarce slept a wink.

Her escape from New York couldn't come soon enough.

When Mr. Travers arrived, she demanded they leave at once, having already said her goodbyes. With a grunt from Mr. Travers, a footman loaded her trunk and Alma's possessions onto the carriage.

"Aren't you a burst of sunshine this morning." Mr. Travers's dry voice harmonized with the gravel under the carriage wheels as they rode along. He rubbed at his red-rimmed brown eyes, and a yawn forced its way through his lips. He shook his head as if to remove his sleepiness.

She ignored his remark and stared out the window at the familiar scenery, but he tugged at her consciousness and refused to leave her mind, like a pestering fly. Alma kept silent beside her, nodding off on occasion from attending to her mistress's whims most of the night and early-morning hours.

Mr. Travers groaned as a light outside passed his vision, and Abigail regarded him with a frown. His skin shone a peculiar shade of gray.

"Are you unwell?" She leaned forward on her seat, unable to keep her concern at bay.

"I'm fine." He braced a hand over his eyes. "In fact, I'm better than fine to be out of this hell-spawn city."

She rested her back on the seat, brows bunched together. "Really? I was under the impression you came here to escape

England."

"After the time I've spent in New York, I'm beginning to see reason." He closed his eyes and rubbed at his face, pulling down the skin into a comical expression.

Her lips quivered as she checked a laugh. She waved his comment away. "New York is the best city in the world." Or it had been until a certain officer ruined it for her.

He blinked at her through his glazed eyes. "Then what're you doing leaving here?" He gestured out the window. "It isn't too late to go back and let me travel alone in peace."

"You would like that, wouldn't you?" A tight pang lodged in her chest. After all their dances, he still saw her as a gushing fool lost in her novels. "No, it's my hometown, and I'm allowed to insult it all I like, but as an outsider, you can't claim the same."

"That's ridiculous."

She gritted her teeth but couldn't keep back her retort at his dismissal. "If I didn't need you, I would've pushed you out of the carriage by now. A pity. Maybe I can find a new escort on the ship and push you overboard." She gave him a stern look.

He only grunted in response and went back to rubbing his eyes. Doubtless he only made his vision worse. His inattention left her free to study his broad shoulders and bedroom-tousled hair. If only he would fall into a deep sleep, then she would run her hands through his disobedient locks. Her heart rammed against her stays.

Alma snored beside her, and Abigail smiled at her fondly before letting her gaze wander back to the man across from her.

"You do look unwell." She gulped before her traitorous mouth could betray her further.

"It's nothing." A small smile tilted his lips. "I merely spent my last night in one of the famed taverns in your fair city."

"That was foolish, knowing you would have to travel." Now she sounded like her mother. Where had this stranger with her voice come from?

He returned her stare, daring her to continue.

She cleared her throat and plastered a smile on her face. She had gone about this all wrong. They would be stuck with each other for weeks. She brightened her tone in an attempt to channel the happy, carefree Abigail. "In any case, thank you for accompanying me. I've never been on a ship. It's quite exciting."

His face twisted up as though she had grown another head. "Exciting, my ass. Sailing is nothing but water and storms. When you think land must be around the horizon, you know what you find?"

She shook her head.

"More water. Water from above and below. If you happen to be in need of a drink, best not run out of ale on board. That water may be wet, but it's only an illusion, a fool's death trap. The ocean is like a siren call to hell."

A laugh escaped her lips at his foul language. Perhaps he didn't see her as a lady at all, and Alma was in no state to correct him. "Then I suppose you hate sailing. Curious you found yourself on the other side of an ocean." He didn't bother to answer her, so she continued to fill the silence. "I don't suppose we will see any pirates or rebel ships?"

He snorted at her hopeful grin. "Madam, your idea of excitement is far removed from mine. Nothing could be better than a boring voyage over the ocean."

"But you said—"

"Never mind what I said. Know what's worse than sailing? Being in battle at sea. At least on land, there's chance of rescue. If the ship sinks, we're as good as dead, and that's the best outcome in a losing battle. Do I need to tell you what happens to pretty women when a ship is captured?"

Her chest expanded at his offhand compliment. She hurried to shake her head, but she was more alarmed he'd called her pretty than he would lecture her about rape and murder. She couldn't decide if it was good or not that Alma hadn't caught a word of their exchange.

She sighed. "I'm sure you're right." As much as it pained her to admit it. "Still, you can't say you haven't imagined such an adventure." She regretted her naive musing as soon as the words left her rambling tongue.

"Miss Riverton, let me reassure you, my service in His Majesty's army is more than enough excitement for me."

"I thought you were simply a secretary? In fact, I don't think you have left New York since you arrived." The corner of her mouth turned up in a smirk. She knew she had him.

"I'll have you know I accompanied my commander into camp on several occasions."

"Indeed? That is something." Her smile grew. "Now, was there any actual fighting not done with a quill?"

He laughed in spite of himself. "We were once set on by rebels on our way back to New York, but it turned out it was only one of our men spooked by a squirrel."

"Ferocious creatures, rebel squirrels." She kept her tone even, serious, and with a hint of false concern. "I hope your man bested the villain or a whole herd of them may very well descend on the city and win the war."

"A drey of squirrels."

"A what?"

A smile spread over his face, and he shook his head. "Never mind. Give me a moment's peace, will you? Besides, we're almost there. You'd better wake your maid."

She huffed but did as he suggested. Alma yawned and blinked out the window but said nothing as was her custom.

Silence invaded the carriage and ran along Abigail's skin like an itch she couldn't scratch.

Relief washed over her when they reached the docks. Not waiting for help, she bolted from the carriage, and they boarded the ship with the few other passengers. The ship was mostly used to transport the much-needed goods to His Majesty's army. Mr. Travers had used his connections to find them passage.

She shared a cabin with Alma, but Mr. Travers occupied his own cabin, much to the dismay of the other cramped passengers.

It seemed the second son of an earl still held the status and money to earn favors. He ignored everyone as he shut himself inside, presumably to sleep off his hangover.

Abigail longed to stay on deck to watch the ship leave, but the captain kindly ordered her to retire to her cabin. The comforting motion of the ship leaving was all that marked the beginnings of her journey. Cornwall may be visible on a map, but her destination remained as intangible as the fleeting wind in the sails.

Mr. Travers's occupation of his cabin proved to be his normal travel state. He seemed to be sick more than well, and she could not imagine how he resisted such open skies. Although their trip bordered on mundane, lifeless, and uneventful, she found plenty to occupy her over the course of the voyage.

Her mind fled her sad reality as surely as she escaped the shores of New York. Her novels embraced her the way her mother would but without the judgment and advice she could no longer tolerate. She was safe among the whims of the authors and her own daydreams.

Once, they spied far-off rebel ships, but the dark forms vanished as swiftly as they appeared. Nothing became of the event except in Abigail's mind. Her imagination conjured whole fleets of French ships bearing down on them. The French accepted no surrender as cannonballs tore apart the ship, board by board. They took Abigail captive as a witness, of course. The handsome captain fell madly in love with her, and she escaped to live a life of luxury in Paris.

When she tired of French captures, her mind traveled to other adventures, fed by the books she'd brought. The waves held secrets of sea monsters, sunken ships, and calling sirens waiting for a willing, or unwilling, ear. Pirates invaded their ship on a daily basis, sparing her and Alma while putting Mr. Travers in his place.

She suspected Mr. Travers escaped to his cabin not just from seasickness but to avoid her fanciful ponderings. She pushed away the hurt and focused on the jewel-toned sea. It was better this way lest her musings give her foolish notions about him.

The fresh breeze on her face was already a cherished friend. A glimpse in the mirror revealed the sea had had an unexpected improvement on her health. Her cheeks bloomed with a peach cast, and her thick black hair held a sheen as it curled around her face. She longed to have the sea breeze move through her hair, but she resigned herself to a few stray curls.

Every night, the rock of the ship comforted her, sending her into a restful slumber after weeks of troubled thoughts of Nigel. Booming cannons and war cries occupied her dreams. She woke panting, exhilarated by the thrill running through her veins. One night, after a spat with Mr. Travers over the inevitability of running into pirates, her dreams took a turn.

At first, the scenario played on the usual theme. Pirates invaded their ship and forced everyone to cower on the deck. The pirate captain held Abigail against him, ready to sacrifice her if anyone moved. This time, Mr. Travers upset the usual balance. He sent a musket ball into the pirate captain's forehead, freeing Abigail to collapse onto the deck.

Mr. Travers rushed to her side and clutched her in his arms like a cherished friend. He kissed her with an intensity beyond her experience, encasing her in a cloud of deep longing. She woke heated and ashamed. After that night, she went out of her way to stay away from Mr. Travers the few times she saw him, afraid he would somehow know about the dream. She broke into a scarlet blush when she ran into him. He regarded her with a sour look every time, seeming to prefer their separate lives.

The weeks at sea turned into years for Abigail as she dodged in and out of her cabin.

At one such time, Abigail was determined to face Mr. Travers. It was just one little dream after all. She chided herself for being such a ninny and braved the deck when she knew Mr. Travers was out.

He leaned on the rail, his skin pale and his hair plastered to his face with sweat. He must have just thrown up into the sea. If his appearance didn't turn her away, she didn't know what would. Yet a tug in her chest prompted her to address him.

"Good day, Mr. Travers. Might I be of some assistance to you? Some ale, perhaps?"

He groaned and spilled what was left in his stomach over the side.

She pinched her nose and covered her mouth as the sour aroma reached her. "I'm afraid I'm not great at this."

He sunk back to the deck and turned a glare on her.

"You should be in bed."

"I was, but it smells like a horse's ass in there. I have one of the men airing it out. What can I do for you, Miss Riverton?"

His question from the ground set her back. She twisted her hands in front of her as she grasped for words. The silence was worse than any answer she could give.

"Nothing, of course. That is, you're already doing enough. I mean to say, you're already ill. Is there nothing to be done?" She knew she rambled but could not help herself.

"Aside from docking the ship? Unless you have a magic carpet or genie lamp stashed away in your cabin, I'm stuck."

"Indeed? Well, I can't say I do." A nervous laugh bubbled up from her chest. Why didn't she just shut up?

His wry smile made her want to crawl into her trunk. "This infernal journey has lasted long enough, Miss Riverton. Let it be known I will kiss the soil of England when we land."

Her gaze flashed to his lips, and his damp pale skin no longer registered in her mind as she remembered the demanding kiss they'd shared in her dream. His soft lips cherished her the way Nigel's never had.

His lips twitched as she watched them, and a scarlet flush heated her cheeks. She cleared her throat and opened her mouth to speak, but no words came out. She tried again with no more success and stood there like a gaping fish. Her feet couldn't take her fast enough back to her cabin, and Mr. Travers's laughter followed her.

At least she had amused him. What must he think of her? Some virginal girl pining for his attentions. To be sure, she was anything but that. Not after Nigel. She had learned her lesson, if nothing else. Mr. Travers was beyond help. Let him wallow in his misery. Alone.

Chapter Two

By the time they reached London, Abigail was much improved. She still slipped into her gloomy thoughts from New York, but now hope shone a light at the end of her heartbreak. Alma faired equally well; seeing her mistress happy improved her own mood. Mr. Travers, however, left the ship with only a faint spark for his homeland in his bottle-brown eyes in an otherwise worn complexion. His skin had taken on a perpetual greenish cast. Still, he was eager to see his brother in Cornwall and got ready for their journey by land as soon as they docked.

Abigail would rather linger in London, but with one look from Mr. Travers, she pushed the idea out of her mind. Spending time trapped in a carriage with him would be uncomfortable. His proximity made her a fidgety mess, and his dominating stature left little space for thoughts of Nigel.

Mr. Travers seemed more at ease than he had been in weeks. He settled back into the cushions of their rented carriage and breathed out his contentment. They had stopped for a quick meal, and he displayed a renewed appetite Abigail was embarrassed to witness. Who could consume so much meat? Then she recalled Delia's amused letter about his brother, Lord Carrington, and decided it was a family trait. Her brothers ate a great deal but nothing compared to this.

Across from her, he appeared asleep, as did Alma. Abigail's gaze traced his features. His unconscious state freed her to study him. He did clean up nicely, having shaved properly for the first time in weeks. The delicious dimple on his chin asked to be kissed. She itched to muss his hair back to its hoydenish state in New York.

His eyes flickered open, and she jerked her gaze away.

His lips tilted up. "You might as well get some sleep. We have at least four days of travel to go."

"That long?" With an infuriatingly handsome and disagreeable man in close quarters. She dropped her head back into the cushions.

He furrowed his brows. "At least. Well, it would've been faster if I'd traveled alone. We'll stop to rest at night and for meals."

"We don't have to stop. We could sleep in the carriage." As much as she longed for breaks, the end of the journey couldn't come soon enough. Every moment, her mouth threatened to pour forth her ramblings, and her skin buzzed in awkward discomfort.

His face loosened into cool patience. "The horses have to stop unless I can change them. I thought you wanted to see the country. You need the daylight."

"I did. I do, but I'm also impatient to see Delia. What was she thinking moving all the way over here? Why couldn't we have docked closer?" Improper things occurred in carriages, like her making a fool of herself.

His gaze shifted to the window. "She was thinking she was in love with my brother. For the life of me, I can't figure out why."

Her face scrunched up. "I don't understand why someone would throw so much away for love."

"You've never been in love, I take it?" He stomped salted wounds with his line of questioning, but he had probably already heard the worst about her in New York. What was one more admission?

"I fancied I was."

He fixed his stare on the passing scene as though he'd never been there. "You weren't?" His tone was unconcerned, bored.

She shook her head, knowing he wouldn't see it. "No, I was in love with the idea of love."

He nodded, and she wondered if he watched her reflection or saw her out of the corner of his eye. She pulled at her skirts to straighten them.

"Your brother is quite handsome and charming. That's why Delia fell in love with him." Her gaze became unfocused. "It's such an adventure to travel across the sea. A distant land, new people. Do you think we'll run into highwaymen?"

He choked on a laugh. "Highwaymen? You better hope we don't. You'll have to kiss your clothes and books goodbye if we meet any."

She snorted and waved a hand in the air. "They can have them. I'm tired of the things I brought."

He shifted his wide eyes back to her, brows raised. "Your books? As much as you read them, I would think they were prized possessions."

"I can only read about the same dashing men so many times before I want to stab someone. Besides, I brought them for Delia as well. She probably has a grand library, but she may not have these. They're from the series she was borrowing from me."

He hid his laughter behind a cough. "Oh, those books. I don't know that the library at Briarwyck has much of that."

"What do you mean, those books?" She narrowed her eyes, ready to pounce.

"Those books. The absurd novels women read."

"They are not absurd." Her voice rose, and Alma shifted in her sleep.

He folded his arms, a spark of amusement dancing in his eyes. "Then what are they?"

She straightened her back against the cushions. The urge to strangle him grew with each word from his mouth. "They are highly entertaining accounts of the plight of women everywhere."

This time, he did laugh. "Plight of women? *The Adventures of the Mismatched Shoes*? Or what about *How to Work Matchmaking to Your Advantage*?"

Her mouth dropped open, and his laughter exploded.

"Those are ridiculous titles and completely wrong." Her cheeks burned as she stared him down. His cruel teasing was the reason she usually avoided him. Well, that and her awful habit of staring at his devilish good looks.

He calmed his laughter with a deep inhalation. A wise decision if he wanted to survive their trip. "Then what are they about?"

She tilted her head, her lip quirked up. "Which one?"

"How about the most recent one you read."

She tapped her fingertip against her lip. "*The Taming of Lord Featherstone*." The book had played out deliciously, and the next installment proved an agonizing wait.

He squinted his eyes. "*The Taming*? Why does he need taming?"

She wagged her finger at him. "Don't interrupt. The heroine is getting married to a man she doesn't love when she's kidnapped by a violent gang of highwaymen. The leader is a strong, handsome man, but he's deeply troubled."

He straightened his lips as though they threatened a grin.

"Anyway, she's able to calm his violent anger concerning his troubled past. They fall in love, and he gives up his violent ways for her. They settle down in the country and marry."

"She marries her kidnapper?" He raised a single brow.

"Yes, she realizes he only kidnapped her to get back at her fiancé. She escaped a bleak fate. Her betrothed was a scoundrel."

"Is this why you want to see highwaymen? To find your true love?" His tone became stern, a mixture of annoyance and concern. He must have thought she'd lost her mind.

"Of course not." She sniffed and trained her eyes on the window to conceal her shame.

"Right." He drew out the word.

A flush bristled along her skin. Who was he to judge her? He got his entertainment from drinking and gambling. At least her vices were healthy; nobody ever got hurt when she was off in her musings or reading a book. Besides, she wouldn't really be kidnapped by highwaymen. It was just a silly story like her dreams of pirates. She gulped and pushed her dream of Mr. Travers to the back of her mind.

The silence nagged at her, and she changed the subject. "Tell me about Briarwyck."

"Last time I was there, it was a crumbling old building with too much dirt. It's in the middle of nowhere."

"When was that?"

He sighed and rolled his shoulders. "About five years ago. My brother claims to have improved it since his marriage, but if you ask me, the place is beyond improving."

"Is it built overlooking the sea?"

He gave her a wicked grin. "Of course. It's a great brooding structure where maidens were known to jump to their death for fear of the unhappy life within its halls."

An alarmed gasp escaped her lips. "Oh my, will Delia be all right?"

He leaned toward her. "She may have a chance if she's careful along the darkened hallways and secret passages. After all, the servants carry secrets that may get her killed."

Her lips turned down. "Are you mocking me?"

"Of course not. Whyever would I do that?"

She shook her head. Must his humor be at her expense? "You're mocking me. Lord Carrington would never let harm come to Delia."

"Are you sure he is who he says? She may already be chained up for discovering the truth." His eyes were pinched at the corners and lit with mirth.

"What truth? No, just stop. I don't want to hear any more."

Her voice held an angry warning, but she feared her inquisitive eyes betrayed her.

His voice lowered. "His first wife's death."

She scoffed. "Delia told me she died in childbirth."

"But did she? Or was there something more sinister at work?" He lowered his voice further to a whisper, and she leaned forward to hear him. "Laura's death was a horrible tragedy."

"Didn't she betray him?" Her voice dropped to match his.

"Yes." His gaze danced in conspiratorial fashion. "That is why some question what really happened to her."

Her breath caught in her throat. "Then what happened to her?"

"She died in childbirth." He leaned back into the seat and surveyed her expression. "Or did she?"

She huffed at his response and settled back, crossing her arms. As much as she knew he was playing with her, her mind wandered over the possibilities. Carrington would not murder his wife; he wasn't that kind of person. What kind of person murdered their wife anyway? Maybe it had been her lover seeking revenge? Or maybe it was a servant that had killed her in some mistaken sense of loyalty to Carrington? That happened all the time, right? It did in her books, anyway, and something rang true about them. Ideas came from somewhere.

All she knew was her visit to Delia would be more interesting than she had thought.

The seeds had been planted in her mind, and not a day passed without her babbling along the drive. After three such days of her constant musings over the mysterious Briarwyck, Mr. Travers found her new books. A group of gothic novels, another ill-fated decision.

For the rest of the trip, she read while Mr. Travers snored against the carriage seat. Barely a word escaped Abigail's lips as she lived her life in mysterious abbeys and ancient graveyards. The occasional sharp inhalation of breath or the sudden jerk of her hand to cover her mouth was all the evidence of life she offered.

Her maid busied herself beside Abigail with needlework and staring at the unfamiliar sights. Immersed in her books and beyond reach, Abigail had a distant awareness of Alma's fond smile.

Time passed without much notice, and the trip lasted the span of a heartbeat. At night, Abigail was too exhausted from the ride to care for anything but sleep. She read through her meals and often forgot where she was, making scenery less of a priority. Once, she caught Mr. Travers with a contented smile on his face as he rested against the carriage wall.

Was she really so unpleasant? She thought to put the question to him but instead swallowed back the leaden words. She could escape him at Briarwyck and banish his opinion from her mind. He didn't need to like her. This trip was about seeing Delia and healing from Abigail's heartbreak. Mr. Travers was a distraction, a beautiful distraction but a barbed one.

When Briarwyck came into view, it aligned nicely with the end of her current book. Mr. Travers hadn't lied about the building, a fortresslike structure overlooking the sea. The house had a modest two stories built in the Elizabethan style in carved granite bricks. The numerous long-framed windows matched the door with its rounded-arch design. To Abigail, the structure was ancient. As they headed up the dirt-covered drive, she marveled at the chipped seraphim sculptures and the gnarled beech trees along the road.

She peered up at the old stonework and shuddered at how such a short building could be so imposing. The structure was sensed more than it was seen. It awoke a tight presence in her chest and an ache in her belly. The carriage stopped near the stairs to the front door, and servants in red-and-yellow livery awaited their arrival. With Mr. Travers's help, Abigail and Alma got out of the carriage.

Abigail's observations were interrupted by the fast-approaching form of her dearest friend. Delia hugged her with unchecked enthusiasm and pressed her rounded belly against Abigail, who gasped at Delia's condition. Her hostess drew back to study her from arm's length.

"Are you quite well, Abs?" Delia studied her face with startled concern.

Abigail sighed, not up to the attention. "It was a long trip. I'm sure I'll be fine. Never mind me—you said nothing about your breeding in your letters. How are you feeling?"

Delia smoothed her gown over her belly. "I'm doing well now. I was sick when I wrote you last, but I didn't want to alarm you or deter you from coming."

She shook her head. "If anything, that would've sped up my visit. How far along are you?"

"About four months. If I'd known you would be here earlier, I would have claimed pregnancy as soon as we arrived." Delia gave her a catlike grin.

"I'll keep that in mind. Where's Lynette?" Abigail glanced around the drive.

"Oh, she's probably off in the garden somewhere. She may join us later." Delia blinked as if she warded off weariness.

"Lynette? In a garden?" The last time Abigail had seen the younger Wolcott sister, she had been nothing but a whirl of mischief and gossip.

"Not making herself useful, mind you. She's either painting or sipping tea. Not that I expect her to do any gardening. She recently took up art and decided the best muse was the gardens. That is, after she tried painting fruit and spaniels or whoever would sit for her. It turns out time passes and life doesn't sit still." Delia's face pinched up.

"Indeed."

Delia faced Mr. Travers, who leaned against the carriage, examining his nails. "I see you've brought my lost brother-in-law. Hugh, are you hiding?"

He looked up at her address. "Only from your constant ramblings, dear sister. Miss Riverton has talked enough for the three of us." He stepped forward to hug Delia.

"My Abby is a great conversationalist, I'll have you know." Delia smiled fondly at Abigail and addressed Alma. "It's good to see you, Alma. Thank you for accompanying Miss Riverton."

Alma gave a short bow, her voice and expression silent. What Alma lacked in speech, her mistress made up for. She returned Delia's kind smile.

"My husband didn't deign to come and greet you in the drive. He's doing whatever it is he does in his study." Delia waved in the general direction of the house.

"Wonderful. I'll go announce my presence to him by mucking up his carpets." Hugh grinned and trotted off to the house.

"You do that. Tell him we'll take tea in the back garden today," Delia called after him, which he acknowledged with a backward wave.

"You must both be exhausted. Alma, Mrs. Evans will show you to your room." Delia gestured to an approaching stout older woman whose lips were set in a perpetual frown. Mrs. Evans nodded to the group and motioned for Alma to accompany her.

"Luckily, I haven't given up the room I intended for you. We have some guests visiting, some friends and family of Carrington. I'm told it's common for people to visit Briarwyck this time of year." Delia placed a hand over her slight belly. "You'll likely meet them at tea—that is, if you're up to it. Things are quite informal here, thankfully. Let me show you to your room."

Abigail smiled gratefully, her trunk already taken away by a footman. She ached from the jostling carriage and yearned for sleep, but her mind buzzed with excitement. She couldn't retire just yet.

CHAPTER THREE

THE HOUSE OFFERED ample opportunity for exploration. The entrance was grand for the size of the building, tastefully decorated in light browns, with accents of the Travers family colors of red and yellow. The center of the entryway housed a table with a large arrangement of matching flowers. Two sets of stairs flanked the room. Delia led her to the nearest staircase, which was carpeted in Persian designs. They continued right when they reached the top.

Their feet pattered over the marble floors as they passed paintings of long-dead Travers ancestors lining the walls. The portraits hung in shadow, revealing little in the candlelight. Delia came to a halt, and Abigail teetered to avoid running into her. The door Delia unlocked was almost at the end of the hall.

To Abigail's amused surprise, the room was decorated in deep blue and oak. A contrast of color from what she'd seen thus far. A large four-poster bed occupied the far center of the room. The other pieces of furniture included a dressing table, her trunk, and a settee overlooking the substantial window.

What drew her attention was the view. She moved closer to the window to appreciate the sight of the crashing waves along the cliffs down the coast. The water was calm below her, but she didn't doubt that was not always the case. The notion sent a rush up her spine.

"Will the room do? I imagine you're tired of the Travers red already." Delia grinned knowingly.

"It's perfect. Thank you." Abigail's gaze jumped over her surroundings.

"Good. I'll have a bath sent up for you. Is there anything else I can get you?" Delia clasped her hands over her belly but looked to Abigail with an air of sincere welcome.

Abigail smiled warmly. "Don't trouble yourself, Dee. I can find my way."

Delia nodded, and her face relaxed. "It's good to have you here."

Her friend left her to ponder the scenery and await her bath. She washed and dressed herself, allowing Alma to rest. She chose a pale, burnt-orange gown that showed off her complexion. Stealing another glance out the window before leaving, she spotted dark clouds moving toward Briarwyck.

Abigail arrived at tea early enough to secure a seat near Delia, who eyed the clouds. They sat at a long table near the gardens. It was not unlike the area reserved for outdoor meals back in New York at Delia's childhood home. The gardens were silent aside from the nearby sea. Abigail suspected the birds were sheltered in preparation for the oncoming storm.

"Carrington, there better not be any rain on my tea. I will hold you responsible for every drenched lemon tart and walnut scone." Delia frowned toward her husband on her other side.

"You're quite right to. I've been warning it off, but if I can't control the rain, then whatever am I good for?" Carrington gave his wife a fond smile.

"Nothing." Mr. Travers shook his head. "How can you ruin my sister's day in her condition?" Mirth danced in his eyes.

"You have walnut scones?" Abigail drew their eyes to her.

"I had our cook make up a batch as soon as we knew to expect you. Imagine, these scones have lavender in them. Lavender. They are divine," Delia said as two strangers joined them.

Mr. Travers raised a brow. "I take it you're fond of walnut

scones?"

Abigail's face split into a wide grin. "The best food on earth."

Delia cleared her throat. "You know full well that lemon tarts are the best food on earth."

Carrington groaned. "Must we?"

"Sorry, an old argument." Delia turned her attention to the newcomers. "Mr. Archibald, Miss Archibald, may I present my dear friend, Miss Riverton?"

They regarded Abigail with a nod but no other sign of interest. They appeared to be siblings, and indeed they were. Delia described them as twins and cousins of the Travers men on their mother's side. They shared the same strawberry-blond hair and brown eyes, but while Mr. Adam Archibald was of average height and build, Miss Alice Archibald was small and dainty. She looked as though she would blow away in the faintest breeze.

Abigail realized with a start that this was a sort of reunion between the Archibalds and Mr. Travers, but they only nodded to each other. Something she didn't quite understand, since her cousins were dear to her, her first companions and friends.

They were joined by three other guests, old friends of the family who often visited Briarwyck. The first to catch her eye was Jonathan Wentworth, Viscount Greymore, a handsome man in the classical sense of a strong, chiseled face and athletic build. He resembled the Travers brothers in height and form but had beautiful dark-auburn hair and deep-blue eyes. Abigail tried not to stare.

A married couple trailed behind Lord Greymore. Mr. Miles Graham was a balding gray-haired man a little older than Carrington. He was stout and paunchy, standing just below Mr. Archibald's height. Mrs. Vivian Graham was closer to Abigail's own age, with honey-blonde hair and shining steel-gray eyes. She was curvy, much as Abigail was, and radiated secretive amusement, giving her the appearance of laughing at an inside joke. Abigail liked the Grahams on sight.

"Will Sir Peter be joining us?" Delia asked her husband.

He leaned back in his chair and regarded his wife. "I don't believe so. He was unwell after breakfast. Maybe we'll see him at dinner. I know he wouldn't want to make you ill."

"Sir Peter Rockwell is a colleague of my husband," Delia explained to Abigail, then addressed Carrington again. "Very well, I hope he recovers soon."

Carrington nodded once. "As do I. We've much to discuss before he departs at the end of the week." His gaze slid to Abigail as he added cream to his scone. "Miss Riverton, I hope your journey was pleasant?"

"It was lovely. I'm fond of sailing, and the countryside is beautiful." Abigail nibbled her scone, the flavors a burst of summer on her tongue.

Mr. Travers frowned at her. "You would. I don't know how you managed it. That ship tried to kill me."

"All ships are trying to kill you, Hugh." Carrington side-eyed his brother. "I hope he wasn't too much trouble?"

She tilted her head, feigning contemplation. "Hmm, not too much."

"All Travers men are trouble." Delia cast a glare toward her husband.

"It's true." Mr. Archibald spoke into his tea. "There is ample proof in the bloodline, especially that scoundrel—"

Carrington cut him off with a glare.

Miss Archibald gave a stiff nod beside him.

Before anyone could elaborate on the matter, the butler approached and said something in Carrington's ear. His eyes widened, but he appeared otherwise calm.

"What is it?" Delia asked when the butler retreated to carry out Carrington's whispered instructions.

Carrington glanced around the guests as if deciding whether now was the proper time to speak. He tapped his fingers on the tabletop and gazed over at his wife. The lines of his face deepened, the weariness slumping his posture.

Mr. Travers covered his brother's tapping fingers with his

own hand. "Out with it."

Carrington slapped Mr. Travers's hand away. "Very well. It seems that Sir Peter has left us."

"So soon?" Lord Greymore raised a lone brow.

"How rude." Miss Archibald sniffed. Her hand shook, and she pushed it under the table.

Carrington closed his eyes and rubbed a hand over his face. "No, Sir Peter has left this earth." He emphasized the last words.

"Oh," came the collective response.

Carrington pushed himself from the table and rose. "If you will excuse me."

Delia attempted to follow, but Carrington held out a hand to still her, his eyes narrowed. "You will stay here."

Delia looked as if she wanted to protest but remained silent as her husband left.

Abigail sensed a thickening disagreement between her friend and Carrington. She edged closer to Delia and took her hand under the table. Delia's head hung above her tea, and a ghost of her unhappy thoughts drifted across her face.

"Was he elderly?" Abigail asked.

"Oh no. In fact, it was a surprise when he fell ill this morning. Sir Peter was always in fine health." Delia looked off in thought. The other guests gave a chorus of agreement.

Lynette strode out from the gardens to join them and took the spot Carrington had vacated. She leaned across Delia and whispered to Abigail, "He was murdered."

Abigail's brows knitted. "What?"

Delia frowned at her sister.

"Keep it down." Lynette waved her hand to shush her. "I overheard the servants. Sir Peter was murdered."

Abigail lowered her voice. "But why? How?"

Delia pushed Lynette back into her chair. "That's enough. We don't know anything for sure. Carrington will determine what should be done, and there's no use speculating at this point."

Lynette smirked at her sister and met Abigail's gaze. "Are you still happy you came to Briarwyck?"

Abigail made no reply as she looked around at the other whispering guests. Could one of them have murdered this Sir Peter? Or maybe the footman who had brought their food? She dropped her scone back to her plate at the thought. She started, seeing Mr. Travers watching her from the corner of her eye, and turned to face him. He met her gaze and shrugged, having overheard Lynette. Abigail noticed he had stopped eating and drinking as well. Though, she didn't know if it was for dramatic effect on his part or if he actually believed there was danger.

She shot him a razor-sharp stare. She wanted to scream at him, to shake him until he told her what he knew. He tilted his head, a maddening grin on his lips, and she had the urge to smother his smile with her mouth. How could he be so amused when a man was dead? Was he insane?

Delia leaned into her ear and whispered, "Yes," making Abigail jump. She hadn't realized she had voiced her question. Indeed, Mr. Travers's eyes were full of amusement at her expense.

A loud rumble signaled the end of tea, and the first of the raindrops followed as the group rushed into the house. By the time Abigail reached shelter, her hair was plastered to her head and her dress was ruined. She noticed too late when Mr. Travers caught up to her, and they walked together on the way to their rooms in the same hallway. Somehow he looked more dashing covered in rain. Next to him, she must appear as though she had rolled in the nearest mud puddle.

"How have you liked your visit so far? Now you have two mysteries to solve." His voice was serious, but she knew he teased her.

She ignored his question and posed one of her own. "How can you be happy about someone dying?"

"I'm not. I didn't even know the man, and my sympathy at his death won't bring him back." He cleared his throat. "Besides, I knew about it before the message came."

"Why didn't you tell your brother sooner?" She threw up her hands in exasperation.

He stared forward as they walked, his hands clasped behind his back. "They wanted to be sure he was dead before notifying His Lordship. My brother has been under a lot of stress lately. I agreed not to say anything out of the slim chance Sir Peter was still alive, to spare my brother an unnecessary burden. It was worth witnessing the excitement on your face."

"I was not excited. A man is dead."

"I didn't say you weren't saddened, but you were certainly intrigued by the mystery."

Abigail bit her lip. "Am I a horrible person?"

Mr. Travers chuckled softly. "Of course not, but you do understand if he was murdered, then the killer is still in the house. We could all be in danger."

Her gaze darted along the hallway. "I don't know any of the guests, so I doubt anyone would have reason to kill me, but I do worry about Delia and Carrington."

He raised a hand to his breast. "Not me? I'm hurt." His face brightened. "Perhaps you need me for protection."

Her heart skipped and faltered. No matter how tempting his veiled suggestion, a rake was a rake. She didn't need any more lessons in misery.

She rolled her eyes and rested her hand above her brow. "Help, Mr. Travers. Arm yourself with your shaved quill and paperweights. The killer is no match for a secretary."

Mr. Travers's brows shot up, and his shoulders tremored as he held in laughter. "I don't know if I should be amused or offended." He lost the battle, and a deep belly laugh burst from his lips.

"Offended, naturally." Giddiness bubbled in her chest and accented her smile.

"You're awfully cheeky." He cleared his throat. "In any case, I'm going to see to my brother. Don't want him to have heart failure before his first child is born."

"Might I inquire what you find out?" She widened her smile for effect.

"I thought you would ask that. Unfortunately, it's improper for me to discuss the events with you."

It took her a moment to realize he was serious. "Since when have you cared about what's proper?"

He nodded in agreement. "You have me there. William wouldn't want me to discuss the matter openly. Muddles up his investigations." He pushed his palm between them. "You'll have to ask Delia about the details. William will likely tell her himself, assuming they're on good terms."

Abigail couldn't imagine what would put the newlyweds at odds, but the tension between the couple had raged at the end of tea. Delia had been tight-lipped about her marital matters—a curious inconsistency in Delia's conversation Abigail hoped wouldn't extend to other subjects, specifically murder.

"All right, if you won't tell me, then I'll have to seek Delia out, but I don't know if she'll be forthcoming. Be prepared to be questioned if she's not."

"You would badger me over Delia? Why?" Irritation snapped in his voice.

Why? To gawk at the fire igniting him when he argued or laughed. Her fool tongue had outpaced her brain again.

"Delia's a dear friend, and besides, who would harass a pregnant woman?"

He sighed, drawing out the sound. "I should have left you back in New York."

A knot lodged in her throat, and she swallowed it down.

"I'd like to see you say that to Delia." She gave him a toothy grin. "I dare you."

He rubbed his chin. "I never back down from a dare. I'll get back to you on that. See you at dinner."

He let himself in his room, and the door shut on her wayward thoughts.

CHAPTER FOUR

DELIA WASN'T FORTHCOMING with further details but not by choice. Lord Carrington refused to discuss the matter with her, and the couple were no longer speaking to each other. Delia fought back tears when Abigail asked her about it, but her friend wouldn't elaborate. All Abigail could gather from the exchange was an old wound between them had been reopened.

Delia seemed as frustrated as Abigail over their exclusion from the inquiry. Her friend even applied to Mr. Travers for answers, but he refused to get into their quarrel. Abigail reasoned she might get more information out of him, since it would allow him to also tell Delia in a roundabout way. Besides, she couldn't back down from the enticing challenge Mr. Travers presented.

The rain continued to beat down on the house. The windows shook with thunder and bursts of wind. Abigail hoped to see more of the grounds, but the downpour limited her to the house, where a darkness persisted. She joined the other guests in the drawing room. Carrington and Mr. Travers were absent, and Delia sat wrapped in her own thoughts with Lynette at her side.

Lord Greymore and Mr. Archibald occupied the chairs beside her. The guests were seated a room's length from Delia and Lynette in an attempt to avoid the tension permeating the air over their hosts like a cloud.

"It's a pity we can't go riding," Mr. Archibald said for the third time. "It's been raining for more than half the time we've been here. I've a mind to go back to town."

"We know," Lord Greymore drawled.

"Why haven't you returned, then?" Abigail barely managed to keep the annoyance out of her voice.

Mr. Archibald drummed his fingers on his armrest. "We may after this storm calms. That is, if Carrington allows us."

"Why wouldn't he let you?"

"He insists we stay until he knows what happened to Sir Peter. An insult to his guests." Mr. Archibald scowled at the floor.

"It's common sense. You aren't being accused of anything." Lord Greymore eyed his vanishing port.

Mr. Archibald glared at Lord Greymore. "The implication is there. Obviously, I'm beyond blame. It's probably one of the servants. Perhaps that insolent boy running around the estate."

Abigail blinked in quick succession. "Felix? I doubt he would murder a houseguest. He has too much respect and loyalty for his employers."

"Respect? There's no respect in that boy," Mr. Archibald said, baring his teeth.

"Maybe not for you," Greymore said.

"How dare you." Mr. Archibald enunciated every word.

Greymore squinted back at him as though looking through a haze.

The men verbally battled. Greymore met Mr. Archibald's remarks blow for blow, massacring him with words. Lord Greymore seethed, his jaw clenched as he reached the end of his patience with the arrogant Mr. Archibald. The storm worked through the house as lightning through their veins.

Mr. Archibald shot to his feet. "I don't care to take more of your abuse." He stomped off to join his sister at the card table.

"I thought he would never leave." Greymore poured another glass of port. He tilted the bottle to her in offering.

She shook her head. "You could have escaped him yourself."

"Where would the fun be in that? One of the advantages of

being a viscount is I don't have to tolerate anyone I don't like. Not to mention, I got the chance to save a hapless maiden from his dull ways." He winked, lips curled up.

A brisk flush warmed her face. "And I thank you, though I wonder about Mr. Archibald's behavior as an untitled man." She hoped she was not breaching some obscure English etiquette.

"I've often wondered the same. He's a second son from an old titled family with money, but it's of little help to him." Lord Greymore's calm demeanor and easy charm made him approachable. Talking to him was akin to reawakening an old friendship.

"How are you acquainted with Lord Carrington?"

"We met during our school days at Eton." His voice slurred. They had yet to eat dinner.

"Were you surprised when he married Delia?"

"No, it seemed perfectly normal for him. I don't remember a time when he followed normal conventions. I wouldn't shock me if he came back married to one of your Native women." He gazed off, a fond smile playing on his lips. Then he turned his attention to her, face solemn. "I don't envy Carrington's predicament now. It will be a blow to him if any of the suspects are guilty." His concern for her friend endeared him to her.

"Who do you think it was?" She attempted to rein in her excitement at finally finding some answers, but Greymore was too far into his cups to care.

He cocked his head and squinted at the ceiling. "I fancy it was Mr. Archibald, though that may be my annoyance and port talking."

She tended to agree he was not in his right mind to judge. As agreeable as his conversation and appearance were, her opinion of him diminished from his fondness for alcohol. At least he seemed sober at tea. His condition didn't improve at dinner, and he grew increasingly difficult to talk to. She resigned herself to converse with Mr. Archibald on her other side.

"I would like to apologize for my behavior earlier, Miss Riverton," he said as they were seated. "I'm not normally so rude, but

I've been on edge since this business with Sir Peter." He held up a finger before she could reply. "Now, I know that's no excuse, but with your permission, I will do my best to win your good opinion."

Her opinion of him did improve over the course of dinner. His pride had driven him to lash out at Lord Greymore. Mr. Archibald transformed into a different person than he'd appeared an hour before. She couldn't say whether his agreeable nature resulted from Lord Greymore's absence from the conversation or her first impression being false.

Mr. Travers arrived late to dinner, grumbled his apologies, and took his place next to his sister-in-law. Carrington had yet to make an appearance. Abigail met Delia's gaze and gave her a comforting smile.

"Poison. Poison," Greymore whispered.

Her gaze flew to him, and she pushed her final plate away. He slurred nonsense, and sweat drenched through his shirt, his half-open eyes shifting along the table. He teetered in his seat as though near collapse or close to losing his dinner.

Abigail shook her head. The man should retire to his room before starting a panic. She attempted to get Delia's attention, but her friend only stared down at her food. Mr. Travers caught her gaze. She nodded toward Greymore, and Mr. Travers's eyes widened as he took in Greymore's appearance. He leaned in to whisper to Delia, who looked up. She hastened the women into the drawing room, putting an end to the matter.

Abigail hurried to join Delia and Lynette in the drawing room. Her own melancholy returned in her friends' depressed company. Soon everyone was uneasy and listless. The entrance of the men cut like a knife through the thick air of gloom. With the absence of Lord Greymore, they seemed in better spirits.

Lynette asked after Carrington, beating Abigail to it.

"He's seeing about the body, making the proper arrangements." Mr. Travers hesitated as though he chewed on his words. "There's been some inquiry, but it hasn't revealed anything other than he was poisoned. Something we already suspected."

Delia paled at his words and rested her head in her hands. Abigail and Lynette attempted to comfort her but with little effect, and Lynette led her sister off to her room. When the sisters exited, Abigail and Mr. Travers remained of their small group, the other guests having paired off around the room.

Mr. Travers frowned after Delia and Lynette. "I hope I didn't upset Delia too much. I didn't realize she would react so strongly, having endured the Foxglove poisonings in New York with such resilience."

Abigail tapped her lips as she considered his words. "Maybe it's because she felt less threatened by Foxglove. This murder happened in her own home. Foxglove seemed to favor my family's parties. I was terrified for much of the year."

"Of course." Mr. Travers shook his head at the memory. "I'm sorry you had to go through that. It must be painful to relive the killing here when you expected to leave it behind you across an ocean." His warm brown eyes soothed her awakened anxiety.

She allowed the calm to wash over her, loosening her muscles. The Foxglove murders had taken a part of New York from her. Nigel had taken the remainder. Cornwall was meant to be her vacation from all the heartbreaking chaos. An escape into the Cornwall of her novels.

He leaned forward as though he would grasp her hand but held back. "My brother and I are doing everything we can to catch this killer. You will be safe here."

"I have no doubt." Her uncertain tone said otherwise. "Do you have any leads?"

"No, but do you think I would tell you if we did?" A hint of a smile graced his lips.

Her mouth twisted to the side. "I was hoping you would, but I doubted it. I seem to have the poor luck of being female in this instance."

"That's not why."

She squared her shoulders. "Oh? Then why? Don't you trust

me?"

"I trust you just fine. I may point out I trust Delia more and I won't tell her." He glared at her, a silent chastisement. "As I predicted, my brother asked me not to say anything. It would be a mess if word spread, and it's much easier just to keep it to ourselves."

Abigail snorted, unladylike. He frowned at her, but his eyes regarded her with amusement.

He cleared his throat. "You seem to have gathered quite a following since you arrived. Short work, that."

"What do you mean?" She knitted her brows in confusion.

"I noticed both Greymore and Archibald are interested in you. Of course, they would be, as they're both broke." He watched her with a steady gaze, and she shifted uncomfortably under his stare. "A match with you would also connect them more firmly with my family. They've both already failed with Lynette. You're the next closest thing to a marriageable sister to Delia."

Her mouth dropped open, and she snapped it shut. She had no designs on either man and didn't welcome a relationship. Mr. Travers must be teasing her. Her thoughts still lingered over Nigel, but the prospect had been as futile during his life as it was after his death.

Nigel had made empty promises and then thrown her away like a common whore when he was done with her. She had been equal parts relieved and shattered when her courses had arrived on the ship. The child would have embodied the only piece of him belonging to her. She had mourned the child that never was and come out of it feeling more alone and hopeless than before.

"Why did Lynette refuse them?"

He raised a brow. "I thought you spent time with them."

"Hmm, you have a point. I was just thinking they're much more agreeable when they're alone."

"Oh, they are." He settled back, crossing his ankles. "But that doesn't make them marriageable. Greymore is a heavy drinker.

Today wasn't the exception but the rule. Otherwise, he's tolerable. Archibald is the opposite. He hasn't gotten over the fact he's a second son. He thinks he was shorted what he's due. I'm surprised he took an interest in a nameless American."

Color flooded her cheeks, and her eyes blazed. "Why is that?"

"The only thing he has to gain by marrying an untitled woman is money. A man like him would want the advantages of marrying as high on the social ladder as he can climb."

She waved his words away. "Isn't that the same with everyone else?"

"True, but more so for him."

She folded her arms across her chest. "What about you? You're a second son."

"Yes, but I'm happy as a second son." He turned toward the footman who brought him a glass of port. "I have no plans to marry, to my mother's horror."

An emptiness shot into her and rendered her numb, distant. She sipped her tea to regain herself. "I have a feeling you'll plague Carrington and Delia for the rest of their lives."

"Quite possibly, but I'll be a doting uncle." His eyes caught over her shoulder, and he sighed. She peered back as Mr. Archibald approached.

"Is this heathen bothering you, Miss Riverton?" Mr. Archibald took a seat between them.

"He bothers everyone." She gave Mr. Travers a mocking frown.

Mr. Archibald favored her with a wide grin. "Too true. Might I suggest a turn about the room?"

"You may suggest it, but I would rather not. You see, my ankle, it pains me." She feigned a weary tone.

"A sad business, ankles. Might I have a look?" He bent over her and reached for her foot.

Her cheeks sparked with heat. "You may not." She squealed and jerked her foot out of his grasp.

"Do leave the lady alone, Archibald." Mr. Travers's eyes

sharpened, and his jaw set.

"I was merely going to inspect the damage." Mr. Archibald fanned his fingers over her ankle, directing his attention to Mr. Travers.

"You need not bother. It's nothing." Abigail hated herself for the lie, since it prevented her from running.

"If it pains you, then it's not nothing."

A wave of nausea crawled up her throat at the thought of him touching her.

"How did you hurt it?" Mr. Travers looked down at her foot with exaggerated interest.

She gave Mr. Travers a flat stare. "I slipped returning from tea."

His brows furrowed. Of course, he'd been with her when they'd returned. "Really? If I had known you were injured, I would have assisted you." Mirth crinkled his eyes.

Her skin tingled as she imagined the prospect. "I have no doubt of that."

"I would've helped you as well." Mr. Archibald's declaration made her wince.

"Mr. Travers, perhaps you would assist me to the hall? Since Delia has made her escape, I would like to rest." She pled with her eyes for him to not give anything away.

"It would be my honor, Miss Riverton." Mr. Travers rose to his feet and offered his arm.

Mr. Archibald watched with a hardened jaw and thinned lips. His cherry-red face looked ready to erupt.

Abigail regretted not exiting with Delia and Lynette. Instead, she would have to ward off Mr. Archibald with the company of Mr. Travers. If only she would forget her dream and the dizzying kiss from her imagination.

Mr. Travers made a point of assisting her with the utmost care. His touch left her light-headed and overheated. Once they reached the hall, she attempted to pull away, but he insisted on escorting her to her room. He mocked her pretend injury, having her lean heavily on him and soliciting the concern of all those they passed.

"You must be exhausted from having to travel such a ways to dine." He tsked. "Whyever didn't you take dinner in your room? And nobody to assist you?" His tone was loud enough for everyone they passed to hear.

"Really, that's far enough." She struggled to untangle herself from him at the top of the stairs. His steady touch carried too much temptation, and her fingertips itched to run over him, but it was more harm than good to her addled emotions. She didn't need to be toyed with after Nigel.

He renewed his grip on her arm. "What would my sister think of me if I didn't assist you the entire journey?"

She forced false ire into a glare. "You know perfectly well I'm all right."

"Do I? Archibald will be overjoyed to hear it." A wicked smile played across his face.

She stiffened. "You wouldn't dare."

"You'd be surprised."

"I better not be." Her gaze darted around in case Mr. Archibald sprung up beside them.

"I thought you liked surprises." He gave her a pained frown.

"Good surprises. Interesting surprises. Not vexing surprises that cause men of undesirable intentions to hinder my peace of mind." She tugged at her arm to no avail.

He nodded solemnly. "Aw, so my insistence on escorting you is vexing?"

"Indeed, yes," she lied.

She stumbled as he suddenly removed his assistance, and sprawled onto the cold marble floor outside of her room. She peered up at him with wide eyes, recovering enough to kick at his legs before he could move out of her reach. The ball of her foot landed soundly on his shin.

He sucked in a loud breath and rubbed at the offending area. "That hurt." His wary gaze prepared for another blow.

"It was supposed to. You're lucky I couldn't reach more sensitive areas." She rolled to her knees. "Help me up."

"Like hell I will." He released his shin and straightened his stance.

She gawked at him. "You're the reason I'm on the floor in the first place."

"It's what you wanted. Is your position any less vexing?" He bared his teeth at her.

"You don't need to worry about the killer getting you. I'll kill you first." She steadied herself on her knees. "What are you doing?"

He cocked his head, mouth half-open. "I rather enjoy seeing you kneeling on the ground."

A flush stormed up her neck, and her jaw dropped. "Go away or I'll scream." She pulled off her shoe and waved it at him.

"All right, I know when I'm not wanted." He stalked off as her shoe landed squarely in the center of his spine. He flinched but continued on.

"I really doubt that."

He made no sign he had heard her.

Pulling herself off the floor took an embarrassing amount of time. At least Mr. Travers was no longer there to witness the spectacle. He must already believe she was a clumsy dolt.

Her skirts tangled, making it difficult to right herself. She wobbled to her feet, her body teetering and threatening to make her injury a reality. She sighed. It was funny the way lies would make their way back to you in the most roundabout manner. Usually she was adept at lying, but she could never rely on other people to properly go along with the falsehood.

Mr. Travers had snuck past her defenses, and she was determined to revert their relationship to its previous state of nonexistence. If she didn't, her heart may shatter like so many raindrops over the Cornish countryside.

Chapter Five

Abigail's injured ankle ruse did not prevent her from the spontaneous idea of eavesdropping on Lord Carrington. Nor did it dissuade her from executing it. She waited, still in her dinner clothes, until the hall was silent of echoing footsteps.

Stepping into the hall with soft slipper-clad feet, Abigail ventured out into the dark, a small, dim candle held in front of her. She was no stranger to eavesdropping, having spied on her parents and brothers a number of times—often learning things she did not want to know, but the payoffs proved far greater than the regretful instances.

Abigail was especially careful passing Mr. Travers's door. His room was quiet from the hallway, but she took no chances. The marble floors made little sound, and she flew past the door, to the stairs without much effort. She'd noted the location of Carrington's study when she'd first arrived, being given a halfhearted tour from Delia on the way to her room. Unfortunately, she would have to traverse the stairs, which groaned beneath her steps. A proper spy would take the time to learn the temperament of the stairs to avoid making any sound. She was not a proper spy.

Abigail skipped steps, taking the edges where she could. The task proved difficult, but she made the landing without much noise. Her satisfaction was cut short when she heard low, angry voices coming toward her. She hurried into a closet nestled under the staircase, where she could just make out two figures through the cracks between stairs. She squinted and identified the familiar forms of her friends, Delia and Carrington.

They spoke in hushed tones, but Abigail was fortunate in her choice of hiding spots. Their voices carried. She crawled closer, and the muffled sounds became audible.

"Won't you listen to me?" Delia didn't bother to hide the hurt in her voice.

"I haven't the time. We can discuss this in the morning."

"When do you ever have time? All you do is go back and forth from here to London. I barely hear a word from you when you're here, barricading yourself in your office."

Abigail slapped a palm over her open mouth.

"I've work to do," Carrington growled.

"You can't spare an hour for your wife, but you can sit and drink with your brother all afternoon?" Abigail pictured Delia with her hands on her hips and her chin raised in defiance.

"We're dealing with cleaning up this mess." His voice became almost a whisper, and Abigail squinted toward him as though it would tune her hearing.

"I'd be more than happy to help you. Why do you shut me out?"

"You know perfectly well why with your history."

"What's that supposed to mean? I'm carrying your child, and you still don't trust me? I told you I'd stop. Didn't you believe me?"

Abigail fought the urge to rush to Delia's defense, but she feared any interference on her part would only make matters worse. They fell silent, and Abigail pictured Carrington rubbing at his face, as both Travers men so often did when they were stressed.

"Keep it down, and yes, I do trust you, but I'm not sure I trust your impulses."

"How's that different? Never mind, I don't want to know. Why don't you go back to London where you'd rather be?" Her friend's angry stomps rushed up the stairs.

"Dee, I didn't mean that." Carrington muttered his words after her, too low for anyone but Abigail to hear. "I don't prefer London."

A heavy weight rested on Abigail's chest from Carrington's words. She allowed that Delia could have her secrets, since Abigail had her own. She'd neglected to tell Delia about Nigel or why she'd accepted Delia's invitation. Her friend had enough things to worry about if her argument with Carrington was any indication.

He shuffled back to his study, and she took the opportunity to exit the closet. The hall was vacant when she emerged, and the study was surprisingly dark for being in use. A light flickered from under the door, and she stationed herself beside the crack. For a few minutes, the clinking of glasses was the only sound, but after moments of loaded silence, even on her side of the door, Mr. Travers spoke.

"Why are you being so hard on her? What could it hurt to have her help?" Mr. Travers sounded annoyed as though they had covered the topic on previous occasions.

She placed a hand on her chest.

"What kind of husband would I be if I had my pregnant wife take part in a murder investigation?"

A snort came from the room and, she guessed, from Mr. Travers. "You've never cared what people think of you."

"It's not what others think of me. I couldn't live with myself if Delia had a shock and lost the baby." Carrington's worried tone sent a shiver down Abigail's spine. She shook herself.

"Delia is no delicate flower, not even in her condition."

"It doesn't matter if she is or not. Do I need to remind you of Laura?"

Glass clinked again. Someone must be pouring another drink.

"There's no comparison between Delia and that witch."

She heard a long sigh that she supposed to be Carrington's. "Sometimes I think she died just to spite me." Abigail pressed herself closer to the door.

"Perhaps she did. I never understood why you married her. I know you didn't love her or even like her." Why indeed?

"It doesn't matter now. She still haunts this place. You can't imagine how relieved I am Delia didn't choose to take up Laura's old room. I wouldn't have denied her anything, but I wouldn't care to visit her there."

A thoughtful pause.

"The blue room?"

"Where else? It was her favorite color, or so she said. I think she only chose it because it wasn't red."

Abigail pressed her hand tightly against her mouth. That was her room. Delia had put her in Laura's room. Had the awful woman died in Abigail's bed? Gooseflesh ran over her skin at the thought of sharing a bed with a corpse.

"You know, you can always redecorate it." The familiar smile altered Mr. Travers's voice.

"I don't have the time. My wife will decide whether to redecorate, but she quite likes the room as it is."

Abigail frowned at the door. If she were Delia, she certainly would have redecorated it, or maybe boarded the entrance. The ghost of Laura needed peace, or possibly a gag.

"Then she couldn't know it was Laura's."

"That may be, but I doubt the servants kept it from her. I know my wife, and she might have kept it as it is out of some misplaced respect for the dead."

Laughter turned into a cough. "For Laura? I don't think so. Besides, she put Miss Riverton in the room. I don't believe she would've done that if she knew it was Laura's."

Carrington chuckled. "Abigail would probably find it exciting. She's most likely holding a séance as we speak."

"You have me there."

Abigail snorted and slapped her hand over her face. For their information, she hadn't had a séance in months. She cocked her head; it wasn't a bad idea actually.

"How did you get on during the trip?" Another clink of glass accompanied Carrington's question.

"You know perfectly well I vomited the entire way." Indeed. At least he hadn't smelled as bad confined to the carriage.

"I mean with Miss Riverton?" Amusement rang in Carrington's voice.

"She was spared the vomiting." Hardly. True, she hadn't been sick herself, but she'd witnessed him slumped over the railing.

"But how did you get along with her?"

"She's alive, isn't she?" His voice went from bored to annoyed.

"She wasn't putty in your hand?" Carrington must be joking. At least, she hoped he was joking.

Mr. Travers scoffed but said nothing.

"I'm amazed at you. Most women would have made it to your bed by now."

Abigail frowned. She wasn't most women, and besides, she hoped she had learned her lesson with Nigel. What made Carrington believe his brother wanted her anyway?

"And displease my sister? Delia's scary as a banshee when she's angry, but I suppose you already know that."

"Good, then I won't need to thrash you on her behalf."

"I was too sick to try anyway, and she was attended by her maid for the journey by land."

"So you thought about it? I should thrash you anyway." Carrington's voice lowered.

"Oh, come now, how could I not?"

Abigail's dream flashed in her mind, and her cheeks heated as she shook it away.

"I'll pretend you didn't say that about my wife's best friend. Stay away from her and Lynette for that matter."

A wave of unexpected disappointment washed through her. She'd barely escaped her poor choices in New York, and already she fancied making the same mistakes. Maybe she hadn't learned.

Mr. Travers groaned. "You're killing me. We're in the middle of nowhere. I'm surprised you didn't limit me from the servants and Miss Archibald."

"You've never shown an interest in bedding servants, and Miss Archibald is a shrew. Your experiences with her will be punishment enough." Carrington snickered. "We do have some unmarried livestock on the estate if that interests you."

"They probably kick less, at least."

Abigail tightened her lips against the building laughter in her chest. Her anger toward Carrington trickled away with his defensive words.

"Who kicked you?" Carrington chuckled, a low rumble.

"Miss Riverton."

Carrington's laugh grew louder. "You probably deserved it."

"Of course I did. That doesn't mean I liked it."

"Another reason to stay away from her, and no, Hugh, that's not a challenge. I can see your mind working." His stern warning marked each word.

Enthralled by the conversation, Abigail didn't notice another form closing in on her until a shadow loomed over her. She shot up her gaze to see Delia blinking down at her. The friends said nothing as Delia took the spot next to her.

"Why do you have all the fun?"

"Hugh, for God's sake, I married her. This is not a game."

A chair scraped across the floor as though someone stood.

"It isn't like I'd be ruining her."

"What do you mean?"

Abigail's cheeks flushed, and she stepped away from the door. She had heard enough—too much, really. She breathed through the hand cupped over her mouth to hold back the tears. Delia's eyes widened at Abigail, and Delia moved to follow her. They left in silence, Abigail leading Delia back to her own room. The blue room.

When they shut the door behind them, Delia grasped Abigail's shoulders and forced her to meet her gaze. "What happened?"

Abigail's fists shook, and her nails dug into her palms. She took a deep breath to steady her words. "I don't know what you heard. He has no right to discuss me." She'd thought they were at least on respectable terms, but he carried on as though she was used goods, unworthy of decency.

"They're brothers. They discuss all sorts of vulgar business, which is why I listen to them. I wouldn't take offense to it." Delia rubbed her palm up and down Abigail's back.

"I thought I was leaving that behind me." Abigail's voice fell soft.

Delia's emerald eyes shone with understanding and sympathy. "You are. Carrington and Hugh wouldn't say anything outside of the study."

Her posture loosened. "Won't they think less of me?"

Delia scrunched up her nose. "I really doubt it. You should hear some of the scandalous business from London. I'm sure your position is tame in comparison."

"You'll have to tell me about that."

Delia shook her head. "Another time. For now, tell me what happened to you? You've said nothing in your letters to suggest anything was amiss."

Abigail sighed. "I hadn't had the opportunity. Then it was too late."

"Who was it?"

Settling herself on the bed, Abigail hesitated. She dreaded discussing the worst events of her life with anyone, even Delia, but she had escaped to her friend's home. Delia deserved to know why. So Abigail bled her story, drop by aching drop.

Abigail clasped her hands together and braced herself. "Do you remember the charming officer I mentioned a time or two?"

"Yes, but you never told me who he was."

"Nigel Weston."

Delia's eyes grew in recognition. "Abs, I'm so sorry. I should've warned you. This is all my fault."

Abigail raised her brows. "What do you mean? Did you know

him?"

"He's a disgusting, horrible man. I thought he was supposed to move out of New York." Delia hesitated as if to consider her words. "It's my understanding he was fond of hurting women." Delia paced the floor.

Abigail swallowed hard. "He was supposed to move out, though it was later than planned. I wish I'd never met him."

Delia halted in front of her. "I ought to travel back to New York and kill him."

"The rebels beat you to it. He died right before I left, an ambush just out of Long Island. It was a slaughter." Abigail couldn't help the weight, like rot, growing across her chest and sickening her stomach.

"How unfortunate. I seem to have poor timing on my revenge plots." Delia frowned to herself. Her friend joined Abigail on the edge of the bed and grasped her hand.

"I wouldn't want you to kill him." She shook her head. "It's as much my fault as it is his."

Delia gave her a stern look. "It isn't your fault, Abs."

Abigail lowered her gaze to the floor. "I made the choice to not wait for marriage."

"Yes, but it was in his character to seduce you into submission. He knew better than to ruin you without the intention of marriage. Did you say no?"

"Repeatedly, but he kept pushing, and then he said he loved me and wanted to marry me. I thought of you and Lord Carrington and drew the wrong conclusions. Here was this handsome, brave soldier, and he wanted me, Dee." She pressed her eyes shut. "How was I supposed to say no to that?"

"My behavior's deplorable, and you should never emulate me. That does not excuse Mr. Weston's actions. I admit you're not without blame, but you had more to lose than he did. He should have known better." Delia squeezed her hand. "We will not judge you here."

"What Mr. Travers said—"

"Was only talk. He's probably trying to rile Carrington up." Delia's patience shifted the weight on Abigail's shoulders.

"I'm sorry I brought my problems to you." She frowned, annoyed with herself. "You have problems of your own, and I don't want to intrude."

"Nonsense, I'm glad you're here." Delia gave her a small smile. "While we're on the topic, I would keep a close eye on the rest of our guests. Something isn't right, but I haven't been able to place it. What makes it worse is my husband refuses to tell me his suspicions. Don't be alone with any of them or accept food or drink from anyone who's not a servant."

Abigail's gaze jumped to study Delia. "Then you're sure it's one of the guests?"

"Our servants don't habitually poison people. Most of them have served the Travers family for generations. The only one of our guests I could say I trusted was Sir Peter, so that doesn't rule anyone out." Delia let out a long breath. "The funny part is we shouldn't have houseguests in my condition, but it was already planned and not even Carrington remarked on it."

"Then you're sure it's nobody in the family? I don't mean to wrongly accuse anyone, but there may be a reasonable explanation behind it."

"I have to be honest with you: I've already investigated that possibility. To my knowledge, none of them have a motive and none of them, save Carrington, spent any amount of time with him. Obviously, my husband wouldn't have killed him. He had too much to lose and it's outside of his character. He refuses to allow me to question anyone, so I'm reduced to listening at doors. I don't suppose you heard anything before I arrived?" Delia favored her with a hopeful smile.

Abigail shook her head.

Delia's smile faded. "That's unfortunate. They must've exhausted the topic this afternoon."

"Who do you think it is?"

Delia stretched out her legs and appeared to relax. "I haven't the faintest idea, though I wonder if Lord Greymore was drowning more than his finances tonight. I don't trust a man who's that attractive."

"You married into a family of attractive men."

Delia scowled at her. "And it took me a long time to trust them. Would you mind if I stayed with you tonight? I'd rather not be alone or with my husband. He seems to have an aversion to this room, so he's unlikely to disturb our sleep."

Abigail considered telling Delia the reason for his aversion but decided her friend had too much to worry about already. Besides, she wanted Delia's company, and scaring her away was the last thing on her mind. It wasn't so much the murder that made her uneasy but the storm beating against the house.

The bedroom windows she'd loved when she'd first seen the room were now a source of anxiety. The waves crashed against the cliffs below her, and the glass shook as if some unholy specter wished to hurl her into the sea. She pictured herself tossed by the violent winds and into the cliffs as she plummeted to the unforgiving waves below, her body never to be found.

Abigail shuddered. "Your company would be most welcome."

"Then it will be like old times." Delia's enthusiasm shone in her eyes. "I warn you, though, Carrington says since my pregnancy my snoring has gotten worse. He assures me it's still as tame as a kitten's purr and never bothers him."

"My dear, your snoring couldn't be any louder than that infernal storm." A crash of thunder roared at the window to emphasize her point.

It turned out she was wrong and Carrington was a liar.

CHAPTER SIX

TO SAY SLEEPING was difficult would be a gross understatement. Delia's snores were not just worse; it was as if she was possessed by a slumbering demon. And like a demon, her friend clenched the covers possessively around her and gave a snort-like snarl whenever Abigail tried to pull them toward her.

Her frustration grew to the point she contemplated suffocating Delia but settled for nudging her friend on occasion. The movement proved enough to stifle the snores for a time but not enough to fully wake her. Abigail continued in this manner until four in the morning, when the storm died down to a light drizzle, and she fell into a blissful sleep during an interval in the snores.

When she awoke, a craving for tea and walnut scones gnawed at her stomach. Her head throbbed through her shoulders, and she longed to stay in bed. Delia, however, thought it would be wise to get an early start, since the storm had cleared. One never knew when another would spring up in its absence in Cornwall.

Once they were both dressed, Delia led Abigail to the breakfast room. They learned Delia and Carrington were not the only ones to argue last night. The Grahams made a pretense at civility, but their conversation was loaded with scathing barbs. The Archibald siblings never attempted to hide their feud and sat at opposite ends of the table.

Abigail and Delia took seats near Miss Archibald and the Grahams, avoiding the gloom that was Lord Carrington and Mr. Archibald. The rest of the party was absent.

With a forced grin, Mrs. Graham suggested the group go on a picnic, while her husband protested it was still too damp. His snappish objections suggested he wanted an excuse to avoid his wife.

"Surely if we brought thick blankets, we could have a pleasant enough time. The sun is out, and the ground should dry in no time." Mrs. Graham's smile wavered. A transformation had occurred in the poor woman since yesterday. She seemed frantic to please her husband, but Mr. Graham fought her every word with the silence he returned.

"We could go on a drive." Delia, no doubt, attempted to be helpful.

Mrs. Graham brightened. "Yes, it would be fine weather for a drive."

Mr. Graham's gaze stayed fixed on his food. "You're forgetting the mud we must travel through. It wouldn't do for us to get stuck if another storm approached."

A unity formed among the women as Miss Archibald joined in. "I wouldn't mind getting out of the house."

Delia faced Abigail. "What do you say, Abs?"

She tried a weak smile. "I'm not afraid of a little mud."

"Fancy four women on a drive in the country. Should we inform any of the others or go ourselves?" Delia glanced across the table.

Miss Archibald shook her head. "Let's go alone."

"Agreed. We don't need the men, and Lynette's off again painting. At least she's found something to do here. I thought she'd be bored senseless in Cornwall."

Abigail didn't relish the idea of leaving without one of the men, though she knew as a group, they were more than capable of driving along the roads. The area seemed untamed and dangerous, but since the others appeared comfortable with their plans, she would not be the one to raise this concern. The guests wouldn't have a chance of leaving without answers about Sir Peter's murder, but a short drive near the estate would do all of them good.

The party setting off after breakfast, Delia drove next to Miss Archibald while Abigail sat with Mrs. Graham. They'd chosen a closed carriage, not taking any chances with the weather. Abigail fought her anxiety until it dissipated into the vibrant green hills.

Mrs. Graham's smile sparked in her eyes. "It's so nice to be out." The relief in her voice made Abigail wonder if she believed she was freed from jail.

"It's only for the moment," Delia called back to them. Abigail pictured Delia's eyes rolling as she exchanged glances with Miss Archibald.

"I don't care. This is the most fun I've had in years." Mrs. Graham settled back against her seat.

Abigail frowned. Could Mrs. Graham be so deprived of entertainment? At least now she would get some distance from her husband.

"We're just getting started." Miss Archibald laughed, and the sound seemed to carry to the rest of the group.

Delia whooped and sped the horses on, causing the women to stop their chatter as they bounced along.

Delia stopped to admire the landscape. The sparse trees allowed a distant glimpse of the sea, and small animals scurried just out of view among the abundant wildflowers. As a botany enthusiast, Delia gathered what she found useful, while the rest of them chose flowers for their beauty.

The drive was an unexpected success, and the ladies agreed to repeat the excursion—that was, until they heard the approaching hoofbeats from behind. The carriage was parked, and Abigail was separated from the other women, where a patch of pale-yellow flowers had drawn her.

Delia shouted from beyond their vehicle, her words muffled by the approaching horses. Abigail froze, and her eyes flashed toward the carriage, but she saw nothing past the branches between them. The leaves seemed to sway with the shouts. Angry male voices yelled over one another, and Delia shrieked back at them.

Abigail shrank in on herself at the unintelligible words. Panic crept through her veins like icy water, and she dove further into the plants along the road, not caring what she landed on. Her arms wobbled as she raised herself on her knees in the mud and away from the brambles lodged into her skin.

The argument near the carriage raged on, and dread took root in her stomach. Her breath caught in her throat as footsteps approached her position. She ducked into the brush, scraping her cheek in the process.

A familiar male voice called out her name, sending a shiver over her limbs. She stared forward in confusion. Mr. Travers spotted her and moved to assist her from the ground, but her hands were encased in mud. He curled his lip and presented his embroidered handkerchief before insisting she keep it once he saw the filthy cloth afterward.

He offered her a gloved set of fingers, and she grasped them lightly, but when he pulled her to her feet, he squeezed her hand. The sensation through the leather left her weightless. Her eyes found him, and her breath caught in her throat as she anticipated his next move.

He released her hand and scanned her form. "Why the devil were you hiding?"

Her cheeks heated as she realized how she must appear. "I heard shouts, and I believed we were being robbed."

"But I thought you wanted to meet highwaymen." He gave her a tight-lipped grin.

She dropped her gaze to hide her face. "That was foolish of me. My fear at the reality was much worse than I expected."

"It was a valid concern, which is why I had to restrain my brother and Mr. Archibald from breaking their necks chasing the carriage down." His voice was worn. The horses had sounded as though the men had ridden for their lives.

The carriage came into view, and the heavy tension in the air must have settled the dust.

"Where's Mr. Graham?" she asked.

"He didn't seem to mind the loss of his wife. I don't know what happened, but I'd stay out of it if I were you." He towered over her, and the warning in his voice forced her to step back.

Her chest clenched for Mrs. Graham. "Then all is well with the Archibalds?"

"I wouldn't say that. Since I know you likely had a hand in plotting this misadventure, I have to ask, What the hell were you thinking?"

She raised her chin to meet his gaze. "Me? I had nothing to do with it. I was only going along with it."

He paused and rubbed his face. "You couldn't at least suggest Delia take a footman or a driver? Or maybe me?"

Her heartbeat pounded a steady march, and her voice hushed at his angry tone. "She acted as if it was perfectly proper, that Carrington wouldn't mind."

"That's far from the case. When we found out where you'd gone, Carrington was frantic. Mr. Archibald wasn't much better."

"And you?" She blurted out the question as if something chased the words. She scanned his face for any reaction while her body froze in time, not daring to hope he cared for her.

He looked away, and she wanted to dive under the carriage. "I panicked as well, but at least I could keep my emotions steady enough to calm them. It didn't help to have Lynette standing there laughing at us. She knew you had left all along but waited and told us in the most innocent manner."

"What of Greymore?"

He snorted. "Our Don Juan was abed. Are you disappointed?"

Her face fell, but he didn't seem to notice. "Of course not. I was merely curious."

As they walked back to the carriage, Mr. Travers took notice of her slight limp. "It seems you got your wish."

"Do shut up." At least he had gone back to teasing her. She couldn't stand another lecture. She was on vacation, after all.

This earned her a grin, but he complied as they approached the others.

"Are you hurt?" Carrington stepped toward her, his arm raised as though to steady her.

"I'm fine, thank you. My ankle is from yesterday." She saw no use throwing more blame on the drive.

"She says she hurt it coming back from tea." Mr. Travers's mocking frown creased his brow.

Carrington glared at his brother and addressed her. "That's unfortunate. My apologies for your injury."

"It's of no consequence." Her face burned, and she faced away, wishing they were back at Briarwyck already.

Mr. Archibald approached her, also noting her limp. "I was hoping your ankle had recovered, Miss Riverton. It's a sad day to see such a pretty girl injured. Are you faring any better?" Concern deepened his brown eyes.

"It's about the same, though my position on the ground didn't help it." Perhaps the injury would strengthen her lie.

Mr. Travers gave her a pointed stare. "Yes, it's better to avoid being forced to the ground." Of course, he implied his dropping her in the hall.

She narrowed her eyes at him, and her voice came out as barbed as the underbrush she'd fallen in. "When it can be helped, I do avoid being on the ground."

She allowed Mr. Archibald to escort her to the carriage, where she joined the other women, who sported matching downcast eyes. At a loss for words, Abigail remained silent.

"So much for fun," Miss Archibald muttered across from her.

Mrs. Graham broke out in tears and grabbed Abigail for comfort.

Abigail patted the poor woman. She couldn't blame her. Abigail wanted to cry herself, but at least she didn't have a neglectful husband.

At their return, the hour was past time for tea. Each of the women took off to their respective rooms and their subsequent arguments. The short token lecture Abigail had received from Mr. Travers appeared to be her only one, and for once, she was thankful her family was an ocean away.

At dinner, Abigail sat near Mrs. Graham. The other guests clustered together. No order or pairing took place at dinner, nor did anyone seem to care. Delia and Carrington had reached some form of peace. They were, to all appearances, happy again. From Abigail's lengthy experience, Delia seemed as if she held back. She didn't quite smile as widely or laugh as loud.

When Lord Greymore finally emerged from his room and stretched out like a cat to dine, he seemed pleased with himself, all smiles and pleasantries. The man was not the same one as the day before. He was fully recovered from his drunken state, and yet he did not hold back on his wine.

At first impression, the seating arrangement seemed fortunate. Mr. and Mrs. Graham were no longer speaking to each other. Mr. Graham glared across the table at Lord Greymore, who seemed unaware of the death stare. Abigail wondered if it would be polite to excuse herself, when the table erupted in chaos.

Greymore flirted with Miss Archibald. From what Abigail could tell, Greymore flirted with anyone wearing skirts, a harmless, habitual pastime for him. What differed tonight was his timing.

"Isn't Miss Archibald's dress a becoming shade?" Greymore asked nobody in particular. The shade in question was an unfortunate choice resembling an unripe banana. Abigail wondered if he was joking.

Mr. Archibald assessed Greymore. "I favor her in pink myself."

"Pink? No, green quite becomes her."

"Either that or red." Mr. Archibald tilted his head as he regarded Greymore. "My sister would be lovely in a brazen red making her the center of admiration and scorn."

Mr. Graham made a sour face. "Pink doesn't look good on anybody." Next to Mr. Graham sat the pink-clad Mrs. Graham, whose dress appeared to brighten as her skin paled. "With one exception: Miss Archibald would look stunning in pink." His wife curled in on herself.

Greymore gestured with his half-empty glass to Mr. Graham. "What do you know about women, Graham? Pink is far too innocent a color for a lady and should be reserved for the schoolroom."

"What are you implying about my sister?" Mr. Archibald rose to his feet.

Mr. Graham stood on Abigail's other side.

"Nothing you didn't already imply yourself." Greymore leaned back in his chair. "All I'm saying is a woman shouldn't wear pink, but perhaps it would look becoming on Miss Wolcott and Miss Riverton."

Abigail stared at Greymore in openmouthed horror. Then a wave of relief settled on her. At least her ruination hadn't spread to the gathered party. What was the man thinking saying such things at dinner? Was he already drunk?

Mrs. Graham fled the room then, followed by Delia and Miss Archibald. Abigail and Lynette, too enthralled to move, watched as the scene unfolded.

"Keep your hands off my sister." Mr. Archibald's fists clenched at his sides.

"I wouldn't dream of touching her, spoiled goods and all."

Mr. Archibald meant to lunge across the table at him, but Carrington held him back. They hadn't expected Mr. Graham to do the same, launching himself and his solid fist into Lord Greymore's proud face. Mr. Travers stood a few paces away from the fighting men, amusement brightening his eyes. He only moved when Carrington yelled at him to stop the fight. Footmen raced into the room but not before Greymore and Mr. Graham had both drawn blood.

Mr. Travers kept Greymore back with little effort, the viscount not being much of a fighter. Three footmen struggled to keep Mr. Graham from renewing his attack.

"You bastard." Mr. Graham spat blood from the open cut on his lip.

Greymore gave a brief bow of his head. "Yes, I know. It's better than being a cuckold though."

Mr. Graham broke free of the footman then, but Carrington and Mr. Archibald caught him.

"Get him out of here!" Carrington yelled at his brother.

"I'm going." Lord Greymore shook off Mr. Travers's hands.

Carrington rounded on Abigail and Lynette. "Ladies, would you kindly retire?" His voice was calm but edged with irritation.

Lynette crossed her arms. "I live here, and Miss Riverton is our honored guest. We have every right to be here." Carrington cast his sister-in-law a dark look, which he then directed to Mr. Travers, who sighed.

"Really?" Mr. Travers obeyed his elder. He gathered Lynette and motioned for Abigail to follow.

The excitement was over, and she figured someone would fill her in later. They exited to the hall, where Lynette stormed off with a toss of her hair.

"What was that about?" Abigail asked Mr. Travers as he led her away.

"I really shouldn't talk to you about this." His halting voice seemed aimed to convince himself.

She snorted. "Who cares? Tell me."

"I don't rightly know. I think we just witnessed the fallout of what happened between the Grahams. It would appear it involved Greymore."

"What of Mr. Archibald?"

"That seems more complicated, and I don't believe Miss Archibald has any interest in Greymore. Yes, quite shocking."

Abigail squinted at him. Why did he insist she was interested in Greymore? The man was nice enough to her, but she couldn't see herself with him. She marveled at the nerve of Lord Greymore for appearing at dinner at all.

"I hope this will keep you away from Greymore. At least be wary until we can get the guests out of the house. William will want to rule everyone out before we can have any peace." Mr. Travers studied her as they came to her door. "That isn't a challenge, Miss Riverton."

Her shoulders stiffened. The man was as dense as a lamppost.

She arched a brow at him, remembering Carrington lecturing his brother. "Why, Mr. Travers? It's not as if I'm not already ruined, didn't you say so?"

Mr. Travers groaned. "You're as bad as Delia. I wanted to alarm my brother."

"Next time why don't you use some other girl's heartbreak to entertain him?" Her otherwise steady voice wavered as her throat tightened. She opened her door. "Or maybe you prefer causing that yourself?" She shut the door on his reply.

She had wanted to hurt him since she had overheard him talking about her. His assumptions about her interest in Greymore only heightened her anger. Yet the echo of her words left a hard pit in her stomach, and the weight festered until tears stung at her eyes.

No matter how she insisted, she couldn't change Mr. Travers's mind. How could she confess to him what she couldn't admit to herself? She was broken. Love wouldn't have her.

She was an adult and knew Lord Greymore was a poor choice for a suitor, but that didn't mean he couldn't be her friend. Greymore knew more than he let on, and she was bound to discover the truth if she befriended him. She could solve Briarwyck's mysteries as surely as she predicted the villains in her novels. She would make Mr. Travers regret his words when he saw she had taken up the challenge, even if she had no romantic interests in the viscount.

CHAPTER SEVEN

INSTEAD OF RESTING, as Mr. Travers suggested, Abigail sought out the one person who may have answers and would actually discuss them with her, Lynette.

Once Abigail was sure Mr. Travers had descended the stairs, she located Lynette's room with the help of a maid. She knocked softly at the closed door. Hurried shuffling came from inside, and Lynette cracked the door.

"Oh, it's you. Come in." Lynette widened the door and walked back into the room to sit on her bed.

Lynette's quarters were decorated in the usual red and yellow, but Lynette had placed bright-green blankets and hangings over every available space, an act of defiance of the tired family hues. Other than the colors, the room was roughly identical to Abigail's, except the view from the windows overlooked the garden instead of the sea.

Abigail hesitated inside the door. "Were you waiting for someone?"

Lynette shrugged. "Only on the chance I'd receive some lecture or other."

"What for?"

"I have no idea, but I seem to get them when I least expect it." Lynette reached below her bed to pull out a wooden box and opened it to reveal a deck of cards. "I take it you're enjoying your stay?" Lynette gave her a slight smile and shuffled the deck.

"It certainly has been interesting."

"It is that. In any case, I'm glad you're here. I find the cards are more accurate with an extra person. Wouldn't you agree?" Lynette patted a place next to her on the bed.

Abigail settled down with keen eyes on the deck. "Yes, of course. It may have to do with more insight, but one never knows. I didn't bring my own deck, a pity, since they would be helpful right now."

"Exactly. We'll do you first. Unless you have questions."

Abigail shook her head. She chose three cards and placed each facedown in front of them. Lynette picked up the first card, which represented the past. She rested it faceup—five of hearts.

"Oh dear." Lynette grasped Abigail's hand. "I wish you had come with us when we first departed."

She remained silent, not wanting to elaborate. The five of hearts was no surprise; it told the story of the past month of despair, powerlessness, and loss. Abigail wondered if the cards could sense the pain through her fingers or if she herself knew on some level which card would tell her story. Lynette hesitated, studying Abigail's expression, and flipped the second card, her current state.

"Eight of hearts. Does that mean anything to you?" Lynette chewed on her lip, her expression thoughtful.

Abigail gave a short nod. "I've put the past behind me"—at least, physically—"but I have some hard choices to make. Though, I don't know what the choices are."

"Perhaps the last card will show us." Lynette turned the third card. "Knave of diamonds? This is interesting. Anyone I know?"

"I haven't the slightest, but that just means I haven't realized his qualities. Maybe we should have done a four spread." Abigail sighed, frustrated with the new questions the cards dealt. "Let's ask about the murder. I hate when the cards are indecipherable until the events have passed."

"Isn't that the nature of fortune-telling?" Lynette sniffed and traced the deck with her finger. "The cards only predict the future so much as we can. The only real accuracy is looking back. We can use them to find clarity and guidance, but we can't know what it's telling us about the future until it has already happened. I'm hopeful for you though. Briarwyck should bring more balance to your life."

"That's the longest you've spoken since I've arrived." Abigail gave her an encouraging smile. Normally Lynette remained silent until a conversation provoked her passion, then she couldn't be kept silent.

"I'm quite serious." Lynette shuffled the cards. "All right, who murdered Sir Peter?" She drew a card and placed it faceup. "Knave of clubs? Really? We already know that. He's a murderer, for God's sake."

"Try again. Maybe ask why he did it."

"Hmm…all right." Lynette shuffled the deck and drew another card. "Five of diamonds. I suppose someone is in need of money. That's half the household, and the other half wouldn't mind having more." Lynette shuffled the deck absentmindedly. "Maybe we should try this another time, when we have more specific questions."

Abigail tilted her head in thought. "Or we could try a séance."

"That's a brilliant idea." Lynette met her gaze with wide-eyed enthusiasm. "I don't know if Delia would be okay with it though."

"Why wouldn't she be?"

"I don't know. She has become a bore since her marriage." Lynette gazed toward the door, a frown creasing her brow.

"Did you know my room used to be Laura's?" Abigail lowered her voice as though they were no longer alone. "She could've died in my bed."

Lynette settled the cards back in their box and turned to Abigail. "Really? Well, now we know where we'll hold the séance. Aren't you afraid to be alone in there?"

"I do feel a bit uncomfortable." Abigail shifted on the bed.

"But I haven't gotten the chance to really be alone in there. I have Alma. It's exciting, to be sure."

"I wouldn't sleep in there." Lynette rubbed her palms over her arms. "You're welcome to join me if you're visited in the night."

"I'll be fine. In fact, I think I'll go to bed now." She rose to her feet and stepped to the door. "It seems nobody had any inclination toward a late supper."

Lynette accompanied her to the door. "We rarely do. Sometimes Delia will get these late-night cravings, and some of us eat to keep her company, but usually dinner is so large we're full until morning. It isn't like New York, where we rationed our flour and meat."

"Then your family fooled me. I was amazed you were able to have such extravagant meals. My mother was always scrambling to make sure we had enough for the parties, but then Foxglove would ruin our plans." Abigail's lips twisted up. "At least that business is over." She opened the door and bid Lynette good night.

"Remember, I have more than enough room in my bed."

"Thank you." Abigail's voice was steadier than her feet as she stepped into the hall. Having made the decision to return to her possibly haunted room, she couldn't back out now.

The quiet hallway emphasized the sounds of her light footsteps, the only noises other than the occasional muffled voices behind closed doors. When she made it to her own hallway, she passed a room where the occupants argued, but she didn't stop to find out what was said. One of the speakers grew louder, and she rushed past the door. It clicked open and closed. Footsteps thudded behind her.

"Miss Riverton, I thought you were in bed." Abigail jumped and peered back to see Mr. Archibald behind her.

"It's too early for me. I was visiting Lynette in her room."

His gaining strides would soon overtake her. An uneasy heaviness settled in her stomach, and she hurried her steps.

"Perhaps you overheard the argument with my sister?" His voice held an ugly bite.

"No, I was merely passing by." Abigail grew cold, and sweat collected on her brow.

He followed her, content to stalk just behind her. "Indeed? Then you have no interest in my sister's troubles?"

"They are none of my business, sir."

"You aren't curious?" Disbelief altered his tone, calling her lie.

"Of course I'm curious, but it's not for me to know." Why was this hallway so damned long? She wished he would take a hint and retreat to his rooms.

He chuckled, an alarming sound in the darkened hallway. "Then maybe you were looking for me."

She took a deep breath. "As I said, I was speaking with Lynette."

"The pretense continues. A girl like you is always playing games with men, but I see right through you. Lead on, Miss Riverton. I've waited long enough."

Abigail stopped midstride and pivoted on her heel. She was not ten feet from her room, but the last thing she needed was Archibald cornering her there. She squared her shoulders, her fists balled up at her sides.

"You're mistaken, sir. I have no such designs. If you'll excuse me, I'd like to sleep now." Her body trembled, but her face was stern, and she stood her ground.

"Girls like you always have designs." He glowered at her, his pupils engulfing his irises. "You come to England to play around where nobody knows you, and you meet your fate at the altar with some unsuspecting man. I've seen it countless times. Then there are the girls who skip the play simply to be married. Whichever you are, I'd like to get down to it. The maids here are little sport."

She suppressed the urge to fall back. "You're delusional. These girls you speak of are products of your imagination."

"I assure you, they're quite real. I'm in an ill mood, but I'm up to the task. Unless you prefer Hugh or Greymore, though I believe the viscount is under guard." He stepped closer, forcing her back. She cursed her weakness but didn't want him any closer.

"Why is he under guard?" Maybe if she kept him talking, he would grow bored with her.

"So you are interested in him. I suspect it's so Mr. Graham doesn't murder him. Poor man. I assume the Grahams will separate soon, and such a happy couple they were. Poorly done by Greymore. Dealing with husbands is a nasty business." He moved closer to her, and she jumped away in alarm.

He scowled down at her. "I'm not Hugh or Greymore, but you won't care in the end." He pounced then, seizing her shoulders and pushing her into her door.

She locked her limbs in front of the closed door and flattened herself against it. "Let me go. I have no interest in you."

"I understand that now, but what you don't realize is I don't care. I've had it with women today, and you'll be the balm I need." He pressed her shoulders into the door and took her lips with his. Whiskey and false importance emboldened him. She tried to scream, but his wet mouth consumed the sound. Her stomach soured at the sloppy, copper-tinged taste of his lips.

A determined rage stole through Abigail. She drew her knee up into his groin and smacked her foot down onto his toes. He grunted and doubled over, leaving her enough time to grasp the handle of her door and open it with a bang against the wall. Archibald regained himself and leveraged his body to stop the closing door.

"Get out." Her breaths came short and hurried.

"After that, there's no way I'm letting you go. You're asking for it." His voice was a low roar as he stepped into the room.

"Please, don't do this." Abigail frantically scanned the room for a weapon. "I'll scream." The only threat that remained to her.

"You do that. I'll be able to tell the whole household you're a husband hunter and a whore. Everyone in Cornwall will know by noon and the rest of England will know at the end of the week how the slut American will throw herself at eligible men, but if that's what you want." He shrugged. "Who am I to judge?"

A tapping sounded in the hall, and they both turned toward it. Mr. Travers stood in the doorway, a pistol aimed at Archibald's head.

"Get out, Archibald."

Abigail stumbled to the side, out of firing range.

"You would shoot a guest in your brother's house? The gun will probably explode in your face." Archibald's lips curled back on a sneer.

"Or yours." Mr. Travers grinned, more tooth than lip, and gestured to Archibald with the pistol. "I believe you're a gambling man. Do you like the odds?"

"You could hit Miss Riverton as well. I'm sure my attentions would be preferable to that."

Mr. Travers sighed and raised his pistol to the ceiling. "Miss Riverton, are you worried about my shooting you?"

"No, sir." Abigail made herself smaller against the wall.

"Do you want me to shoot him with the chance of your being shot, or would you rather he rape you?"

"I'd rather die than have him touch me."

"Very well. There you have it, Archibald." Mr. Travers aimed once again.

Archibald raised his hands. "Wait. I'll leave. I'd rather not disturb Alice by destroying my clothes."

"I'm sure she would be more distressed over your mangled face and missing brains. Oh, but she must be used to that." Mr. Travers gestured for Archibald to move to the door. Archibald did as he was told, and once he'd passed Mr. Travers, he jumped into a sprint.

Abigail slumped to the floor and gasped out her breath.

Mr. Travers gazed down at her. "Are you all right?"

"Fine. Go get him."

Without a word, Mr. Travers rushed after Archibald, and a

crash down the hall followed. Shouts and thumps echoed back to her, and Mr. Travers returned to her room. He looked disheveled but not much more than usual. His blond hair dangled over his dark eyes. She wanted to soothe away the concern etched around them.

She fought between embracing him and crying under her bed. The dirty sensation burrowing into her skin seemed more than enough for her heightened emotions.

"He won't be any more trouble." He set his pistol down on a table outside of her door.

"What did you do?" She attempted to see past him into the hall.

"I knocked him out. The footmen will drag him back to his room and lock him in. It was a good thing I came in time."

"You were going to shoot him." Her body shook, and she crossed her arms over her knees.

"Of course I wasn't going to shoot him. I'm not a fool."

"Then what were you doing with a pistol?"

"Threatening him. He didn't know I wasn't going to shoot him. It wasn't even loaded, since I barely had time to grab it." He leaned over her, and she flinched away from his searching eyes.

"What if he had called your bluff?" She gulped and tried not to picture the possible aftermath if Archibald had gained control.

"It worked, didn't it? Let me help you." Mr. Travers offered his hand.

She stared at it but didn't reach out.

"It's over now. You're safe." Why did their encounters always result in her on the ground?

She accepted his hand, and he brought her to her feet. A shock of awareness moved between them, and a sharp tingle spread over her skin. Abigail jerked back her hand and brushed at her skirts.

She inhaled deep breaths and spoke again. "I'm sorry. I do appreciate you coming along when you did. It was..."

He shifted his weight and looked as if he wanted to reach out to her, but he refrained. Instead, he cleared his throat. "I only wish I'd come sooner. I saw him kiss you in the hallway, and I thought it was mutual until you attacked. I had to run back to my room. It wasted too much time."

She dropped her gaze to the floor. "I would never. He disgusts me. You were just in time, and I'm in your debt."

"Nonsense. I wouldn't have left you to Archibald. Besides, it was quite liberating to have an excuse to punch him. Wasn't it?" His smile reached his eyes, and she grinned in return.

"Yes, it was good to hit him."

Rapid footsteps grew near in the hallway.

"My reinforcements have arrived," Mr. Travers said as Carrington and Delia rushed into the room. They arrived in messy robes thrown over nightclothes. Delia curled a protective arm over her shoulders, and Carrington stood close in front of her.

"Did he hurt you?" Delia leaned into Abigail, who shook her head. "I'm going to kill him."

"I thought we would have some relief now that we have Greymore out of the house." Carrington regarded Abigail with a concerned frown creased between his brows.

"Greymore left?" Mr. Travers's gaze focused on Abigail.

"I ruled him out after learning he was with Mrs. Graham during the time frame of the murder. I thought it would be wise to have him leave for the sake of Miss Riverton and Lynette. It seems our problems are bigger than that." Carrington's exhaustion deepened his crow's-feet.

"What kinds of guests are you subjecting the women to? For God's sake, man. Miss Riverton could've been killed. What will her parents think?" Mr. Travers raised his voice and widened his stance.

Abigail shrank into Delia. "Please don't tell my parents. They'll never let me go anywhere again." Delia reassured her with a nod and squeezed her shoulders.

"You're right, of course." Carrington regarded his brother. "I didn't think they would be a problem, since they've been guests for years."

Mr. Travers's nostrils flared. "Clearly you were wrong. Already a man's dead, a marriage is ruined, and Miss Riverton has been attacked."

Carrington's face darkened. "I'm aware."

"I'm all right, no harm done." Abigail straightened in Delia's arms and forced her widest smile at Mr. Travers.

"What would have happened if I hadn't been around?" Mr. Travers's tone grew solemn. He nodded when her face fell. "We must make sure nobody is alone until we find out what's happening."

"That would be a smart plan." Delia lifted her fist to her mouth in thought. "I'll have Lynette stay with me, and Carrington will be in his adjoining bedroom. Hugh, you take the empty bedroom next to Abigail. The Grahams and Archibalds have each other to worry about."

Mr. Travers opened his mouth as if to protest, but she continued, "You promised me, and we can't sleep three to a bed." Abigail knew this wasn't precisely true, since Delia's bed was enormous, but she said nothing, preferring her own snore-free sleeping arrangement.

Carrington studied his wife, and a small smile crept across his face. "It's fine with me. My dear, perhaps you'll give Abigail the use of one of your knives?"

Delia brightened at the suggestion. "Of course, and maybe Alma could also sleep in your room?"

Abigail groaned. "Alma keeps odd hours. She barely sleeps at all. It took me years to get her not to rustle about in my room before dawn. Besides, she's usually nearby."

"Very well. I'll make sure you're fully armed." Delia directed a stern look at her brother-in-law. Mr. Travers frowned at her in response.

Carrington nodded to his wife as she left the room.

Abigail studied her host. "What will you do with Mr. Archibald?"

"If my wife got her way, we would castrate and hang him. He'll be confined to his room until we've ruled him out. I've sent for assistance in investigating the murder, but it could be as much as a week before anyone gets here." He paused. "After that, it isn't up to me to decide."

Abigail paled. "Then he could go free?"

"He may if he isn't a murderer. The court in Truro will side with him without solid evidence his advances were unwanted. Even then…"

Abigail's knees became unsteady, and she stumbled a step. Mr. Travers grasped her arm. This time, she didn't draw away. Something seemed right about the gesture, familiar.

"You'll be safe as long as I'm around." Mr. Travers looked down at his hand and released her. His lips turned up into a wicked smile when Delia reentered. "My dear sister has some deadly steel that will comfort you as well. She's quite a collector."

Delia held up a blade clenched in her fist. It was at least six inches long, excluding the hilt. She handed it to Abigail, who noted the intricately carved garden of flowers on the wooden handle. The double-edged blade was sleek and sharp. Abigail loved it on sight.

Delia must have noticed her approval. "It was a wedding present from Carrington's father."

"An odd gift."

She gave Abigail a wry smile. "Somebody told him I like a good blade." Delia turned to Mr. Travers. "Remember your promise."

He nodded. Delia and Carrington took their leave once they were satisfied with Abigail's safety.

"Do you need anything else?" Mr. Travers was half-turned to the door.

"I can manage."

"Well, scream if you're in any danger. Knock if you need anything else. Try not to stab yourself." He raised an eyebrow and considered her. "Do you know how to use that?"

"I assume you stab with the sharp end."

He laughed. "Basically. Point the blade at me." With slow, deliberate movements, he guided the point to rest at his abdomen. "This would be a good target for you." He moved her hand this time and adjusted the dagger over his heart. "If you get close enough. You need to hit as hard as you can."

Her own heart thudded through her grip. He was close now, his breath tickling her hair. Pressure built in the air between them, and his touch left a whisper behind.

"Now, if you're in bed or on the floor." He adjusted her hand to hover over his thigh. "If you strike here, it can be deadly."

Her breath quickened as their eyes met. She bit her lower lip.

He released her hand, and her air left in a whoosh.

"The goal is not to need the dagger." Her gaze faltered. "Are you a sound sleeper?"

"I don't plan to do any sleeping." He cleared his throat and backed up a step to put some distance between them.

"No, you must rest. Mr. Archibald is locked in his room."

"I would feel better if he were dead." He moved the rest of the way to the door. "Get some sleep. You've been through an ordeal. Put your mind at ease."

She was at ease. Strangely, she felt safe for the first time since she had arrived at Briarwyck. Murderers, ghosts, and thunderstorms were no match for Mr. Travers's presence. She didn't want him to leave, but she couldn't think of a reason to detain him.

It would never work.

"Thank you, for everything." She gave him a gracious smile.

He nodded slowly. "I'll try not to wake you. We wouldn't want you to get startled and stab me."

She clicked her tongue. "Nonsense, you don't frighten me."

"I should." That mischievous Travers grin played across his face, adding a spark to his eyes. "I should." He closed the door behind him.

Chapter Eight

When abrupt noises outside her window startled Abigail awake, the sounds Mr. Travers made, from the rustling of paper to his shuffling across the floor, were like a lullaby easing her back to sleep.

Once, faint footsteps scuffed in her room, and she grasped the dagger with white knuckles, but she was alone. She wondered if Laura watched her and hated Abigail for sleeping in her room. She fancied the ghost had sent gusts of wind pounding like fists in a wordless warning for Abigail to stay on her guard.

Her mind tangled with possibilities.

Mr. Travers was a shout away, and since she had never met Laura, the ghost couldn't have a grudge against her. Yet maybe the ghost had lost all sense in death and needed no reason to plague the living. This line of thought proved her undoing when the moonlight through the curtains cast shadows and took demonic forms that crept across the walls to hover over her in bed.

She cried out.

Mr. Travers cursed and scrambled about next door. A knock tapped at the adjoining door. "Is everything all right?"

"Yes. Sorry, I had a nightmare." She hadn't been asleep, but she wouldn't explain that to him.

He grunted. "All right, go back to sleep."

"Mr. Travers?" She spoke before she thought better of it.

"What?"

"Is Briarwyck haunted?"

A long pause followed, and she wondered if he'd heard her. Then a low rumble disturbed the silence as he laughed.

"Never mind." She thanked the door between them for hiding her scarlet face.

"Stop troubling yourself. No ghosts will get you." The laughter chimed in his voice.

She fell back against her pillow and sighed. Could he find her more ridiculous than he already did? Strangely enough, their exchange reassured her more than anything, and she drifted off into a deep, dreamless sleep.

Hours later, her eyes flew open, and she glanced around the room to the source of her disturbance. Sun peeked around the sides of the curtains, lighting her empty room.

A high-pitched scream echoed from the hall and vibrated off the walls. She threw herself out of bed and wrapped her nightdress in a robe. Her feet bare, she hurried across the cold floor to peer out the door. A small group of people gathered at the doorway of one of the rooms down the hall. She couldn't quite tell whose quarters it was, so she ventured to join the assemblage.

Mr. Travers intercepted her approach, shaking his head and holding up his palms to prevent her advancing. "You don't need to see this. Go back to your room."

Carrington guided a white-faced Miss Archibald, who was the source of the scream, from the room down the hall. Mr. Graham gazed into where she'd come from, his face hard and expressionless.

"Why? What is it?" Abigail pushed Mr. Travers aside and dodged his efforts to pull her back. Curiosity had gotten the better of her, and she made it to the door before anyone had the chance to block her view. She stood transfixed and unblinking, unable to comprehend the scene.

Archibald's naked form sprawled across the bed horizontally.

The usual red-and-yellow bedding was obscured by a dark shadow behind his head. She took a step closer and gasped when she recognized a thin red ribbon cut jaggedly across his pale throat. She slapped a hand over her mouth and allowed Mr. Travers to guide her from the doorway.

He leveled his lips at her ear, and his warm breath heightened her awareness. "You shouldn't have seen that."

She trembled at the image imprinted on her eyes, and he pulled her against his chest to shield her from the horror she had seen. His quickened heartbeat did nothing for her nerves, but his slow exhales and his soft caress over her hair kept her from mindlessly screaming as she fled from the hall.

She closed her eyes tight. "What happened?"

"We don't know. The footman who watched his door is missing. Mr. Graham discovered Archibald after finding the door open. He went to get Carrington, and when they arrived, Miss Archibald had found him. Her screams alerted me."

"Why is he naked?"

"Apparently he slept that way."

Abigail blinked up at Mr. Travers's face, and he arched a brow. "Is that normal?" Her curiosity got the best of her at the worst of times.

"I can't speak for all men, but I do as well."

"Really?" She realized how close he was then, smelling traces of salt and coffee. He studied her. The corner of his lips quirked up and drew her attention. Her tongue made a sweep of her own lips.

"I mean, I'm surprised it's that common." Her voice came out a whisper.

"Why is that?"

She knew he was teasing her, playing with her flustered emotions. She uncoiled from his protective arms and secured her robe more firmly. How did she get herself into these situations? What gave her the foolish idea of discussing nudity while embracing an annoyingly attractive man in the hallway? She had narrowly escaped that trap with Nigel. Never again.

The others appeared too preoccupied to have noticed the embrace.

She spoke to fill the silence once she regained her composure. "I suppose you're quite abnormal." She stepped around him with the intention of returning to her room. He caught her arm, stopping her midstride.

"I'm abnormal in all the best ways." He released her with a low laugh.

Her eyes widened at him, and she scurried back to her room. His faint chuckle faded out behind her. She pushed away the heat that crept up her cheeks and focused on straightening her walk to escape in a somewhat dignified manner.

Once she reached the privacy of her room, she lost all composure and dropped back to her bed. The soft down of the mattress did nothing to ease the image of Archibald's lifeless body. He was almost unrecognizable as the same person.

He was gone. In death, the features remained the same, but something was missing. Life itself left an imprint on the body and disappeared with one's demise. Almost the absence of a glow, but Archibald had never glowed. His was the lifting of a shadow, or the removal of a parasite.

She would have preferred his disappearance and not this horribly violent end. The search for regret proved futile in her tangled emotions, but the loss of human life nagged at her heart.

Poor Miss Archibald.

Abigail remembered how the loss of Delia's brother had eaten away at her friend. Losing a twin must be like losing a limb, a constant all of your life only to be ripped away, forever throwing everything off-kilter. She didn't know Miss Archibald well, since it was impossible to avoid the brother without avoiding the sister, but she resigned herself to being kind to the woman.

The timing of his death highlighted the motives of many of the household. She had doubts of anyone's innocence but her own. Then there was poor Sir Peter. Was this murder somehow connected to his? Perhaps homicide was a normal occurrence at Briarwyck or Cornwall in general. Maybe she should have stayed in war-torn New York.

Briarwyck had promised a distraction, something to shake up her life and thrust her into the best of her novels. Unfortunately, the upheaval had become a hurricane, the reality proving far more uncomfortable than she'd imagined. The house made her startle at every creak and rattle, and the other guests failed to put her at ease. All but Mr. Travers, who was out of her range.

This was not the Cornwall of her cherished stories.

A short while later, the remainder of the household scattered around the breakfast table. The air was thick with suspicion. Strangely enough, everyone was present for the meal, as though their absence would proclaim guilt. The party had broken into two groups, the women clustered together at one end of the table and the men at the other.

When Abigail attempted to take a seat next to the puffy-eyed Miss Archibald, the woman glowered at her. Abigail froze, taken aback by the rebuff. Stepping away, she gazed along the table to look for any type of welcome, but her options were limited. She settled for a seat between the two groups by a grim-faced Mr. Travers and a sarcastic Lynette.

"Don't take it personally." Lynette gave her a slow smile. "Half the household thinks you murdered Mr. Archibald. The other half doesn't care if you did or not but thinks you would be justified."

Abigail frowned at her. "What side do you take?"

"The third side: if you killed Mr. Archibald, then I wish you'd at least let me in on it. Did you?"

"Of course not." If so many thought she was a murderer, how would she eat with them? What if they turned on her? Poisoned her food?

"Well, I've known you for years, and even I questioned your innocence. You, Abs, have a problem." Lynette pointed her fork at her.

"Mr. Travers can attest to my whereabouts. I was in my room all night."

He sighed beside her in answer.

"Even he admits he could have dozed off, and there are those who believe you acted together." Lynette smirked toward Mr. Travers.

"Why would we do that? Mr. Archibald was subdued in his room."

Lynette rolled her eyes at Abigail. "Who knows how people come up with these things? It could be from revenge? A love triangle? Out of spite? The ideas get wilder as the clock ticks."

The skin creased between Abigail's brows. "Who would believe such things?"

"Miss Archibald, for one. The Grahams seem to share the same belief but for different reasons. We've all at least thought of the possibilities."

"What about Delia and Carrington?" She could do without Miss Archibald and the Grahams, but her friends believing her a murderer?

"Delia is of the same mind as me, but Carrington seems to believe his wife is at fault. Apparently she made threats last night."

Clearly Briarwyck had gone mad. "I can't imagine Delia slitting anyone's throat, let alone overpowering Mr. Archibald. Wasn't she with you?"

"Yes, but that also doesn't mean I'm presumed without guilt. I'm sure you know I didn't kill him, nor did Delia leave me during the night."

"Would Carrington bring Delia up as a suspect?" The idea sent an icy shock through her, leaving her chest hollow.

"Goodness, no. At worst, he would scold her for being sloppy, but as far as I can tell, he's the only one who suspects her. A bit backward, might I add."

"So as the newcomer, the blame shifts to me?" Her shoulders

slumped as she contemplated hiding under the table.

Lynette patted her hand. "That's one reason, the other being your conflict with him shortly before his death. It was more peaceful here prior to your arrival, but you simply have poor timing. It's more likely Hugh would cause chaos."

He directed a half smile at them.

Abigail gazed back at him. "Do you believe I did it too?"

Mr. Travers kept his voice low. "Not particularly, but I don't have proof otherwise. I can only rely on my own ears that you didn't leave your room. Remember, I also saw your reaction to his corpse. The others didn't have that luxury. They've only our word. Somebody's lying, but all I know is it isn't the two of us."

"Then you don't believe me, brother?" Lynette's voice came out a melodic hum.

"You and Delia are the most adept liars I've ever had the pleasure of meeting. I don't know what to think, but I trust my brother's judgment." His attention went back to his meal.

Abigail picked a piece of bacon off her plate and chewed it thoughtfully. She'd never been accused of murder before. She had no way to prove her innocence other than locating the real killer and getting a confession. The bacon tasted wrong in her mouth, and she left it half-finished. This wouldn't do.

"Abs? Are you still up to the séance? I was originally going to invite Miss Archibald and Mrs. Graham, but the idea seems tasteless now. I think I can convince Delia to join us, at least."

Mr. Travers choked on his drink.

"Yes, but wouldn't it be better if we had more people?" Abigail asked.

Lynette tilted her head and tapped her spoon on the rim of her cup. "Hmm, I believe you're right. Maybe we can bring Delia's maid, Hope. Would Alma be up to it?"

"I really doubt it." Abigail exhaled a stream of breath. "Alma isn't at all sociable, and she wouldn't be comfortable mingling with us. I know; I've tried. She's a valuable maid but nothing like Delia's Hope."

"Then we've only one other option. Hugh, will you come?" Lynette's gaze settled on him.

He made a strangled noise. "No."

Lynette leaned toward him, over Abigail. "Please? We'll forever be in your debt."

He avoided their eyes. "It's foolish, and I'm sure William won't approve."

"Then you'll have something to laugh about. Don't you think you need more fun in your life?"

"I'll admit I'd enjoy irritating my brother, but this is hardly the time for it. I even know it's in poor taste." He attempted to return to his last few bites.

"Your whole personality is in poor taste, Hugh. If you won't do it for yourself, do it for Abigail. Don't you want to cheer her up?" Lynette petted Abigail as though she was a child.

Mr. Travers seemed to sense a trap and hesitated before responding. "I'm not sure this is the best way to go about it. Miss Riverton, wouldn't you rather spend your time walking the grounds or reading one of your infernal books?"

"I don't know. I enjoy a good séance. Last time, Delia and I were scared senseless when their dog, Pierre, knocked into the table. It was quite fun. I haven't yet seen the grounds though." Her excitement and hope shone in her voice.

"Well, I doubt I can talk you out of it in any case. I might as well see what the fuss is all about." He paused with the interruption of exclamations from the two excited women. "I'll only do it if Delia is all right with it. Also, I suggest you don't mention it to my brother. We don't need to create a larger rift between them."

This sobered them, and their faces settled into small, controlled grins.

"Tonight, then?" Lynette gained her feet.

"If we must." Mr. Travers stabbed at his plate without much enthusiasm.

Abigail nodded happily and returned to her own plate.

Lynette rushed off in determined strides.

"You know, I've never seen her this excited." Mr. Travers watched Lynette pull Delia out of the room. Indeed, Lynette seemed to have found new purpose.

"She only gets like this when she's passionate about something. Otherwise, it's like she's bored with life. Maybe she is." Abigail regained her appetite with something to look forward to, and she devoured the rest of her meal.

"You said you would like to see the grounds. I'd be happy to show them to you. I can arrange for an escort as well."

She analyzed his expression. He spent so much energy teasing her that she couldn't imagine any other motive. "Why?"

"I don't have anything better to do, and I made that ill-advised promise to Delia." His face was humorless. "Really, my brother's a better choice, but he has been preoccupied of late. He takes pride in this estate, and if he's unavailable, then I'd be doing him a favor by showing you around."

She winced inwardly. He regretted his promise to protect her and only saw her as a distraction from boredom. She would be his burden to carry for the sake of his brother and Delia.

"Very well. If Lord Carrington isn't available, then I'll take you up on your offer. I'm getting a bit crazy not leaving the house."

"Then it's settled." He rose to his feet. "I'll see who will accompany us, and we can meet in the parlor in an hour."

They parted ways, and Abigail went to change into more appropriate attire. She settled on a smart light-brown jacket and dress with boots. Alma arranged her hair securely to keep it from blowing out of her wide hat. She donned her leather gloves on the way down the stairs and noticed she was the last to arrive.

Mr. Travers had managed to assemble not only Carrington but Delia as well. He had tried to solicit Hope as a chaperone, but she had stayed in bed, sick since last night. Delia filled in for the maid, but when Carrington had heard of the proposal, he'd insisted on showing Abigail the estate himself.

Abigail thanked them and grinned to herself. Mr. Travers

winked at her. A thrill traveled over her flushed skin. Had he manipulated this whole tour to recruit the duo, bringing them together? She suspected he wanted to mend the bridge between the usually happy couple.

They headed out, Delia's arm linked with Abigail's and the men flanking them. Carrington walked beside Abigail to better narrate their journey. Briarwyck had a long, mostly forgotten history. The house and grounds had come into the Travers family through their great-grandmother's marriage and stayed neglected until Carrington had taken up the renovations. Nobody else in the family had an interest in living so far from society. The nearest village was almost a day's ride, and it had little in the way of people or goods.

The newly cultivated gardens were not quite finished to Carrington's standards, but the wild, rustic look of them emphasized the house's enchanting appearance nicely. The beech trees hung over the grounds like doting nannies. The vibrant green of the yard was edged by abundant wildflowers in an artist's palette of colorful splotches from bright red to pale purple.

Abigail inhaled deeply as if she could become a part of the beauty around her. Her eyes drank in the view before the path met with the coastline and the sparkling waters below.

Carrington suggested they walk along the coast while there was time and fair weather. Everyone was in agreement of the proposal, and Carrington led the way down the path with Delia at his side.

Abigail trailed behind to take in every sight and smell of the landscape. Her fingers graced over the pale-pink heath as a grassy scent floated along the wind. Mr. Travers kept her company but left her to her silent contemplation. It was a comfortable silence, and yet his presence carried a lightness and a steady hum between them.

Her boots sank down as the party descended to the sand, and she had to work harder to stay upright. She laughed, stumbled over the little hills, and fell to her bottom on the soft earth.

Delia sped off down the coast with Carrington's long strides closing in on her. Their playful shouts drowned out the waves as Delia kicked off her boots and waded into the water.

The sea air nudged at Abigail's memories of the trip across the ocean. Her dream no longer seemed foolish. Misleading and farfetched, maybe. Embarrassing for sure. Mr. Travers couldn't help that, and she should have spent the trip understanding her guide better.

Mr. Travers puffed out his breath when he stopped beside her. He watched his brother and Delia, and a weight lifted from his posture. He beamed, accenting his handsome profile.

"Thank you for planning this." Abigail stared up at him from beneath her hat. "The fighting was destroying them. I don't think it could have gone on much longer." She had judged his motives for the outing unfairly. She wasn't a distraction but an excuse to bring her dearest friend and his brother together. Nothing could be closer to her heart, and his actions resonated deep inside her.

"Agreed. My brother can't resist his wife when there's laughter and sunshine. Too much of this summer has been wasted in storms." Of course, he wasn't just talking about the weather.

She accepted his help to stand, uncertain of her own footing. Her breath caught as she tumbled into him. Their eyes met. A moment passed in a still world. And another moment shifted the heavy air between them.

He blinked and steadied her upright.

He kept a hand on her arm as they neared the water's edge. Their contact held a tingling thrill behind it. She chided herself; he was only making sure she didn't make a clumsy mess of herself.

So much beauty surrounded Briarwyck, but not the cultivated beauty she was accustomed to from her neighborhood in New York. Cornwall left her spellbound. She didn't think she would be able to leave.

"What's the matter?" Mr. Travers watched the light flee her face.

"I left a great deal of trouble behind me in New York, and I met trouble here. This place is more wonderful than I had imagined, but I fear I'll have to run away from it as well." She would leave her family and friends behind.

Leave him behind.

She pushed the thought away. Her novels were clouding her judgment. She had as much chance with him as King George had of accepting the independence of the colonies. None at all.

He studied her. "Where would you go?"

"I don't know." She shook her head. "I have cousins in Virginia, but I don't know if that would be wise right now with the war. I wish none of this had happened. Curse Archibald."

"My brother and I won't let them arrest you."

"How can you be so sure? Even you aren't above the law." As much as she admired his positive outlook, she took little comfort from his confidence.

Mr. Travers shrugged. "The constable on the way is a family friend, not to mention we're the ones paying him."

"I don't know whether to be relieved or disturbed by the legal system in this country. Of course, New York isn't much better off right now. Today I think I'd prefer the Traverses' sense of justice."

Carrington called to them. Delia was fatigued and wished to return. They agreed, and Mr. Travers helped his brother assist Delia back to the house. Abigail trailed along behind them, lost in her own thoughts.

Chapter Nine

Fortunately they returned just in time. A storm formed swiftly to overtake Briarwyck with enough force to make the last storm appear a slight breeze. The effect worked on the atmosphere of the séance that night. Delia was hesitant to hold it in Abigail's room, an improper location for Mr. Travers. What would Carrington think if he knew the reason for the choice of location? After constant pressure from Lynette, Delia gave in, and a table was set up for the occasion.

The room was left in shadow, candles dotting the space just enough for visibility. Mr. Travers was the last to arrive and snorted at the three women shrouded in darkness at the table. He shut the door behind him, and they welcomed him to sit down.

"Let's get this over with." Mr. Travers grasped hands from Delia and Abigail. "I have a new bottle of port needing my attention."

Abigail tried to focus on anything but his warm grip on her hand. How would they summon spirits if she couldn't even concentrate?

Delia side-eyed him. "You didn't drink enough at dinner?"

He glared at her. "Not nearly enough for this."

Lynette shushed them and gazed into the lighted candle before her, her eyes becoming unfocused. She mumbled to herself, her words unintelligible. Abigail narrowed her eyes at Lynette.

Since when did Lynette know Latin?

"Where did you get that nonsense?" Mr. Travers was the only one with any education in the language.

Delia leaned toward him to whisper. "She made it up."

Lynette leveled an icy stare at her sister. She swept her hand over the candle flame and retook Delia's hand, her attention on the flame as if it was an idol on an altar to the spirit world. Her deep breath made the flame dance, and her voice filled the room as if the spirits were deaf. "If there are any spirits with us, give us a knock."

Silence.

"Don't be afraid. Spirits, tell us you're here."

Again, silence.

"Maybe they don't want to talk to us." Mr. Travers gave Lynette a mocking smile.

"Quiet." Lynette shot the word at him. "Spirits, give us a knock."

Abigail squinted at the candle, worried she might miss some ghostly transformation in the flame. "We should've hired a medium."

Delia glanced her way. "With such short notice?"

Lynette shushed them again and turned her attention back to the dancing flame. The wind beat the glass in the window, which rattled like shaken knuckle bones. Mr. Travers glanced toward the noise as if he wished to hurl himself to the mercy of the sea.

Lynette cleared her throat. "Please, spirit, if you're here, answer my call with a knock."

A loud knock reverberated through the room, and the party jumped as one. Four sets of eyes searched the space.

Lynette shifted in her seat. "Spirit, are you there?"

Another knock, this one from behind Delia.

"Spirit, we want to ask you some questions. Two knocks for yes and one for no. Do you understand?"

Knock, knock. The disturbance came from behind Abigail and sent a chill down her spine. She grasped Mr. Travers's hand tighter.

"Spirit, did you die at Briarwyck?"

Knock, knock, behind Delia.

Mr. Travers peered at the location with his mouth agape. He shook his head as if to dispel the sound and glanced down at Abigail's hand in his. She forced her gaze onto the candle.

"Spirit, are you the ghost of Laura Travers?"

Knock, knock.

The group fell silent, all eyes now focused forward. This time, the knock had come from a new location near the window. Abigail had never witnessed such an active spirit, but Mr. Travers's grounding presence made the experience bearable.

Lynette raised her voice. "Laura, did you die in this bed?"

Knock.

"In this room?"

Knock.

Lynette frowned at the candle. "Somewhere else in the house?"

Knock.

"Did you die outside?"

Knock, knock.

Abigail sucked in a breath, and the candle wavered at her abrupt action. The rapid drum of her heart consumed her, and the hair on her arms and neck rose at attention. Mr. Travers arched a brow, and she squirmed beside him. Must he judge her here of all places?

Lynette paused and glanced toward the covered windows. "In the sea?"

Knock, knock.

"Did you fall?"

Knock. Lynette gasped but hurried on with her questions. Abigail and Delia leaned forward.

"Did you jump into the sea?"

Knock.

Abigail's grasp went white-knuckled. Her frantic gaze flew to

Mr. Travers, who watched the flame as if it was an annoying insect. He glanced up at her, and she hid her stare. Maybe now he would believe her.

Lynette's voice was strangled. "Laura, were you...were you thrown off the cliff?"

Knock, knock.

Mr. Travers yanked at his hands. "We need to stop this now."

Lynette stared him down. "Keep your hands where they are. We can't break the circle just yet."

He sighed and leaned back as far as his grip would allow. He made no further protest.

"Laura?"

Knock, knock.

Lynette gulped in a breath. "Do you know who killed you?"

Knock, knock.

"Was it a friend?"

Knock.

Lynette's gaze darted to her sister. "Was it family?"

Knock, knock. Delia gasped, and her eyes darted toward Mr. Travers.

"Did your husband kill you?"

Mr. Travers groaned, but a single knock echoed loudly through the room. Everyone's gaze fell on Hugh.

"Did Hugh push you?"

Knock, knock.

Mr. Travers rolled his eyes. "This is insane. I didn't kill Laura."

Lynette ignored his interruption. "Laura, are you sure?"

Knock, knock.

"Hugh?" Delia's face was a picture of confusion.

"I didn't." His jaw tightened. "Why don't you find out something useful like who killed Sir Peter or Archibald? Why would I kill Laura?"

"Guilty." A faraway voice rose behind Delia. They turned as one in the direction of the voice but once again, nobody was there.

"Guilty." From near the window. The voice trailed off as though it sounded from inside a tunnel. It was high-toned, more feminine than masculine.

"Murderer."

Mr. Travers rolled his head back. "That's quite enough."

"Murderer."

He pulled his hand from Delia's and massaged the bridge of his nose. "Really, any longer and they're going to turn on me."

"Coward."

"You have me there." Mr. Travers laughed. The women glanced around the room with matching frowns. Abigail inspected Mr. Travers. The man had no fear, but any sensible person wouldn't laugh when a spirit spoke to him. Something was off, and she opened her mouth to ask what was going on when the voice sounded again.

"Witless Tory."

Mr. Travers stood, freeing Abigail's hand, and his chair clattered to the ground as he strode to the bed and aimed a kick below the mattress.

"Ouch. No need for that." Through the faint light, Carrington pulled his tall frame from the ground. His blue-black hair shone, tousled, in the candlelight.

Abigail sat speechless, her eyes wide and unblinking.

Lynette scrunched up her nose. "How did you…?"

Delia groaned. "Felix, come out."

Movement rustled the curtains, and the sandy-haired boy appeared. He was barely recognizable, having grown at least three inches since Abigail had last seen him. He favored them all with a wicked grin he must have learned from the Travers brothers.

"Is there anyone else?" Anger singed Lynette's voice.

Delia folded her arms over her chest and glared at the two offenders. "They don't need anyone else. Felix is quite adept at throwing his voice. Carrington didn't even need to be in the room."

"Yes, I did. I wouldn't have missed this for the world. For the record, neither I nor Hugh were around when Laura died. I believe I've said as much to my wife." Carrington threw Delia a hard look.

"I wasn't asking the questions." Delia shifted her stance. "Honestly, I thought we were going to ask about the murders."

Carrington gave her a grim smile. "Then why use the blue room?"

"I'm sorry, Dee. This was my idea." Lynette didn't sound the least bit guilty.

"I somehow doubt Miss Riverton was completely innocent." Mr. Travers's eyes met Abigail's. His scrutiny pierced like a blade embedded in her sternum.

Abigail let out a puff of air and nodded. "I may have encouraged the plan. I'm sorry." She pushed her brows together. "Does this mean you weren't worried about Lord Carrington's reaction?"

"Quite the opposite." Mr. Travers's eyes brightened. "The idea has been a source of amusement since I told him about your plans. Felix overheard us and came up with the idea of interrupting your little ritual. We didn't take much convincing. I must say, it was a great success." His face tugged up in silent laughter, deepening the dimple in his chin. If only they were alone, she would slap him senseless for scaring her, and then she would kiss away the pain she'd caused, with abandon. She would have done the same thing.

"Well, traitors, Felix did an impeccable job." Delia regarded the boy with a half smile. He dropped a deep bow, a grin still splitting his face. She mussed his hair fondly and turned to her husband. "You could've let me know."

"Why spoil the fun? Although, I must add, accusing my brother of murdering my first wife was in poor taste, Felix." Carrington sobered. "I hoped one of you would at least reveal your thoughts on these murders. I'm at a loss here. Felix hasn't found any clues."

Felix's smile fell. "It's true."

"Does that mean you don't believe I had anything to do with it?" Abigail glanced from face to face. Heads shook around the room.

Carrington met her gaze, his kind bottle-brown eyes so like his brother's. "We didn't believe you would resort to such measures, and I trust my brother's observations."

"And mine." Felix's grin returned. "I'm a bit disappointed you didn't kill him. I considered it myself."

"He's joking." A nervous laugh bubbled from Delia's throat.

Felix folded his arms. "No, I'm not."

"It's fair to say most of us were thinking of murdering the man. For our own good, we probably shouldn't meet like this. If the guests find out, they might believe we're plotting something." Carrington ushered them to the door.

"We needn't care what they think. I can't wait for them to be out of the house," Delia said as she trailed after her husband.

Carrington placed a supportive hand on his wife's back, and an emptiness answered deep inside Abigail's chest. "I got word from the constable. He should be here tomorrow depending on the weather. He'll arrive earlier than I expected, a small mercy." Everyone followed them through the doorway, and Abigail moved to see them out.

Carrington stopped Hugh in the hallway with a hand on his shoulder. "Are you going to stay next door?"

Mr. Travers ran his fingers through his hair. "Do you think it's still necessary?"

"More so than ever. She may not be in danger from Archibald, but we still have a killer loose. At this point, I wouldn't be surprised if any one of them attempted to harm her. This house and its guests are a recipe for madness."

"Very well." Mr. Travers addressed Abigail, his face expressionless. "I'll be right next door as before."

She managed a small smile, and they left her to her room

only to be replaced by Alma.

Her maid was as quiet and uninterested as ever. Abigail had never heard an instance of her maid gossiping, an unexpected bonus to her diligent work. No better maid existed. Yet however much Abigail appreciated Alma's work, she longed for an ease in their conversation. Her maid undressed her in routine-like fashion, and it wasn't long before Alma asked if she wished for anything else. Abigail dismissed her; there was nothing more her maid could give.

Alone, Abigail allowed herself to experience the full weight of her foolishness. She no longer fancied she heard Laura in her room. At this point, if she were haunted, it would be by Mr. Archibald. The prospect did not frighten her. What was a ghost to a murderer? Any of them could be next, and she would be damned before a harmless spirit scared her out of the safety of her room.

The three women had long experimented with different forms of fortune-telling, communicating with the dead, and dream reading. This time had seemed different from the start, but she assumed that was due to the presence of Mr. Travers tugging at her senses.

The women had been able to summon their usual enthusiasm, but with Mr. Travers in the room, it had seemed, well, a bit stupid. He must have a bad influence on her. It wasn't like he didn't have fun, but he lacked the kind of awe making up much of her personality.

Abigail struggled with how to act around him. He was only a couple years her elder, but his experience and education made him seem older. What was even more maddening was when he showed an immaturity that baffled her. Most confusing of all, she longed for his company and hoarded her memories with him to relive in her head.

Every experience was enhanced when he was around. Mr. Travers was far above Nigel in every way but well out of her reach. The way the war seemed headed, she hadn't even a dowry to excuse her lack of titled relations. She would take what she could get and not form an attachment.

She carried these thoughts with her to breakfast the next day, determined not to lock herself in her room for meals. Last night's dinner before the séance had tortured her, and she didn't see how breakfast would be any different. Besides, she wanted to see Mr. Travers again. His occupancy of the room next to hers was an exercise in self-control. She wanted to converse with him for no better reason than to hear him speak.

To her disappointment, the seats next to him were taken. Now that she sought him out, he was deep in conversation with Miss Archibald. Instead, Abigail accepted a seat next to Delia. The Grahams didn't greet her but didn't snub her either. Miss Archibald kept her attention on Mr. Travers.

Abigail stabbed at her eggs as Mr. Travers laughed with Miss Archibald. The woman's giggles made Abigail flinch, and her fork handle imprinted into her palm. Didn't the woman's twin just die, or had Abigail missed something?

"What did your eggs do to you?" Delia's amusement was palpable in her voice.

Abigail inhaled a deep breath and slowed her movements with the utensil. "They are merely there."

"I see." Delia dragged out the words. "Perhaps you'd like to go riding with me? That is, if the weather remains favorable." The strong storm from last night had already cleared, leaving as fast as it had come. When she'd woken, the sky had been clear outside her windows.

"Should you be riding?"

Delia waved her off. "I've been assured I can ride for another month. I don't know where Carrington's grandmother gets her numbers, but if they allow me to ride, then I don't really care. That reminds me, I forgot to mention she arrived this morning to help me with my pregnancy. Terrible timing, but she was already on the way when the murders started, and she insisted she would stay despite the danger."

"Yes, unfortunate timing. I hope she can avoid this nasty business." Abigail couldn't understand why they would subject an older woman to this cursed house.

"Indeed. She was annoyed at her grandsons' lacking welcome and took herself off to her usual room after giving me unwanted pregnancy advice. So we'll ride while we can."

"That sounds sensible." Abigail glanced around at the click of the breakfast door. She dropped her fork when the beautiful form of Lord Greymore entered. The room fell to a hush until Lord Carrington arrived, and everyone spoke at once.

He raised his hand to silence them. A squat, wigged man appeared behind him in the door and took a seat beside Mr. Graham.

"Why is he here?" Mr. Graham's face bloomed purple, and his squinty-eyed glare followed Greymore.

"Lord Greymore and Constable North crossed each other's paths. Mr. North insisted Greymore return with him for the full story." Carrington settled on Delia's other side next to Lynette, and Greymore sat in the vacant seat next to Abigail. Dark circles rimmed his eyes, but a smug smile creased his lips.

"If I'm needed, I'll be in my room." Mr. Graham wiped his mouth, threw down his napkin, and hastened out the door. Mrs. Graham stumbled behind him, though they all knew by now the couple had separate bedrooms.

"Hypocrite." Greymore spoke under his breath. He gave Abigail a bright smile. "Did you miss me?"

She tilted her head to the side. "Well, you certainly make things interesting." In truth, she liked Lord Greymore. He had a way of lightening her vacation, and he never accused her of anything.

"Alas, I've returned to entertain you and your womanly companions." He made a seated bow.

Abigail's cheeks heated, and she shifted in her chair. "I have male companions too. Wouldn't you like to entertain them?"

"You know." He tapped a finger on the table. "The notion

hadn't occurred to me. Maybe if they were to ask."

She scrunched up her face. "Don't you usually do the seducing?"

"My, but you are direct. To be honest, I don't have to seduce them. Oh, I do flirt from time to time, but nothing ever happens unless the lady wishes it to."

"You certainly have a bad reputation for ravishing women."

"And it serves me well. Keeps the undesirables away." He winked and poured himself tea, an odd choice considering his usual preference.

"Yes, I've been warned away from you already." She twisted her lips to the side and indulged in another walnut scone.

"That's to be expected. May I ask who I have to thank?"

In answer, Abigail cast a furtive glance at Mr. Travers.

"Mr. Hugh Travers, naturally. We haven't been on good terms for some time." He seemed enamored with the roll he buttered.

"Why is that?"

"You could say we're rivals. Though, as I said, I don't make conquests. It seems I paid attentions to a certain lady he was interested in. Really, I had no idea, but he has taken to believing I steal women right from under him." Greymore shook his head. "I don't blame him, and if I could take it back, I would. I'm afraid I'll never have his friendship again."

Briarwyck must be a lonely place for Greymore. The other women seemed to avoid him, and his only ally was Carrington. Their host was busy with other matters. Well, he could count her as a friend. His situation as a pariah was not unlike her own.

"Lord Greymore, do you like horses?"

"I should say I've one of the most envied stables in England. In fact, I was on my way back to my babies." His gaze narrowed toward the constable.

"Perhaps you'd like to go riding with us today. I'm sure Delia wouldn't mind the company."

Greymore's eyes lit up. "That sounds delightful. It's certainly preferable to sitting around here while Graham plots my demise."

Abigail favored him with a wide grin. "It's settled, then. We ride at noon."

CHAPTER TEN

ABIGAIL WAS INEXPERIENCED with horses, but both Delia and Greymore assured her the horse she would be riding was a tame animal. The dappled gray mare certainly looked the part. The horse, Soot, had a dark, flowing mane and an overall silver quality to her coat. Delia's horse, Starlight, was a shining white mare that blended with her friend's light hair. To Abigail's surprise, Greymore's horse was not a large, intimidating stallion but a sleek flame-colored Arabian mare named Ember.

Constable North argued against their leaving, but Delia reasoned they were in no state to flee. Delia and Abigail had nowhere to escape, and Greymore left priceless valuables behind at Briarwyck in his trunk, including a family heirloom he had been entrusted with keeping safe. Passing the time pleasantly while waiting on Mr. North and Carrington's investigations was harmless. The dispute was settled when Greymore emptied all his pockets and handed Carrington all his banknotes and his treasured gold watch.

With no supplies and little opportunity in the middle of nowhere, they set off.

On the ride, Abigail was out of place with her basic horsemanship and soon fell behind them. They rode single file with Delia in the lead, and no one noticed Abigail slowing. She urged her horse on, but Soot sensed Abigail's fear of falling and proceeded cautiously. They trotted along the sand as she gave in to the view and slowed her horse further.

Up ahead, Delia and Greymore stopped to wait for her. Guilt crept up her chest and into her cheeks. Then two other riders came into view. She soon recognized Mr. Travers and Miss Archibald. A nagging urge to turn around almost won until Delia shouted for Abigail to catch up. She groaned and rode up next to her friend.

Miss Archibald, once again, ignored Abigail's existence. She appeared worn, her usual pale nose a bright red and her eyes swollen and tired.

Yet Mr. Travers was all smiles in the woman's company, and the sight sent a blow to Abigail's stomach. A preposterous reaction, since he had shown little interest in her other than a few suggestive comments and looks. The man was a helpless flirt, which only drew her to him. If she continued to seek his company, she would have to remain guarded to keep her heart intact.

The group was arguing about horses when Abigail arrived, and soon the topic gravitated to horsemanship. She stayed silent in her ignorance and amused herself by listening to the men's self-importance express itself.

"Mr. Travers is an excellent rider." Miss Archibald favored him with a fond smile. "Rarely do I see such fine riding."

"I thank you, ma'am, but I'm sure that's an exaggeration." Mr. Travers beamed through his false modesty.

Abigail reined in a growl, and pinpricks raked across her skin. This drivel between them had to stop. "Really? I was just admiring Lord Greymore's horsemanship. Ember's a beautiful horse." She gazed over at the animal. "I don't pretend to know ridership, but he makes a stunning figure in the saddle."

This got Miss Archibald's attention, and she directed her horse closer to Mr. Travers. "I'm quite fond of Mr. Travers's beast, Coffee." She motioned to the muscular brown stallion Hugh rode. "A fine horse and as fast as any Arabian."

Delia glanced between the women. "Perhaps we should have a race, then? Ember against Coffee. The names alone practically cry a good time. Now, if Soot were a faster horse." Delia's thought seemed to trail off. "What's your horse called, Miss Archibald?"

"Her name is Lady." She patted the butter-colored mare.

"Oh well, I was hoping for cream. What say you, gentlemen?"

Mr. Travers and Greymore eyed each other, and a long pause followed.

Greymore pulled back on his reins as Ember tugged forward. "What are the terms?"

"Ride around the large outcropping down the coast and back. If we have a tie, we'll take a vote on the winner."

Greymore gave a short nod. "Agreed."

"What about you, brother?" Delia looked to Mr. Travers, who studied the chosen course.

He frowned at the women. "There's a great deal of things for Coffee to stumble on."

Delia considered the area and tapped her reins in thought. "Hmm, maybe you're right."

Miss Archibald agreed it may not be the safest choice for a race. Perhaps she didn't believe Mr. Travers could win after all?

Greymore regarded Mr. Travers with a wry grin. "It's a simple enough run."

"Are you afraid of a little rock, Mr. Travers?" Abigail batted her eyes. If Greymore was willing to take his prized horse on the path, it must be safe enough. "If you forfeit now, then we'll simply assume Greymore wins."

Mr. Travers's brows crinkled as he shot her a sharp look. "I don't have to prove my skills to know I'm the better man."

Miss Archibald nodded along with him.

Delia tilted her head in confusion. "I thought we were judging horseflesh."

"Is there a difference?" Abigail smiled wide at Mr. Travers, but she wondered if she had gone too far. Seeing Mr. Travers with Miss Archibald had brought out the worst in her. No use turning back now.

Greymore threw his head back in laughter.

Mr. Travers watched her with lowered brows. "All right, Miss Riverton. You'll have your race." His voice was like gravel.

Delia cleared her throat. "What does the winner get?"

"Why, a kiss, of course. All race winners are rewarded with a kiss." Greymore's laughter still echoed in his amused voice.

"From whom?" Mr. Travers's mouth tugged to one side, and Abigail's heart jumped in her chest.

"Anyone you like. Winner's choice."

"Excluding Delia." Mr. Travers's firm tone left little argument. "Carrington will murder you if you lay a hand on her."

Greymore raised a hand to his chest. "How little you think of me. My host's pregnant wife is naturally off-limits."

Abigail fidgeted in her saddle.

The men lined up according to Delia's instructions. Abigail's scanned the scene with shifting eyes. She would never forgive herself for insisting on the race if something happened to either of the men.

She didn't dare move as Ember and Coffee dug at the sand.

"Are you ready?" Delia met the gaze of each man in turn.

Both men bobbed their heads and stared forward. Delia waved them on, and their burst of speed summoned a tide of sand. Coffee's longer strides thrust him into the lead, but Ember's sure footing on the sand gained her ground, and soon the horses were neck and neck.

Abigail bit her lip as she clenched her reins. The horses were almost to the outcropping when Coffee stumbled. The women gasped, but Mr. Travers righted the horse. Ember gained ground and rounded the rock. She shone like the sun when she emerged on the other side, and Abigail stared in awe at the vision of the flaming horse carrying Apollo toward them.

Coffee put on a burst of speed and cleared the rock. But it was too late. Mr. Travers eased up, appearing to concede the race to the other man.

Ember slowed and pulled up in front of them. Greymore dismounted, the rest of them followed suit, and Mr. Travers joined them, his posture loose and resigned.

Without any preliminaries, Lord Greymore took Abigail in his arms and dipped her in a passionate kiss. She squeaked in surprise at his dramatic actions, thinking the prize implied a chaste peck. Her hands grasped behind his neck to keep her from falling, and her heart gave an erratic thump while he explored every bit of his award.

When he brought her back up, she was breathless. She blinked at his smiling face and moved her hands firmly to her sides. Her skin blazed from her scalp down to her chest. For once, she couldn't summon anything to say.

"Now that was a kiss," Delia said through her laughter. "I wish I hadn't been out of the running."

"Lady Carrington, I would die before disappointing you, but your husband is a scary man to cross." Greymore winked.

Abigail regained her senses and caught a glimpse of Mr. Travers's hardened stare. She snapped her gaze away and noticed Miss Archibald had gone off to Briarwyck. The kiss had been beyond improper, but it was a game all the same. Still, she couldn't help but think Mr. Travers was disappointed in her.

They rode in pairs back to the house, Abigail and Greymore taking the lead. The viscount fawned over his horse after the win, promising her all manner of treats. The horse seemed to understand him, and when she broke into a proud strut, Greymore turned his attention to Abigail.

"I don't think I've had that much fun in months." He beamed. "The look on Hugh's face was worth all the danger of killing myself."

Abigail's mouth dropped open. "You implied the route would be fine."

"I was goading him."

She scowled at him and wondered if he was drunk. "He certainly hated losing, but what if one of you had been hurt?"

"We weren't, and I wasn't talking about his losing. He took that better than I thought he would. I was referring to the look he gave me while I kissed you."

She squinted at him. "What look?"

"Something between hopelessness and murderous rage, if you can believe it. Who knew he could show such a range of emotions in one look?"

She shook her head and turned her attention forward. "I didn't see anything."

"That's because I was keeping you preoccupied." Well, that was one way to put it. "Of course, now I'll have to watch my back even more. I don't suppose Hugh is the killer?" He sounded wistful. She couldn't fathom his reasoning.

She chose her words with care. "I don't believe so."

"Well, if he's not, he may be now."

"You're exaggerating. It was a game. I doubt he holds my virtue that highly. His obligations to Delia will only take him so far." She made a sour face.

Greymore regarded her with silence as they arrived at the stables. Delia and Mr. Travers dismounted beside them while Greymore helped her down, grasping her waist. His gaze shifted to where Mr. Travers stood, and he gave her a conspiratorial smile. She arched an eyebrow at him as he held her.

"I'll see you at dinner, dearest Abigail." Greymore leaned in to peck her cheek and bowed before departing.

Her mouth went dry, and she raised her hand to her cheek. His motives for showing her such attention left her frustrated. He wanted to poke the hornet's nest, but she couldn't prove to herself she was over Nigel if men kept playing these silly games with her.

Mr. Travers stormed off, and Delia stared at her as she would an exotic plant.

"What?" Abigail shut her eyes against the world.

"You gave him permission to use your name?"

"No, I didn't. He took the liberty to irritate your brother-in-law." She hadn't even noticed, too consumed with shame for accepting Greymore's false advances.

A groom collected the horses, and the group started toward the house.

Delia pursed her lips. "Right. In any case, I've never seen Greymore take an interest in having an actual conversation with a female or even initiate contact with one. Do tell me if you need me to make you a tonic."

"A tonic?" Abigail's mouth fell open. "No, I don't need one of your potions. I've no intention of ever needing one." Not anymore, anyway.

"You were lucky the first time back in New York with that awful man. I wish I'd been there for you. Then I brought you to Cornwall, and you have men flocking to you." Delia shook her head. "I don't understand what it is."

"Maybe it's my fallen woman allure?"

"I was going to say money, but that works too. Maybe I'll put a footman on your door, but he'll probably be seduced by your siren call." Delia giggled at her own joke. "Hugh should be enough protection, though I believe he thinks he's already failed. Do be nice to him. The poor man isn't getting enough sleep as it is."

"Fine, but I can't speak for those who follow my enchanting song into shipwreck," Abigail said in a dry voice.

"I just hope there won't be any more casualties."

She couldn't be sure whether her friend meant casualties from Abigail or the murderer or both. A change of topic to murder proved safest. "Did they ever find the footman?"

Delia sighed and slowed her step. "No, and all his belongings are still here. Carrington is worried it will spook off his staff. Some of them have worked here for years."

When Abigail reached her room, exhaustion took over. The day's events left her confused and indecisive. Alma suggested a bath, which she gladly accepted. The hot waters worked on her conflicted mind.

She didn't like being the subject of an ongoing male feud. Her novels glorified love triangles, but to her, they resembled being used in a game of tug of war with no clear winner. As the rope, she was ripped to pieces. Abigail already resisted the strain of their conflict. She would have to learn to distance herself and prevent being torn into some broken mess as she still bled from the wound left by Nigel.

The memory of Nigel made her want to curl into bed and forget dinner like the coward she was. She had been distracted since her arrival, but the hurt still ached when she was left with her own thoughts. She knew, alive or dead, he wasn't worth her energy, but every time she thought she was recovered, the ache returned like a weeping hollowness in her breast.

Nigel wouldn't have mourned her death, having embraced a life without her until he was killed. Why couldn't she do the same? She had invested so much emotional energy into him that she wondered how she felt anything at all.

But she did.

Abigail appreciated her time with friends and relished Mr. Travers's company. Yet her happiness fell flat. She had avoided his charms since she'd met him back in New York, and now she couldn't get enough of him. During her more hopeful times, she sensed he enjoyed her company too.

His new interest in Miss Archibald put everything in doubt. Not just Abigail's attraction but her friendship with him and by association, her friendships with Carrington and Delia. Miss Archibald had accused Abigail of murdering her brother, and Mr. Travers kept company with the hateful woman.

This vacation was supposed to offer her something other than heartbreak and loss. Cornwall was a whirlwind adventure molded to emulate her novels, but with or without romance, her novels had never failed to whisk her away. If Mr. Travers preferred Miss Archibald to her, it was his problem. She would quit mooning over the man and find something better to do.

As she left her room in a brilliant blue gown the color of the summer sky, she was intercepted by the man in question. Mr. Travers regarded her with thinned lips and a set jaw. His clothes were clean, but his waistcoat was buttoned askew, and his cravat was tied in a firm knot.

He looked as dashing as ever. This would never do. "Did you just crawl out of bed?" she asked.

Her heart pounded as if it would close the distance between them. The thought of him in bed sent tingling desire between her legs.

He glowered at her. "I didn't have time to deal with fripperies."

"Oh, well. I'm sure Miss Archibald will look much the same, so you'll be safe."

He stopped in the middle of the hall, but she moved on without him. He rushed to catch up to her. "She just lost her brother. Give the woman some time."

"Why should I? Oh, that's right. I murdered her brother, so she needs her space. How thoughtless of me." She hurried her steps.

He regained her side again. "There's no need for that. Miss Archibald is simply misguided. You're the most obvious explanation for his death."

Tears stung in her eyes. She took a deep breath and kept her posture steady. "Plenty of other people could have killed him. Why am I being blamed for being attacked? I didn't ask or encourage his advances. In fact, I repeatedly told him no. Was I expected to let him violate me without a word?"

"Of course not. You did the right thing."

Confusion scrunched her brow. "Tell that to Miss Archibald and the Grahams."

"They won't believe me when they see you with Greymore. It'll be a reminder of Archibald's attentions."

"Are you calling me loose?" She froze in place and gawked at him. One innocent kiss and already Greymore was another Nigel.

He regarded her with his mouth agape. He made a strangled sound, and his hand rose as if to summon speech.

"Fine, I'm not going to argue." She left him to stare mutely after her.

"Abigail, please listen."

Her name on his lips was like a branding rod piercing her heart. She stopped and pivoted to face him. "You've no right to use my name."

"I'm sorry, it slipped." He met her gaze. "It's not you I worry about but Greymore. You should stay away from him. Look at what he did to the Grahams."

"The Grahams did that to themselves. Whatever this animosity is between you and Greymore, I want nothing to do with it." She raised her palm out to ward him off, but the pang lodged deeper until her hand shook. "Leave me alone."

His face and shoulders fell.

A shadow descended on her mood, but nothing she said would improve the situation. Delia was right: the man thought he had failed. But he had gone too far with criticizing Abigail's choice of friends. She didn't stop him when he turned back down the hall and disappeared behind his door.

Chapter Eleven

MR. TRAVERS DIDN'T come to dinner.

The atmosphere at the table was like a dense fog the guests endured with sullen expressions. The talk hushed with the arrival of the newcomers. Carrington's grandmother, Mrs. Eddings, a practical silver-haired older woman with a willowy figure and knowing amber-brown eyes, cast a more subdued tone, while Constable North followed their every movement with his slate eyes.

Delia leaned toward her. "Abs, have you seen Hugh?"

"I believe he stayed in his room." She kept her attention on her soup for fear her features would give away her concern.

"How odd. He never misses meals without making his excuses. Do you think he's ill?"

"I wouldn't know." She lowered her tone and breathed in through her nose.

Abigail sensed her friend studying her like insects crawling over her skin. Her eyes shot to Delia's. From Delia's other side, Carrington watched Abigail with a frown, unblinking. She glanced away to dispel their censure.

"William, where's Hugh? I haven't seen the boy since I arrived," Mrs. Eddings shouted across the table.

"I don't know, my dear. I'm sure he doesn't mean offense."

Was the whole dinner going to be like this? Already her argument with Mr. Travers twisted her mind into unforgiving knots. Maybe she should plead a headache and retire.

"He's probably just sore from losing the race." Greymore sipped his Madeira from beside Mrs. Eddings.

"My Hugh rarely loses. When he does, he takes the loss poorly. William, do you remember the time Hugh pouted for days after the Stirling girl threw him over? That woman was a waste of tears and good port," Mrs. Eddings said.

Carrington gazed over at Greymore, who tipped his glass to Carrington. Carrington shook his head and turned his attention back to his grandmother. "Yes, I remember it clearly, and I'll have to agree with you. She was never serious about him. Hugh is going through something a bit more complicated this time."

Mrs. Eddings sniffed. "I hope it's worth neglecting his poor grandmamma. You tell that boy I expect to see him at breakfast. There'll be no pouting on this visit." She gestured to Delia with her spoon. "Dear, don't overindulge or you'll lose it all later."

"Yes, grandmamma." Delia took another bite.

Mrs. Eddings shook her silver head. "I don't see why you can't take up residence in London. Cornwall is such rough country, and this old house is too far out for comfort. I advised your father to sell the place, but he's never listened to good sense."

They ignored this. Mrs. Eddings could say anything, and nobody would contradict her. Her conversation bordered on crass, but those around her showed a deep fondness and respect for her.

Mr. Graham muttered something beside Abigail.

Abigail tilted her head toward him. "Excuse me, what did you say?"

Mr. Graham raised his voice for everyone to hear. "I said Cornwall is the pit of hell."

Miss Archibald nodded from across the table. "I'll have to agree with you. I can't wait to get back to London." The vile woman addressed Constable North. "When can we leave?"

The constable heaved a great sigh as if even the question proved too much work. "I'm making little progress. Unfortunately, I also need to get going. Our killer will make his appearance soon, but I don't think I can wait it out."

"You haven't even questioned the killer." Miss Archibald's face blazed scarlet.

"Ma'am, I'll get to everyone soon." He paused as though to collect his thoughts. "It baffles me there are no witnesses in a house full of servants. My time is cut too thin to unravel this mess."

"She killed my brother, and she'll kill us all if you don't do something."

Abigail went still, her eyes fixed on the table as the open assault continued.

Constable North's voice held firm. "I assure you I've looked into Miss Riverton as a suspect. I pride myself on being impartial in all my work."

Miss Archibald snorted. "Prove it."

"I'll not have Miss Riverton involved in this." Carrington's eyes darted from Miss Archibald to the constable.

Mr. North gave Carrington a firm look. "I have to treat Miss Riverton as a serious suspect. With your permission, my lord, I would like to move past the servants to the guests."

Carrington drummed his fingers on the tabletop. "Miss Riverton, would you agree to this?"

"You're asking her?" Miss Archibald's voice sharpened into a shriek.

Carrington shot his words toward the woman. "Be quiet."

Abigail straightened her spine and raised her chin high as she glared toward Miss Archibald. "I welcome anything that will end this misery. I've nothing to hide."

"Bravo, Miss Riverton. I'll drink to that." Greymore raised his glass. She gave him a slow grin.

A frown scrunched between Mr. Graham's eyes. "You'll drink to anything."

"You have me there, old pal." Greymore chuckled and gulped down the rest of his glass.

"I'm. Not. Your. Pal."

"Really? We have so much in common. No matter. Where's your lovely wife, might I ask?"

Abigail's jaw loosened, and she snapped her mouth shut.

"You most certainly may not." Graham wiped his mouth and stood. He excused himself, not waiting for a reply, and left midmeal. Nobody tried to stop him.

"William, this house you keep is highly volatile. Do be a dear and invite me more often. It will wake up my tired old bones." Mrs. Eddings stared after Mr. Graham.

Delia let out a barely audible groan.

Carrington's lips quirked up. "I assure you, grandmamma, this situation isn't the usual at Briarwyck. The most excitement we face is the occasional violent storm or the birth of a healthy colt."

Once they reached the final course of their meal, Abigail fidgeted in her seat with nothing left to distract her. Relief washed over her when Delia led the way to the drawing room, and the rest of the women followed her. As Delia, Abigail, and Mrs. Eddings settled in the room, Lynette and Miss Archibald made their excuses and left. The three remaining women sat together sipping coffee.

Mrs. Eddings fixed her intelligent eyes on Abigail. "What's your story, my dear? My new granddaughter speaks highly of you, and William assures me you're not a murderer, though I'd like to judge that for myself."

Abigail struggled to find her words. "It's good to hear that, and no, I didn't kill anyone." Except her chances of finding a husband.

"A pity. Mr. Archibald was an awful man. He was almost as bad as the sister. The whole family was raised by wild boars."

"Hugh has been spending time with Miss Archibald," Delia said over the lip of her coffee cup.

"My Hugh?" Mrs. Eddings crinkled her forehead. "I don't believe it. He has some explaining to do when he sees fit to speak to me. Entertaining such a woman."

Delia nodded. "I was surprised myself. Of course, Carrington won't speak of it, but he couldn't possibly approve, since he despises her."

"I don't suppose we could kill her off and blame whoever the real killer is." Mrs. Eddings puckered her face and glanced at the other women.

Delia choked on her coffee and swallowed hard. "Of course, that would make us the real killers too."

Mrs. Eddings arched a brow at Abigail. "Miss Riverton, why do you think everyone believes you're the killer?"

Abigail studied the older woman's eyes and found a warmth she hadn't seen before. "I wouldn't know."

"Oh please, you must have some idea."

She hesitated, not sure how much she should reveal. "He attacked me the night he was murdered."

Mrs. Eddings's eyes widened a tiny fraction. "Indeed? Then I'm doubly glad he's dead. However did you escape?"

When she didn't reply, Delia came to her rescue. "Hugh arrived just in time and saved her. If it weren't for him, we might've had an even more violent outcome."

"That's not surprising. My Hugh is the savior of the family. That's quite a motive for those loyal to Miss Riverton. Are you sure you didn't kill him, Delia?"

"And destroy my pretty new clothes with blood? No, thank you." Delia smoothed a hand over her lilac silk skirts. "If it was one of us, it's more likely my husband or Hugh. I find that improbable though."

"Agreed. William has no stomach for killing, and Hugh wouldn't have hesitated in the first place if he intended to kill him. What of the other guests? I'm only familiar with Greymore, and he's harmless."

Abigail's lips curved to the side.

Delia shook her head. "Greymore isn't harmless, grandmamma."

"Hmm, yes. He has ended many a failed marriage. How awful for them," Mrs. Eddings said in a dry voice. "The man's no killer unless you count the murder of his own person by drink. It's shameful, ruining such a pretty face. What of the Grahams?"

"I don't know much about them. Mrs. Graham was unfaithful to her husband, but other than that…" Delia shrugged.

Mrs. Eddings set her coffee down and settled her hands in her lap. "I think you'll find Mr. Graham isn't what he says. The failure of a marriage goes both ways. From what I saw of the man, his wife must cling to the edge of her happiness."

Abigail leaned forward, her voice lowered. "Dee, she's right. Mr. Graham seemed like a different person when I arrived. It's as if we're seeing the darkness in him. What if he's the killer?"

"I like this one." Mrs. Eddings tilted her head toward Abigail.

"Thank you. I like you too, ma'am."

"Please, call me Evelyn. We're family, since Delia maintains you're a sister to her."

Abigail burst into a wide smile. "Then I have to insist you call me Abigail."

Delia beamed at them. "I'm so glad you get along. Abs, I was going to ask you to stay on for my delivery. My mother isn't here, and I'm afraid Lynette will faint. I'd like to have you and Grandmamma assist me."

"Of course I'll stay. Hopefully I can keep alive until then. Let me speak with Alma to make sure she's comfortable with being away from home so long. Aside from these murders, this is the happiest I've been in some time." She knew her parents would have no trouble with her absence. After all, she had escaped the fighting in the colonies, which was one of the reasons they'd agreed to the trip.

"For me as well, and I'd like to go riding again before it's too late."

"Don't let me keep you. I'll busy myself with bothering my

grandsons and arguing with that sister of yours, Lynette. A quiet thing, but once you draw her out, there's no stopping her." Mrs. Eddings chuckled to herself.

Delia echoed her laugh. "Your description suits her. She'll warm to you in time."

Their attention wavered with the entrance of the men, or rather, the entrance of Greymore and Mr. North. Carrington was called away when a footman brought him a message. The constable seated himself next to Delia, while Greymore melted into the chair, catlike, between Abigail and Mrs. Eddings.

"You seem pleased tonight, Greymore." Mrs. Eddings eyed his casual posture.

"Always in the company of you, ma'am." He gave her a flashy grin.

Mrs. Eddings made a sound that could only be described as a cackle. "I'm sure it isn't me that excites your fancy, but I'll take it. I'm old, but I'm still a woman."

His eyes danced over Mrs. Eddings. "Old? Nonsense, you're as spritely as ever. Your beauty knows no age."

The footman came in with a message for Delia and Mr. North. After a whispered exchange, they hurried out into the hallway. Abigail stared after them, an itch tugging at her to follow.

Mrs. Eddings nodded toward the closed door. "I believe we're missing some excitement. A pity. I was enjoying this ongoing entertainment. Should we retire?"

Abigail's brow furrowed. "If we're to learn anything, I think it's likely someone will return to share the news. I do hope everything is all right."

"I'm in agreement, Miss Riverton. Besides, all the good company is already here, and so are the refreshments." Greymore sloshed the contents of his drink.

She watched the red tide swirl in his glass. "How do you think clearly with so much drink?" Abigail studied him.

"I don't think. That's the beauty of it. You'll find thinking is overrated and helps nobody. You should try it more. Let me get you some port." He poured them all glasses.

Mrs. Eddings took a sip. "This is much better."

Abigail gazed up from her wine as Delia entered. Her friend's shoulders hung as she asked to see Abigail in the hall. With reluctance, she set her drink down and followed Delia out.

Delia rubbed at her temples. "What did you do to Hugh?"

"What do you mean? I didn't do anything."

"He requested someone else watch you, and he wants to change rooms. He's insistent, but I don't know who will replace him. Did something happen?"

Abigail averted her eyes, blind to her surroundings.

"You can tell me. He may be my brother-in-law, but you're my oldest and dearest friend. Please." Delia grasped Abigail's hand.

She blinked, and a sigh escaped her lips. "Really, it's nothing. We had a fight, and I told him to leave me alone."

Delia's brows lowered over her emerald gaze. "That's not nothing. Why did you wish him away?"

As much as Abigail loved Delia, she couldn't handle this conversation unearthing her shame. "I don't need a nursemaid. He kept warning me off Greymore. It isn't that I don't appreciate all he's done, but I can choose my own friends."

"That's understandable." Delia paused. "For the record, I agree with him about Greymore. Be careful with him. With his history, he's likely to turn into another Nigel for you. Why risk it?"

"I want nothing from Greymore, and I suspect he feels the same. My reputation is already in tatters, and I've no plans for the future aside from being here for your delivery. It's refreshing and liberating. Nobody expects anything from me now. If it pleased me, I could shrivel up as an old maid." Tears filled her eyes, and she blinked them away. "It doesn't matter anymore." She pulled her hand out of Delia's.

"Don't say that." Delia reached out after Abigail and held her firm. "It does matter. You deserve to be happy. I know you, Abs. You won't settle for being an afterthought in someone else's story."

"Don't you get it?" Abigail's cheeks flamed. "My chance at happiness has turned from a torrent of opportunity to a small trickle tainted with disappointment. I've accepted the consequences of my mistakes, and I don't need borrowed hope. Why don't you go back to your perfect life and leave me be?"

Abigail flew up the stairs to her room to escape Delia's pained, openmouthed shock.

Abigail buried her sobs in her pillow, the shaking gasps bursting from her throat. She'd never fought with Delia like this. Their arguments ended before truly starting. The recurring memory of Delia's horrified expression kept Abigail's cheeks awash with tears.

After the sobs wore themselves out and her pillow was drenched through, she fell into a fitful sleep. She woke to fresh dampness coating her lashes and a faint knocking at her door. She wiped at her face but gave up at the pretense, since whoever was at the door had no doubt heard her crying in her sleep.

She steeled herself. "Come in." She dropped her guard when Alma entered. Her graying head bobbed as she shut the door behind her.

"Can I do anything for you, miss?" Alma's kind slate eyes filled with worry. "Perhaps you would like to change?"

Abigail let out a long breath. "That would be nice. My stays are pinching me terribly."

Alma nodded and gestured for Abigail to stand. Alma's deft motions released Abigail from the torment of her daytime apparel. Moments later, she lounged in her favorite flower-embroidered nightdress as Alma brushed out Abigail's midnight hair. She sighed in contentment as the brush worked out the tangles and massaged her scalp.

"Alma, do you think I'm a fool?"

"Ma'am?" Alma paused the brush on its path.

"I've done some stupid things since you've come to work for me. Do you think I'm stupid? I think I must be."

"I've never thought you stupid." Alma continued her strokes.

"Really? I seem to be making a mess of my life."

"You're young and maybe a bit misguided."

"I'm not so sure I'm learning from my mistakes."

"Indeed you do. Maybe too much so. Don't be so hard on yourself." Alma's voice was as soothing as cream in bitter coffee.

Abigail leaned into the brush like a cat, her eyes sealed shut. "But what I said to Dee and Mr. Travers… They'll never forgive me. I've been cruel and ungrateful to them."

"Lady Carrington's a kind woman and will understand. I can't answer for Mr. Travers, though I believe he's a reasonable man. He treats the staff well. I'm afraid his type of hurt will be more difficult to overcome."

Abigail bit her tongue as she fought back threatening tears. No more crying over her past wrongs. She would fix this. "What should I do?"

"Apologize to Lady Carrington," Alma said without hesitation. "In time, you can apologize to Mr. Travers as well, but for now give him space. I saw the room after he moved, and it took them hours to clean up the broken glass."

Abigail peered back at Alma with wide eyes. "Broken glass? That doesn't sound promising."

"True, but he was remorseful afterward and offered the servants bonuses for the trouble. Everyone was more than happy to clean the mess."

"Dee saw this?" The incident would explain Delia's earlier mood toward Abigail. She could have put an end to this sooner.

"Yes, I saw Mr. Travers send for Lord Carrington. They argued for a time, and Lord Carrington sent for Lady Carrington."

"I don't suppose you overheard them?" Her stomach twisted at asking her maid to disclose such information, but servants overflowed with forbidden fruit.

Alma stilled. "I didn't listen in. All I know is Mr. Travers was unreasonable, since Lord Carrington kept yelling it and some other words I won't repeat. They calmed down when Lady Carrington arrived."

Abigail couldn't ask any more of her maid—not now, anyway. "Thank you, Alma. You've been a great help to me." She reached around to squeeze the woman's hand. Alma stiffened but returned her squeeze.

"If you don't mind my saying, ma'am, I hate to see you this way and right after suffering such an ordeal." Alma moved around to face her. "Do you need anything else? Some tea?"

"That would be nice." Abigail smiled gratefully as Alma rang for tea. "Do you like it here?"

"It's a beautiful country, and the other servants are good people. Aside from the fear of dying, it's paradise."

Abigail brightened at Alma's words. "Then you won't mind staying for Delia's child?"

"You don't have to ask me that. I go where you go, ma'am." Alma's voice was soft, shy. Her maid kept to herself, needing some coercion to express her opinion.

"Oh, but I do." She tilted her head. "I so wish you to be happy if it's in my power."

A smile whispered over Alma's lips. "Thank you. I'd like very much to stay here. I've been happy since entering your employ. It's a great improvement from my last situation."

"You'll tell me if something disagrees with you? And save me from myself when I become a blundering fool?" She gave Alma what she hoped was an encouraging look.

Alma's smile grew, still barely noticeable but there. "I'll agree to that, but I still don't think you're a fool."

"Will you tell me what happened in your last job?"

Alma's gaze darted away. "It's in the past, and it should stay that way. I worked for a cruel man, and I'll leave it at that."

Abigail's face fell. "I'm sorry. If you ever need to talk about it, I'm here. I do understand. I'd like to bury my own past." She suspected she would never know what happened to her maid, but she believed she had finally broken through the wall Alma had erected between mistress and servant.

Now she would discover how badly she had destroyed her bridges.

Chapter Twelve

Morning dawned, not with the startling light Abigail expected of summer but with the escalating household sounds around her. She frowned at the blanket of clouds canvassing the sky and hoped she could still spend the day out of doors.

She dressed with the help of Alma and found the room Mr. Travers had vacated was already taken up. She stood in the hallway in front of the door when Delia exited the room to provide explanation. Her friend eyed her with a strange shyness, and Abigail's gut wrenched.

"Dee, I apologize for what I said. You know I've always valued and sought your good opinion. I don't know what has gotten into me." She watched her hands as she wrung them in front of her.

"I've a bit of an idea. You've been through such a difficult time, and you came here to get away from all that. Instead, you find more of the same. From now on, do what makes you happy. You'll hear no judgment from me."

She shook her head in a quick burst. "You've every right to judge my poor behavior. In fact, I count on you to be the voice of reason for me. I don't know what I want anymore."

"Getting out of this investigation alive would be a good start." Delia offered her a bright grin.

Abigail met her with an uncertain half smile. "Is that what this is about? Are you my new neighbor?"

"No, Carrington would never allow it. You had a few volunteers, but we decided on the most sensible one."

Abigail's brows came together. "Who?"

"Well, my husband was at first insistent he take his brother's place, but as you can imagine, Mrs. Eddings was adamant he stay with me. Then Greymore offered, but Carrington flat-out refused him." Delia watched Abigail's face. "Hugh would've changed his mind if Greymore were the one to replace him. A missed opportunity, I think. Felix also volunteered, but I assume he just wanted the room. Finally, Mrs. Eddings insisted she'd do it. She's in there now arranging her things."

"Mrs. Eddings is going to protect me?"

Delia laughed. "I said much the same thing. Carrington assured me the old woman is a deadly shot with a pistol, quite a feat with those tricky things. Apparently she can scream like a banshee as well."

"I suppose she'd act as a deterrent, at least." Abigail paused to nibble her lower lip. "Who would try to kill an old woman?"

"You'd be surprised." A wry smile twisted Delia's lips. "In her own right, Mrs. Eddings isn't someone you want to cross. Add her family and connections, and she's a dangerous foe."

"Thank you for this. I'll be more comfortable with Mrs. Eddings."

"Of course," Delia said. "We missed you at breakfast. Did you sleep well?"

"Not really, but I decided I'd have to face the world eventually."

"Or not." Delia cocked her head. "Did I tell you I've collected some of the most awful books while in London? You really must read with me today. We needn't travel far to read out of doors, in case there's rain. I've already had some refreshments prepared, but there's always more than I need."

Abigail readily agreed, and Lynette joined them with her

paints. It wasn't long before the trio fell into a companionable silence as they were engrossed in their respective amusements. Delia and Abigail lounged across a blanket, while Lynette stood off with her easel. The novel Delia lent Abigail turned out to be a frivolous romance with a delicious hero, and she couldn't put it down to save herself. It was because of this that she didn't hear, at first, the footsteps toward their sanctuary under the wide branches of an old oak tree.

"Why wasn't I invited to this rendezvous?" Carrington stood beside his wife, smiling. Mr. Travers waited off to the side, gaze toward the house.

"Maybe because you're too distracting?" Delia's focus rested on her book.

"I'll take that as a compliment."

Delia nodded. "Sure."

Carrington lowered himself to the blanket and gazed over his wife's shoulder at the book. "Another one? I was sure the author must be dead from boredom by now. Hugh, can you understand how they read these things?"

Mr. Travers moved closer to the couple and peered obediently at the novel. "No, they give people an unhealthy view of reality. Imagine all the drama and unhappiness we could avoid if people didn't read novels. Frankly, I'd like to set fire to the lot of them."

"I'm sorry, but that's just untrue." Abigail met Mr. Travers's gaze, and his knowing grin stoked her ire. "Novels allow readers to escape their unhappiness in an otherwise hopeless situation."

"I prefer not to avoid my problems. The last thing someone needs is to delude oneself about their unhappiness." He returned her stare and crossed his arms over his chest.

Her expression tightened. "That may be the case for problems with solutions. Of course, you're a man and don't face the same restrictions."

Delia cleared her throat, interrupting the beginnings of their argument. "Why are you here?"

Carrington gave his wife an exaggerated frown. "Do I need a reason to visit my wife?"

Delia narrowed her eyes at him. "You do when you bring trouble and interrupt my book."

"Trouble? Oh, Hugh. Well, we happened to see you ladies while strolling the grounds."

Lynette snorted. "Unlikely."

Carrington's gaze darted to Lynette. "My own house is a toxic wasteland, and I wanted to escape. Does that suit you, dear sister?" Carrington pushed Delia's book aside. She favored him with a murderous stare.

"If it helps you cope, dear brother." Lynette's attention never left her canvas.

Delia gazed over her shoulder at Hugh. "Do come join us. I've some wine here you might enjoy. I believe we still have quite a few pastries as well. Imagine, this book's so exciting I've only eaten half a lemon tart."

He hesitated and lowered himself to Delia's other side, the furthest space away from Abigail. She swallowed her hurt with a scone and went back to her book. This wasn't a promising start to seeking his forgiveness.

"Who's that coming from the house?" Delia squinted at the figure.

They all turned to the silhouette. Mr. Travers groaned and made to rise.

"Don't you dare go anywhere, Hugh." Delia shoved him back down. "What was all that talk about avoiding problems?"

Mr. Travers frowned at her but stayed seated.

The subject in question, Lord Greymore, eased down next to Abigail. Carrington raised his glass in greeting, and the women murmured their welcomes. Mr. Travers made a sour face but said nothing. They offered Greymore a drink, which of course he accepted.

Recognition sparked in Greymore's eyes when he spotted the book in Abigail's hand and favored her with a toothy grin. "What part are you on?"

Abigail's brows shot up. "You mean you've read it?"

"Of course I've read it. Only a fool would avoid the lessons in that treasure trove. Not to mention how entertaining it is."

"Really?" Abigail glanced toward Mr. Travers, who made a show of ignoring them. "In that case, they've just arrived at the house party. Tell me something scandalous happens."

He leaned in as if to tell her a secret. "I won't give anything away, but what's a house party without a scandal?"

"Peace of mind," Mr. Travers said under his breath.

Delia tsked. "Hugh, that would be the most boring book."

Mr. Travers looked to Abigail, and mirth accented his wicked smile. "I thought the idea was to avoid unhappiness?"

Abigail rolled her eyes. "Your own unhappiness." She let out a long breath. "There's something refreshing about reading about someone else's problems that are worse than your own. It's even better if there's a happy resolution at the end, something we may never have in the real world."

"No woman should have to face such unhappiness." Greymore's tone was gentle yet chiding. "It's a crime for you to need to escape when happiness can be yours."

She blinked, and her gaze dropped to her lap. "I'm afraid happiness isn't so easy. We can't always have what we want."

"Are you speaking from experience?"

She nodded, and Delia saved her from elaborating. "This is a rather depressing conversation for a summer day. I'll need more wine. Lord Greymore, would you hand me that bottle?" Delia gestured to the wine beside him. "I mean, before you consume it all."

Greymore laughed and handed her the bottle. "You know me well."

"Luckily not too well." Mr. Travers stared into his own half-empty glass.

"Hugh, what's wrong with you? Greymore's my friend and guest." Carrington pinched his lips together as if he held on to his anger.

Greymore's halfhearted smile was wistful. "It's quite all right, William. Hugh has never liked me, and I would expect nothing less. It's well deserved, as you know."

Carrington regarded his friend. "No, it's not. All of it happened so long ago, and holding a grudge at this point is just childish."

Delia tugged at Carrington's sleeve and whispered something in his ear.

"Really?" Carrington asked. She nodded, and he continued, "Hugh, it's time you stop putting off visiting Grandmamma. Come with me." He rose to his feet and pulled at Mr. Travers's coat to follow. Mr. Travers shot Greymore a sharp look and followed his brother back to the house.

Abigail squeezed her eyes shut. "What did you tell him?"

"Nothing important."

"Since the fun is over"—Lynette stretched her arms above her head—"I think I'll go back as well. My back's cramped." Abigail eyed Lynette's painting, barely half-finished. Her attention had obviously been elsewhere.

Delia watched after her sister and spoke when she was out of earshot. "Lord Greymore, I've asked Abigail to go riding with me again. Perhaps you'd like to join us? Preferably when we're sober and the sky is clear." Greymore readily accepted, and Delia went on, "It's a shame we've had such frequent storms. There isn't much for us to do indoors without too much conflict."

Abigail nodded solemnly.

"Perhaps some music?" Greymore seemed far away as if he were speaking to himself. "I can be civil if they can. You may be overlooking the advantages of Constable North observing our collective behavior. A conflict can reveal a lot."

"I hadn't thought of that." Delia ran a finger along the lip of her glass. "Maybe we shouldn't be avoiding this. Maybe we should try to get everything out in the open so we can finally move on. A little concert is a fine idea. We live as outsiders to such a musical people as the Cornish. It's a shame we don't celebrate our environment. I believe there's some musical ability in our group."

"Don't forget: everything sounds better with alcohol." Greymore downed the last of his glass.

"Indeed." Delia passed the bottle back to Greymore.

He regarded her with a raised brow. "I thought I didn't get any more."

"That was when we had other competition."

Abigail handed her glass to Greymore, which he refilled.

"Madam, is that your third?" He passed it back to her.

"There are other ways to forget." She brought her glass to her lips.

"This happens to be my favorite one. Cheers." He closed his eyes and took a big gulp.

Delia lay back into the blanket and sighed.

Abigail started and stared down at her friend. "Are you having pains?" She faced Greymore. "Should we fetch Carrington?"

Delia waved her off. "I'm fine."

Abigail studied her friend. "I don't think she's been sleeping much."

"I'm not sure any of us have." His heavy eyes searched hers. "What troubles you so?"

"I'd rather not talk about it." She sipped at her wine and formed a plan of escape if he continued to press.

"Was it back in New York?"

She closed her eyes and gave a short nod.

"Then I hope we can make it up to you in England. I hate to see you unhappy."

A loud snore answered him. Abigail fought back her giggle as Greymore looked upon Delia's sleeping form.

"It's a wonder William gets any sleep." Greymore's lips quivered.

"I've thought as much myself."

His tone grew solemn. "Miss Riverton, I hope you count me

as a friend. It isn't often I find someone I enjoy spending time with, and even fewer people enjoy my sense of humor."

"It can't be all bad." The man must attract women by the townful. He couldn't have any want of companionship.

"It is. I've few friends."

"I don't believe that. Women seem to adore you." The words were out before she knew she'd said them. Perhaps she'd had too much wine.

"That's very much the problem. Few women want me for my conversation, and even fewer men want me around because of it. Lord Carrington knows me well enough, and he trusts his wife. He's the exception."

Abigail fell silent. His jokes and heavy drinking no longer marked him as the carefree viscount but revealed the sadness beneath. Greymore carried an unhappiness not unlike her own, a shadowy loneliness only a kindred spirit would understand.

She held his gaze. "I'd be honored to count you among my friends."

"Good, then we shall have no more seriousness for the day." His smile reached his kind blue eyes. "I haven't had nearly enough to drink for such topics."

"That's hard to believe." She gazed down at the form of their snoring hostess. "Should we wake Delia?"

"Let her sleep for now. There's still more wine."

They drank for a time and allowed the alcohol to dull their senses. Conversation poured from them like warm syrup until they were roused from their hazy world by the arrival of a footman. Abigail shook Delia to get her attention.

The footman handed Delia a note, which she studied with blinking, sleep-filled eyes. "Oh dear." Her voice was slurred from sleep and wine. "I'm needed back at the house."

Abigail made to rise. "Do you wish for me to accompany you?"

"If you'd like." Delia seemed deliberately vague.

Abigail took her friend's answer as an affirmative and to avoid

Delia's lecturing her about being alone with Greymore. The three of them packed their things with the help of the footman. They walked in silence. Greymore was too far gone for conversation, and Delia's mind appeared to be on the business ahead.

Abigail wondered at the message her friend had received, but her thoughts were occupied by the man beside her. With her newfound knowledge, she studied him as he was and not as he had appeared: the man poisoning himself with drink.

His dark-blue eyes were dull with intoxication, set out of place on his flawless face by his tired red eyelids. He hid behind his witty remarks and cultivated reputation. She couldn't recall a time when he'd been sober for long, but perhaps his drunkenness had become his natural state.

Sadness clouded her mind—whether from alcohol or her overworked emotions, she couldn't say. Her realizations about Greymore had shed a light on the rest of her false perceptions. Her recent crimes tugged at her heart and forced their way to the foreground of her mind.

She had wronged Carrington, even if he didn't realize it. He had invited her to his home, and she had entertained horrid notions about the death of Laura. What was worse, she had been discourteous to his brother. Her actions toward his well-meaning behavior had been unwarranted.

If Mr. Travers chose to befriend Miss Archibald, it wasn't Abigail's place nor her right to judge him. What was Abigail to him but an unwanted guest whose care had been thrust upon him? He had saved her life, and she had repaid him by turning her back on his friendship. Alma was right. Abigail would keep her distance from him and bear his hatred as the oxen carried the weight of his yoke, trudging forward with the purpose of plowing ahead another day.

Her throat tightened, and she steeled herself as they reached the house.

Inside, Mr. Travers waited with an impatient frown. "William didn't want to include everything in the note, and of course, he's having me tell you about the commotion." He cleared his throat, drawing Abigail's unwilling gaze to him. "We've located the missing footman."

"I'm pleased, but must I be fetched to hear this? The note said the matter was urgent and of some importance. I don't see how." Delia shifted her weight and leaned on Abigail.

Mr. Travers appeared to shrink under Delia's sharp stare. "It's the manner in which he was found that's of concern, though I don't know why William considered it urgent other than letting you know at the earliest possible time. You and the guests must avoid the upstairs until Constable North says otherwise."

"Where was the footman found? Wasn't most of the upstairs searched yesterday? Why must we refrain from going to our rooms?" Delia's questions were more demands. Carrington had wisely chosen to send his brother instead of facing his wife's wrath.

Mr. Travers combed a hand through his hair. "We did search everywhere upstairs, or so we thought. If it hadn't been for the smell, he would've rested there forever. The poor man was pushed to the back of the linen closet, buried deep. The linen was piled on him in such a way that a hasty search wouldn't have revealed his body."

A chill crawled up Abigail's spine, and she flinched.

Delia heaved a sigh. "Such a horrible fate, but that doesn't explain why we can't go upstairs."

"For one, Constable North is examining the area. He doesn't want to lose any clues or be distracted by our 'puttering about,' as he called it. William had to assure him nobody would hamper his work. Also, the smell isn't something anyone should suffer through. Several people lost their breakfasts, including Felix, and that boy has the strongest stomach I've seen. Would you really want to go up there?" He looked between Delia and Abigail, ignoring Greymore.

Delia groaned. "I'd rather hoped to change. I swear these shoes are tighter than they were yesterday. There can't be any harm in my changing."

"I'm afraid it goes beyond that. I'm told he's searching the bedrooms as well. The man's impatient to be away and seems to have found the excuse he wanted to go through our things."

Abigail's stomach lurched as she imagined Constable North pawing through her private undergarments.

Delia seemed to have similar thoughts. "The nerve. Did Carrington approve of this?"

"You know he did. He wants this over and done with as much as North. The loss of trust and a few bad friends is a small price to pay for peace of mind and the safety of one's family."

Abigail wondered if she was included as one of those bad friends. Mr. Travers would lump Greymore into that group, though it was likely the search wouldn't bother the easygoing man. At this point, the invasion of privacy was unpreventable. Carrington's actions were understandable. She would have done the same in his place.

"Very well. Let's take tea in the library today. I'd rather not let my imagination wander over the contents of the closet." Delia stepped forward as if she would leave the problem behind her.

Mr. Travers stilled her with a hand. "There's one more thing. Miss Riverton."

Abigail kept her gaze lowered, and her heart leaped in her chest.

"I've been tasked with taking you to my brother's study. It seems Constable North has found damning evidence in your room."

Chapter Thirteen

Abigail could no longer avoid Mr. Travers's eyes, but what she saw there was worse than not knowing. Pity etched over his gaze and frown. She could handle disappointment or sadness but not pity. It meant whatever had been found wasn't something they could ignore. He must have given up on her. She looked away.

"Hugh? What do you mean?" Delia stood in front of Abigail like a protective wall.

"Just that. North thought it prudent he search Miss Riverton's room first. I can't provide any other details."

"I'll come with you." Delia laced her arm into Abigail's.

Mr. Travers stopped her with a raised hand. "You can't be there. It's important she goes alone."

Delia squared her shoulders, and her grip became iron. "I won't have it."

He glanced between Delia and Abigail. "You know she'll be fine. William and I will be there." At his words, Delia loosened her grip.

"Miss Riverton shouldn't be left without defense. I shall accompany her." Greymore moved to block Mr. Travers from Abigail.

"Certainly not." Mr. Travers shot Greymore a hard stare. "North won't be there this time. This is William we're talking about, and I'll be more than enough defense against my brother."

"Your actions tell me otherwise. How can you question her without also presuming her guilt? She needs a real defense by someone who doesn't suspect her." Greymore reinforced his stance, crossing his arms over his chest.

She paled. Greymore's words thrust like knives into her chest. Mr. Travers suspected her?

Mr. Travers eyed Greymore up and down. "That's out of the question, especially from you."

"I'm the best defense she has here besides Lady Carrington."

Mr. Travers snorted, dismissing the viscount. "I sincerely doubt that. I'm perfectly capable of facing this matter objectively. There's no need for you to involve yourself."

"Who are you to her that you have her best interests at heart?" Greymore's voice lashed out like an adder attack.

Abigail stilled at the unexpected angry tone from the usually placid man. She wouldn't have wanted to be in Mr. Travers's place. Indeed, Mr. Travers stood frozen into silence from the verbal assault. She placed a trembling hand on Greymore's shoulder, and he faced her.

Abigail softened her voice. "I appreciate your support, my lord, but I'll have to face this alone."

"Are you sure?"

Abigail sighed. "Yes, I want this finished."

"At least send word to me if you're in need. I'm sure Lady Carrington will agree with me to come at the first sign of trouble." Greymore stepped closer to her as though his presence would provide comfort and protection.

"That's enough." Mr. Travers's outburst sliced between them. "We aren't the villains here. I'd have thought you had a higher opinion of William."

Greymore's gaze snapped to the other man. "There's no question that William's intentions are honorable, and he's aware of my loyalty to him. It's you I doubt."

Mr. Travers's fist shot forward, giving Abigail just enough

time to intercept the blow with her shoulder. She cried out with the lance of pain through her arm and reeled back. She grasped the stinging muscle with her other hand.

Mr. Travers stared at her with a dropped jaw and blanched face. She couldn't stop the tears from coming to weep out her foolish heart. The pain shocked her more than anything else. The surprise from his punch brought the tears. The blow had been an accident, but at that moment, it didn't matter so much as the reasoning behind it.

"Look what you've done." Greymore showed admirable restraint at not returning the blow. "If you weren't William's brother, I'd have your hide."

Delia came to Abigail's side. She examined Abigail's arm and stroked her back. "Does it hurt?"

Abigail wiped her tears and straightened herself up. "It will be all right. Can we get this over with?"

Everyone fell silent at her quick recovery. Mr. Travers led her to Carrington's study, posture abashed. If he had a tail, he would be hiding it between his legs. Delia and Greymore did not attempt to follow.

He continued to glance back at her as though he wanted to say something. Finally, when they reached the room, he faced her with halting movements. His hand rubbed at his neck as he spoke.

"I'm deeply sorry for hitting you. I've never once hit a woman in my life." The pain in his eyes left a twist in her chest. "I can't even begin to express my regret at having let Greymore anger me. It was an accident, but that doesn't excuse my loss of control." He paused to gauge the effect of his words.

Abigail lowered her lashes and nodded, saying nothing.

"Please, if you could only—"

"What's taking so long?" Carrington swung the door open before Mr. Travers could finish. "What happened?" Carrington's gaze searched the pair as if he sensed conflict.

"I hit Miss Riverton." Mr. Travers's voice grew muted like a chastised boy's.

"You what?" Carrington straightened to his full height to glare down at his brother. "Have you gone mad? I only asked you to bring her here, not beat her."

"I was aiming for Greymore."

Carrington shook his head. "Hugh, I assume you've already given your apologies to Miss Riverton, but now it's time you make amends with Greymore." Mr. Travers started to protest, but Carrington gave his older brother a deadly stare. "I know you haven't bothered to apologize to him, because you never do. It's long past time you make peace. He's one of my oldest friends and a guest of mine. Leave Miss Riverton to me."

Abigail angled her body away from them, looking everywhere but at the brothers. Being in the middle of this argument would only make her situation worse, and she needed all the good opinions she could get.

"How can you side with him over your own blood? You don't even know what the argument was about."

Carrington clenched his jaw and massaged his forehead. "I don't have to know. I'm merely asking that you set aside your grievances so we can live in relative peace. If you can't do that without shedding blood, then so be it. Thrash each other until you're unconscious, but when you're done, this ridiculous feud should be over. It's bad enough when you're trying to kill each other, but when someone else is harmed in the process, it's inexcusable."

Mr. Travers hunched in on himself. The difference in the brothers' ages spanned only a few years, but it seemed like a dozen. She suspected Carrington had often taken a fatherly role to his brother in the frequent absence of their father at home.

Mr. Travers caught her gaze and parted his lips as though he wanted to say something more to her. She couldn't imagine what remained to discuss. Instead, he settled on a weak smile and headed off back down the hall.

Carrington's gaze followed him, and a smile grew across his

features as his brother's form retreated.

"I have to thank you, Miss Riverton. I've been waiting for years to do that. At last one of them snapped. I regret you were harmed in the process. Does it hurt?" Carrington ushered her into the study.

The room had the usual red-and-yellow theme, but the resemblance to the other rooms stopped there. The furniture was constructed from a light oak with matching leather upholstery. Books lined the wall behind the large desk scattered with papers and odds and ends. It had a clean, masculine smell that seemed at odds with the disheveled appearance. There was no dust in sight.

She perched on a chair in front of the desk, and to her wide-eyed surprise, he took the chair beside her. His face was grim, and he leaned forward with his hands resting on his knees. An uneasiness crept over her at what he would say, but she refused to let herself fidget as she ached to.

"This is a nasty business, Miss Riverton. I think you'll remember it from the Foxglove investigations. Regardless of the evidence against you, I tend to believe you had nothing to do with the murders, but I can't dismiss what has come to my attention." He watched her closely. "Do you know what I'm referring to?"

She shut her eyes and shook her head. "I haven't the slightest notion."

He sighed. "I thought not. It appears the murder weapon has been found at the bottom of your trunk."

She blinked at him in confusion. "You mean the murder weapon wasn't already found?" She inched forward in her chair. "What was it?"

"A letter opener."

Her jaw dropped.

The side of his mouth tilted up. "I was astonished myself. It appears to be a very sharp letter opener. North found it among your things, wrapped in a shirt belonging to Mr. Archibald and covered in blood. We think it's the same weapon used to kill my footman, Henry."

"I don't understand. A letter opener? And how did it get in my things?"

"I assume someone planted it there. They've had ample opportunity since the murders. Let me assure you, anything can be a weapon if one is creative and desperate enough. I once witnessed a rebel prisoner force his jugular open with a wooden spoon. It was unpleasant, but it had the desired effect."

"It couldn't be mine. I forgot it at home and had to borrow one from Delia when I arrived."

"That's reassuring. The wounds match the blade perfectly. I wonder at the choice of weapon, since there are far better options around the house. Even the poison used on Sir Peter would've served better. It would take a great deal of rage to inflict that kind of damage with such an inferior weapon."

"Why are you telling me?" This conversation was the longest she had spoken with Carrington, their only common interest being Delia. If she had known he was such a font of information, she would have consulted him sooner.

"I wanted to prepare you for North's interrogation. That may sound unfair, but so is your situation."

"You've certainly been forthcoming. What did you mean by the damage done? I thought Mr. Archibald had his throat slit." No sense letting this opportunity go to waste.

He widened his eyes. "I see what you have in common with my wife. When we turned Mr. Archibald over, there were dozens of stab wounds in his back. The throat wound was the final cut, an act of mercy after the assault on his back. The footman fared better, but it was hard to tell through the decay. I think the killer just wanted him out of the way."

Abigail clutched the arms of the chair, digging her nails into the leather. "What are you going to do?"

"I'm afraid we'll have to see this through. When Miss Archibald hears the news, there won't be much time. Our cousins are from an important family line, and you've little chance against these accusations." His frown creased his brow. "I'm hoping we can discover the truth before you're called in front of a magistrate. I sincerely regret having this search, but I can't ignore it. Too many people are already aware of what we found. For now, I want you to pretend everything is as it should be. It would be wise to stay away from Miss Archibald."

She leaned back in her chair, studying the ceiling in an attempt to distract her mind from the shaking fear inside her. "Naturally. I'm not particularly fond of her company. I don't know what your brother sees in her."

"Indeed. Unfortunately, they're also family, and it's my obligation to welcome them here. Maybe if I hadn't been so tolerant, Mr. Archibald would be alive. Anyway, I've taken up enough of your time. Say nothing of our talk." His last words made her think of nefarious conversations in shadowed alleys. She suppressed a giggle; now was not the time.

"Not even to Dee?"

"Especially not to her." His tone held a stern warning. "My wife prefers to control these situations, and I'd rather she didn't upset herself while in her condition. If you must speak with anyone, Hugh already knows everything."

She nodded. Delia was capable of judging for herself what was best for her, but Abigail stayed silent on the matter. Since the quarrel with Greymore, Mr. Travers was the last person she wanted to talk to. She would keep her worries to herself. The bubbling pot of her emotions would find no relief.

Her promises to silence made, she went in search of Delia. Her friend wasn't in the library as intended but instead had gathered the guests into the drawing room for music. Their hostess must have decided the idea had merit as a form of distraction. Bread and circuses.

Not everyone was happy for the excuse. Mrs. Graham seemed especially ill at ease. The woman spent most of her time confined to her room, and she looked the part. Her usual rosy complexion had become wan and pale. Delia sat with her, a protective force in case of attack.

Everyone sat in small groups, far enough away for privacy but close enough to share musical pursuits. Miss Archibald stiffened next to Mr. Travers as Abigail entered. Mr. Graham sat with them, pointedly ignoring his wife. Lynette and Mrs. Eddings appeared to be bickering next to Lord Greymore, who rose at seeing Abigail. She made her way to them.

"I see everyone has been forced into one room," she said to Greymore, drawing the attention of Lynette and Mrs. Eddings.

"To my disappointment, there have been no fisticuffs. Imagine, we'll actually have to hear the dubious talent of those around us." Mrs. Eddings scowled at the people in question.

"There already was fighting, my dear. You missed it," Greymore said in a dry voice.

Mrs. Eddings's brows shot up. "Really? Why was I not informed of this? What happened?"

"It's no longer my story to tell. A tentative peace has been made, and I'd rather not interrupt it. Perhaps Miss Riverton would care to tell you."

"Miss Riverton, what's he talking about?" The older woman sounded personally offended she had been excluded from her entertainment.

Abigail aimed a pointed look at Greymore and faced Mrs. Eddings. "It was a trifling matter."

Greymore pursed his lips. "I would hardly call being punched 'trifling.'"

Mrs. Eddings sucked in a breath. "Who punched you? Any man who hits a woman doesn't deserve to be called such. Tell me who hit you. I'll have a word with him and perhaps set my Hugh on him."

Greymore burst into laughter but didn't supply any explanation. The conversation aroused Lynette's interest, and she raised an inquiring brow at Abigail.

Abigail didn't know whether to laugh or cry. "I'm afraid it was Mr. Travers himself. An accident. He tried to punch Lord

Greymore, and stupidly, I got in the way." Seeing Mrs. Eddings's openmouthed horror, she added, "It was nothing. A glancing blow. I hardly feel it anymore."

Mrs. Eddings glared across the room at her grandson. To Abigail's relief, she kept quiet, a frown etched into her face. She wondered if the woman's disappointment was in Mr. Travers or in herself. Mrs. Eddings didn't hesitate to assign blame where it was due, and Abigail doubted the public setting would prevent her from shaming him.

A hush fell over the room as Delia stood in front of the room. "Since I've forced you all here, I find it only fair that I begin. I'm no great musical talent, but as Lord Greymore would put it, there's plenty of drink to go around to drown out the noise. I hope some of you will join me."

A murmured laugh echoed through the room as Delia took up the harpsichord. Abigail knew how difficult this was for her friend, and she sat attentively silent. Lord Carrington arrived just in time and seated himself next to Mrs. Eddings. He gave Delia an encouraging smile.

Abigail mirrored his grin and cast her gaze at Mr. Travers, who caught her eye. He inclined his head to her and brought his attention back to Delia.

The first notes of Bach traveled across the room. Abigail let out a sigh of relief for her friend, as starting was always the hardest. Delia played tolerably well, and when she completed the song, polite clapping followed.

The gathering debated who would go next, until Mr. Travers urged Miss Archibald to sing. "You have a sweet voice. It would be a shame not to hear you tonight." He beamed at her solemn face.

An encouraging murmur went up for her acceptance. Abigail suspected nobody else wanted the pleasure of performing.

"What's Hugh playing at? Is he trying to put me in my grave?" Mrs. Eddings spoke just loud enough for her neighbors to hear. A faint smile tugged at Abigail's lips at the woman's words, but she wondered much the same.

Miss Archibald agreed at last and glided to the front of the room. "I'll take no pleasure in this performance. but I feel it's what my dear brother would have wanted. He so loved music. I'll sing this for him. I regret I don't have my harp here to accompany me."

Remembering Carrington's warning, Abigail forced herself to look up from staring at her hands as Miss Archibald began. The song was unfamiliar, but she guessed at the stunned silence that the rest of the party knew it. The singer kept her attention on Mr. Travers, and she sang as though nobody else was in the room:

> She was a sight, my darling fair, her satin lips and golden hair.
> Never there was a rose so pure, never there was a love so sure.
> We met one evening down a vale, our song sweet o' her maiden tale.
> Lost is my maiden o' that night, as a dream, vanished come sunlight.
> My heart sings o' my darling fair, my heart bleeds o' my darling fair.

Abigail's cheeks burned as she tuned out the words and studied the buckles on her shoes. The bawdy undertones of the song made her question the choice of a proper drawing room. When the song completed, the silence became a living being cocooning the room. Finally, to the relief of everyone, Lord Carrington clapped, and they followed his lead. Abigail glanced toward Mr. Travers, but his back was to her.

"Well, that was unexpected." Greymore took a long gulp from his glass.

Delia broke into a nervous laugh. "Who would care to go next?"

Abigail leaned into Greymore. "What was that all about?"

Mrs. Eddings clicked her tongue. "An invitation, my dear. I

suspect things will get interesting soon."

Abigail's nerves hummed for her to flee the room, but she held fast and allowed the sensation to wash over her. Miss Archibald couldn't get the upper hand. Besides, Abigail hadn't a breath of a chance with Mr. Travers. Her angry outburst had ruined any possible relationship.

Greymore poured himself more wine and offered her some, which she gladly accepted. The viscount gave her a fond smile. "Miss Riverton, I'll make a drunk out of you."

"Bite your tongue," she said and downed a mouthful of wine.

Miss Archibald had set a new standard, and Mr. Graham followed her performance with a racy drinking song. The lyrics were even more difficult to listen to, and Abigail hung her head low to keep from showing her scarlet cheeks and shifting eyes. The song overshadowed Miss Archibald's performance, and Abigail's emotions quieted for a moment.

Lynette gave the song her full attention, and she tittered when it was done. Mrs. Eddings shook her head to stop from laughing. Had they all gone mad? Only Greymore seemed calm, but he had probably heard worse.

A commotion ensued, and Mrs. Graham rushed from the room, her cries echoing as she ran. Lord Greymore watched her flee, pain plain in his eyes. Nobody moved until Lynette sighed and followed her out.

Mrs. Eddings studied Greymore. "Having regrets, handsome?"

"You know as well as I do I had nothing to do with that. Their marriage has been a lie from the start. Graham's a horrible cad." He directed his displeasure at the disappearing contents of his glass.

"Does that make you feel any better?"

"Of course not. I still don't like to see it fall apart."

"A romantic, are you?" A small smile creased Mrs. Eddings's lips. "I'd no idea you had it in you. Do you see yourself as some reverse cupid?"

A smug smile played over his lips. "Madam, I'm cupid incarnate. One of these days, I'll demonstrate to you the powers of my unerring arrows. For now, suffice it to say I'm always hard at work on the betterment of my peers."

"I'm sure you are." Mrs. Eddings patted his hand. "Who will be the next to humiliate themselves?"

Delia gazed around the room, hopeless for volunteers, when Lord Greymore raised a hand to get her attention.

"Tell me, Miss Riverton, do you play?"

She shook her head violently. "There's no way you're getting me up there."

"How about a duet?" He seemed unconcerned by her refusal as Delia approached.

"Yes, Abs, do come and play. It's much easier when someone accompanies you, and Greymore has a pleasant enough voice." Delia's brilliant green eyes pleaded with her.

Abigail looked to Mrs. Eddings, who waved her off. "You're on your own. I'm only here for the entertainment."

Abigail groaned and allowed Greymore to lead her to the harpsichord. Her hands shook as she turned the sheet music. The viscount leaned over her and pointed out a song in French by a composer she'd never heard of. This wasn't a promising start.

She squinted at the music. "I don't know this one."

Delia squeezed her arm. "It's easy enough, Abs. You're a better player than I am, and it wasn't challenging for me. Nobody will judge you for making a few mistakes, since it's your first time playing the piece."

Abigail tried the initial notes experimentally. She'd rather get this over with and make a fool of herself than sit here another minute. "Fine, but I've some reservations about playing a song with lyrics I don't understand fully. My French is miserable."

"As is mine. It can't be any worse than Mr. Graham's song." Delia stepped away to give them room. Greymore cocked his head and smiled at their hostess, but she ignored him.

The song had a slow, haunting melody, and Greymore's

tenor voice went beautifully to the music. She warmed to the performance, and her fingers danced as though the tune guided her. Greymore moved off to the side, allowing the audience to see her play. It was too late for her to be nervous; the music had captured her, and the progression of the song came naturally now. She closed her eyes and let the sound pulse through her. As the music closed, the notes continued to echo, and she was transfixed, mesmerized.

Silence swept over the party. She followed Greymore's gaze to Mr. Travers, whose mouth had fallen open. His warm brown eyes called to the music within her and captured her attention. She couldn't look away. A nameless message crossed the span of the room. The rest of the world was unfocused, remote.

CHAPTER FOURTEEN

MR. GRAHAM JUMPED to his feet and broke their trance, leading the others into applause. "Well done, Miss Riverton. Not the choice I would've made, but well done."

Miss Archibald smirked and folded her arms over her chest. "I thought it was a fitting choice for her."

Greymore grinned down at Abigail's confused frown. "Pay no attention to her. You played beautifully."

They rejoined Mrs. Eddings. The older woman met her eyes with a grave face, and she squeezed Abigail's shoulder as though to comfort her.

"I've always loved that piece. It almost moved me to tears this time." Mrs. Eddings's gaze was fixed forward as though she was lost to another time.

"Goodness, whatever was it about?"

Mrs. Eddings appeared not to hear Abigail's question. When Abigail asked Greymore instead, he shushed her and directed her attention to Mr. Travers, who had taken up the harpsichord. She'd had no idea he played, but then again, she'd had no opportunity to find out. Her heart skipped when she recognized the song, the sounds of his baritone voice stealing her senses.

I've been lost to the world since I met you,
And I'd give my soul just for your gaze,

You're the pulse of my blood to my heart,
I want you for the rest of my days.

I know that I've lost my moment,
And I don't think I'll come out right,
Now I'm consumed with such darkness,
I ache for the warmth of your light.

My heart weeps that you can't see me,
And tears burn my eyes with my want,
Your voice echoes my every moment,
I live with the sound of your haunt.

I die that I can't embrace you,
And our bodies, lips lie apart,
I die it can't ever be me,
You're the pulse of my blood to my heart.

When the song's last chords faded, Mr. Travers grew still and fixed his attention above the harpsichord. His shoulders rose and fell as he breathed, like the song weighed across his back. He ignored the applause as he returned to his seat. All eyes focused on Miss Archibald and Mr. Travers. The hateful woman seemed to glow at the attention.

An expectant air filled the room.

Abigail slumped in on herself. The song had awoken unshed tears to her eyes. The lyrics were too close, too soon. After Nigel, she would never have love in return. It had been months, and she had come to terms with her spinsterhood. Yet the reality crashed down on her in the form of a soft, heart-aching melody from Mr. Travers's lips. His perfect, kissable, and unobtainable lips.

She had experienced the words of the song as they'd crept through her bones to the root of her pain. Her breathing came fast as she tried to control the overwhelming sensations pulsing beneath her skin. Her stays tightened, and her chest strained against the fabric. She needed to get out. Now. Before she passed out, or worse, lost control of her tears.

She pushed to her feet and stumbled to the doors of the drawing room. Delia murmured her intentions to follow, but Mrs. Eddings stopped her. "Not now, dear. Let it come."

Abigail's feet led the way, but she couldn't go back to her room. She lost the battle with her tears when she reached the hall, and wiped at them frantically as she half ran, directionless.

A distant rustling in the drawing room announced the party had broken up. Their food must be ready, but she rushed on. When her feet finally stumbled to a halt, she stood outside under a towering willow. She broke into chest-shaking sobs and fell against the tree.

The sun had set, and the wind blew her hair to catch against her tears. Still she cried. Why had he chosen the one song guaranteed to rip her apart? He couldn't have known, couldn't have imagined the force his voice would have on her. Though she thought she cried for Nigel, she mourned for Hugh.

The emotion in his voice rippled in her still. He'd sung from a place of loss with which she was all too familiar. The ache sat deep in her chest, ready to suffocate her. A different pain than the disappointed emptiness from Nigel.

Her life crumbled in her captive state. They thought she was a murderer, and the victim was the very man who had assaulted her. With luck, she would be sent away, but she was just as likely to hang. Her panic consumed her as if the noose already crushed the life out of her. Abigail's sobs became hiccups. She rubbed at her throat and chest, an attempt to ease the building tightness. She closed her eyes to focus on her next breath.

Footsteps scuffed along the ground behind her, and she hurried to right herself. Whoever it was hesitated before speaking. She dared not turn around for fear of revealing her tearstained appearance.

"I've been looking for you. Dinner wasn't the same without you." Mr. Travers's voice was like an echo from his song.

Abigail slapped a hand over her mouth as she cried out at the sound.

"Come, you need to eat."

"Did Dee send you?" she asked in a hoarse whisper.

"Delia? No, I was concerned." His shoes shuffled along the ground. "Are you well?"

She swallowed, buying time to consider her words. "I…I don't know. It's all too much."

"Would you turn around? Let me look at you." His soft words were like a caress she couldn't dream of ever feeling, an offered embrace without fulfillment.

Safety required avoiding his eyes, but she couldn't think of a believable excuse to refuse. She turned slowly, looking at the ground. She sensed his measuring gaze and peered up to meet the frown creased at the corners of his eyes.

"What's troubling you? Is it that fellow in New York? Because he isn't worth your tears."

"No, but I hadn't realized you knew Nigel." Somehow the knowledge made everything worse, and she released a breath to school her features.

"I met him only briefly, but I know his reputation. When I heard him associated with you, it was far too late to say anything. I didn't know you well enough to bring up the topic anyway, though I believe Delia partially blames me." He watched her face. She wished he would look away and stop witnessing her wretched state. "I don't say this often, but I cheered for the rebels when they ambushed him that day. A lot of young women were spared."

"Funny, your caring about the colonies." She bit her tongue. She hadn't meant to sound so sour, but his steady attention unnerved her.

"I don't base my empathy on birthplace. No matter how high- or lowborn, we all bleed the same. I've a lot in common with the Americans. We both value independence and despise tyranny."

"Then why did you come back here?" She chased the conversation further away from her. The wound was already open, and she didn't need salt poured over it.

"England's my home, and no matter the lunatic sitting on the throne, it will always be my home. My family may not be able to escape the atrocious taxes, but we have it easier than most of the citizens. People are starving on the wages—that is, when they can find them."

"Then why don't you do something?"

He sighed. "We've done the best we can. Briarwyck can't take on any more servants, but they're paid better than the miners. If the estate had been taken up by anyone else, it would've been sold off long ago. William was determined to keep the property and employ as many as he can take on. It loses money, but he shoulders the losses without complaint." He frowned, and his voice lowered. "You still haven't answered my question."

"What question?"

"Why are you upset?"

"It's nothing." She made a pretense of studying the tree beside her. With any luck, he would take the hint.

He stepped closer, not letting her back out. He was close enough for her to reach up and pull him to her lips. "Are you worried about the investigation? I meant what I said before. Nothing will happen to you."

She swallowed. "I'm not sure there's anything you can do to prevent it."

"Then that's what's troubling you? Please, put your mind at ease. Have I ever lied to you?"

"I don't know." She shrugged, a heavy lift and drop of her shoulders. "It isn't just the investigation."

He frowned, and she traced the contour of his mouth in her mind. She needed to get ahold of herself.

"If you won't tell me what's troubling you, can you at least let me know how I can make it better? How can I ease the pain in your eyes that twists my heart?" His words set her own heart pulsing through her veins, a drumming echo in her ears.

"Your song." Her lashes dropped over her eyes as though to hide her thoughts. "Your song for Miss Archibald."

The air stilled between them. His brows were twisted up as he studied her face. A new tear streamed down her cheek, and he reached out to wipe it away with his thumb. A shiver ran up her spine at the familiarity.

"Why would you think my song was about Miss Archibald?"

"Wasn't it?" Her breath caught in her throat as she anticipated his answer.

He shook his head, the movement slow and deliberate as he kept her gaze. "She'd like to think so, and it would be better if she does. Any attention away from the investigation is a blessing."

"Why?"

"I thought I could change her mind, or at least divert her anger. I've had some success, but it'll be hard to avoid her intentions."

"Then you mean to follow her wishes?" A sharp pinch grabbed her chest. Disappointment dawned like a cloud covering the sun in thick shadows.

"Not as far as I can help it. I don't like it, but for now, it's necessary."

A wave of relief lifted some of the shade from Abigail's mind. Then distress gripped her stomach as she realized how far he might be willing to go for the sake of diverting his cousin. She wanted to scream at him, to pound on his chest until he saw reason.

The distance between their bodies was mere inches now. One or both of them must have moved closer, or the pull between them had come alive. The scent of wine drifted over her as the closeness of his skin vibrated over hers. His mouth was slightly open as if to breathe her in.

"Tell me." His whisper carried with his scent. "Did you listen to the words? How could I sing for Miss Archibald when my heart belongs to another?" He leaned in, his head only a breath away from her. His eyes held a new look, a dangerous stare that sent her pulse racing in her neck.

"Who?" Her question came out on an exhale.

He smiled down at her lazily. His hand grazed over her cheek, and he pulled her to his lips. The kiss was slow, almost a question, and it held a heat behind it that coiled away as he held back. He stepped away to study her face.

She let out a short laugh.

"What amuses you?" He raised his brow. "Did I answer you sufficiently?"

"That was no answer at all. A breeze, perhaps, but not an answer." Her lips twitched as she fought her smile.

He chuckled. "A challenge." He leaned in again, his lips no longer hesitant, his hands cupping her face. An urgency took over, released from their previous kiss. He backed her against the tree trunk in his need, his lips capturing her yelp of surprise.

Molten fire swam through her body as she pushed into his embrace and returned his kiss with equal hunger. She tasted tart wine as he groaned into her mouth. The scents of leather and cedar consumed her and turned her to jelly in his arms.

A deep-throated laugh sounded behind them, and a throat cleared.

Mr. Travers shooed the other person away.

"I don't mean to interrupt, but it's a pressing matter." Carrington's amusement brightened his tone.

Mr. Travers pushed away, but Abigail tugged him back down to her lips. He rewarded her efforts by pressing her fully against him, forgetting his brother.

"I must insist," Carrington said in a firm voice. "There's been another death."

Mr. Travers continued to ignore him, but Abigail stopped dead, and Mr. Travers had no choice but to turn to his brother. He sighed. "If you don't mean to interrupt, then why do you? Have you any idea how much I want to hurt you now?"

Carrington's lips formed a half smile. "Yes, I've some idea. It's nice to be on the other side of things. Painful, isn't it?"

"I'll show you painful." Mr. Travers growled and stepped forward, but Abigail held him back. He faced her. "I was only going to thrash him."

"I need you in one piece." Her lips curved into a coy smile.

Carrington laughed and shook his head. "She has you there."

He scowled at Carrington. "Was there something you wanted?"

"Right. I thought it best I inform you Mrs. Graham has left us this evening."

Abigail's jaw slackened. Mrs. Graham? The sweet young woman was dead? "But how?" Her cheeks heated in shame as she wondered if they would blame her for this.

Mr. Travers must have thought the same thing, as he angled his body in a protective stance in front of her.

Carrington's gaze wandered over them. "It appears you'll escape blame this time. Mrs. Graham killed herself while we were all at dinner. The servants can attest to your whereabouts."

Abigail sighed in relief, and her conflicting guilt rose to contradict her. "The poor woman. I knew she was upset, but to kill herself? I don't understand it."

Mr. Travers's voice lowered. "You think you know somebody." He let out a breath. "William, as much as I regret the loss of Mrs. Graham, if the danger is clear, why tell us now? You could have waited until we were back inside. Can't we have a break from death for one evening?"

"I quite enjoyed ruining your fun." Carrington cleared his throat. "Also, we're supposed to be chaperoning Miss Riverton, not ravishing her."

"Of course you aren't supposed to ravish her, but I'm sure that I am."

"Get in the house, Hugh."

Mr. Travers held his ground and gestured with the sweep of his arm. "After you."

Carrington paused before he led the way. He looked back to make sure they followed, and they did so reluctantly. The space between him and them widened as they walked.

"We can't let them know what happened between us." He spoke in a hurried whisper. "It'll make things worse."

She nodded. "It won't be easy."

"Just go on as you have and don't think anything of my relationship with Miss Archibald, because there isn't one." He paused, waiting for her to respond. "I must insist you keep some distance from Greymore."

She stiffened. "You have no right to make demands of me, especially after justifying your friendship to Miss Archibald. Besides, I have no interest in Greymore, nor does he think of me that way."

"Excuse me if I don't believe that."

She craned her head to the side to glare at him. "You can ask him yourself, without your fists."

He released a shivering breath. "I'm deeply sorry for that. I can't tell you how much my guilt has eaten at me. Seeing you hurt by my hand was the worst thing I've ever felt."

"You can make it up to me." Her brain remained back at the tree, since her lips were now talking for her.

He appeared to measure the distance to the house with his eyes. "When can I see you?"

"Obviously not right now. Later, maybe." She left her answer vague as her reasoning floated back to her bit by bit.

He grasped her hand and kissed her wrist. "Are you sure it can't be now?"

She glanced around the darkened yard and motioned with her head to Carrington. As if he had sensed the gesture, Carrington stopped and looked back. He rubbed at his face as he walked back to them.

"Do I need to tie you down, Hugh? Release Miss Riverton so we can go back in." He nodded at their clasped hands, and she pulled hers back. After that, Carrington made them walk in front of him the rest of the way. There was no talking then, and they returned to the house without incident.

Carrington addressed her when they reached the building. "Mr. North has completed his search. You may return to your quarters if you wish. A few of us have gathered in the drawing room if you'd like to join us there." He insisted his brother accompany him to the drawing room so he could keep an eye on him.

Abigail headed for the stairs, at last capable of avoiding the others. Mr. Travers started as if to follow, but his brother held him back. She left them behind her.

"How would I explain both your absences? Aren't you trying to avoid suspicion?" Carrington's voice carried behind her.

"William, I swear when this is over, there will be no peace for you. I'll never walk on again when I come across you and Delia."

Their voices faded, and her footsteps brought her back to the ground. Kissing him had been a mistake, and being upset was no excuse for her rash behavior. He had only given her the answers she wanted to hear. She was just another girl to him. Another dalliance to hold him over until he returned to civilization.

She snapped her door shut behind her and pushed her trunk against it to barricade herself against the world.

Chapter Fifteen

Late into the night, footsteps tapped along the hallway outside of Abigail's room. Expecting another murder, she rose to check the door, when voices came from the hall. Her hand froze on the doorknob.

"Hugh? What are you doing up so late? Stop stomping outside my door. I need my rest." Mrs. Eddings's voice was clear and wide-awake.

"Go back to bed, Grandmamma," Mr. Travers said, irritation edging his tone.

"I don't think so. Leave the girl alone, Hugh."

The footsteps stopped. "Or what?"

"Or I'll have your father reduce your inheritance."

Steps shuffled over the hall floor. "You wouldn't."

"Try me. I've been given specific instructions to watch out for you. Leave the girl be so I can go back to sleep."

Muffled grumbling about Carrington that Abigail couldn't quite make out came through the door. She stared at the wood with wide eyes and covered her mouth with her hand to stifle her giggle.

"This is not William's fault." Mrs. Eddings's voice hardened. "You've shown yourself to be a scoundrel, and we've drawn a line with Miss Riverton."

A warm appreciation filled Abigail's chest at Mrs. Eddings's concern for her, and her skin heated at the shame of their earlier kisses. England was a clean slate, and she had taken every opportunity to destroy it. What was worse, this was Nigel all over again without any plans attached. She had wanted the taste of desire on her lips. It had been so long since she had experienced that passion, the longing. It wouldn't last, and she would be alone and broken again.

A long, melodramatic sigh came from the hallway, and retreating footsteps faded away. Abigail poked her head out at Mrs. Eddings, who stood in the hall with her hands firmly planted on her hips as she watched her grandson's retreating form.

"Miss Riverton, I adore Hugh, but I wouldn't trust him to be alone with an old, withered nun. Please be careful." Mrs. Eddings's gaze never left the hallway.

"Thank you, ma'am. I appreciate your concern." Abigail suspected the woman had eyes on the back of her head.

In truth, if Mrs. Eddings hadn't intervened, Abigail would have invited him in just as she had opened her window to Nigel on their final night together. She had fancied Nigel as her Romeo, whispering secret declarations of love, but she'd conveniently forgotten *Romeo and Juliet* ended in tragedy.

The next morning, avoiding Mr. Travers proved easier than she'd imagined. He wasn't at breakfast when she went in, and Delia renewed their plan of going riding. Greymore seconded the idea, and the trio made an early start out into the sunny Cornish countryside. Soot seemed to recall their previous outing and was eager for the exercise. Her intentions clicked right into place.

They rode in silence with the exception of the pounding horse hooves. Delia took a path along the cliff face, giving a chilling view of the fall below. Once, Abigail's gaze wandered to the crashing waves below, and dizziness swept over her. She kept her distance from the edge after that. Visions of falling to the rocky waters below were enough for her.

They traveled in a roundabout way from their last ride, and the path descended along to the beach. Among the brilliant yellow wildflowers, Abigail spotted a cluster of black forms scrambling about the ground. When she got closer, she recognized them as ravens fighting over some poor creature's body. Their high-pitched cries broke the stillness of the ride. Her stomach churned, and she shuddered as one of the creatures pulled away a mangled gray wing.

The event cast an uneasiness about her she couldn't shake for the rest of the trip. Her senses became hypersensitive. The flowers shone too bright, the water too murky, the salty air too putrid. She greeted the sight of the stables with a relieved sigh.

The returned party met with the anxious stares of Carrington and Mr. Travers. Carrington grabbed the reins of Starlight and helped his wife down. Greymore beat Mr. Travers to Soot and did likewise.

"What's the matter? Grandmamma said I was able to ride still." Delia straightened her back as though she expected to defend herself.

"It isn't that. There have been some startling developments." Carrington faced Abigail. "I don't want to alarm you, Miss Riverton, but Miss Archibald's calling for your arrest. She claims you're the sole murderer of Mr. Archibald, Sir Peter, and Mrs. Graham."

Abigail steadied herself on Greymore's shoulder. "How would this not alarm me? I thought Mrs. Graham killed herself."

"That's what we believe, but Miss Archibald claims there's enough evidence to charge you for all three deaths. We've been trying to persuade her otherwise, but I'm afraid we'll have to send you with Constable North if we don't find evidence to the contrary. Proving your innocence of killing Sir Peter and Mrs. Graham will be easy enough, but there's too much against you concerning Mr. Archibald's death. It's more than enough to bring you before the magistrate."

She blinked under her lowered brows. "Why would she accuse me of the other deaths?"

"To her, the faster you're away for the murder of her brother, the better. She may even believe you committed the other murders, since she has little reason to believe otherwise."

"So that's it, then?" Her fists tightened at her sides. "It's her word against mine?"

He shook his head. "It's not so easy as that."

"Of course it is. I'm an outsider. An untitled daughter of an untitled father. Not to mention I'm a colonist. It isn't much of a stretch to blame me for murder, because my people are rebels and traitors to the Crown. I've no chance against Miss Archibald or her family. You'd all be better off abandoning me to the gallows." Her voice was steady compared to her quaking fists.

"We're not abandoning you." Greymore set his jaw. "I'll be there for you, and I'm sure the Travers family will as well."

"Of course." Carrington shifted his weight as he rubbed at his neck. "There's one thing Constable North brought up that may help. If you were to become an Englishwoman, it would make things go easier."

"What do you mean?" Her forehead scrunched up. "I'm attached to my home."

"Dear, he means you could marry an Englishman." Delia's gaze snapped to Carrington. "That's a bit extreme."

"I'd be more than happy to fill the role if it would keep you free." The solemn offer from Greymore made her doubt her own ears. "Being Viscountess Greymore will carry weight with the magistrate."

"Like hell." Mr. Travers's protest was more growl than words. "I may not bear the title, but my family name holds just as much sway."

"You can't be serious. Marrying Miss Riverton will only antagonize Miss Archibald further. The woman will probably have you drawn and quartered."

"I'm willing to take my chances to keep you from Miss Riverton."

Abigail closed her eyes and rubbed at her temples. "I appreciate your enthusiasm to be the sacrificial lambs, but I'd rather not marry anyone. Don't be so quick to impale yourselves on the altar. I take marriage seriously, and these proposals are for all the wrong reasons."

Carrington studied her expression. "Are you sure? If we delay, it will be too late."

"Quite sure. I'm not ready for marriage." She had been quick in her desire to wed Nigel, and she had narrowly dodged ruining her life. A hasty marriage without happiness was as good as hanging.

Mr. Travers made to protest, but Greymore interrupted him. "I know what you're going to say, Hugh, and I suggest you respect her decision."

"I want only what's best for her." Mr. Travers stepped toward Greymore, but Carrington held him back.

Greymore's face grew blank. "It's her choice to decide what's best. Nobody can decide for her."

"And you think you're the better choice? Excuse me if I fail to agree with your assessment. I'll be damned if she chooses you."

She flinched at his words and blocked him from Greymore. "How dare you speak for me? Lord Greymore's a friend, as I told you before. Of course he'd want to help me, and it's appreciated. Since you continue to be pigheaded, maybe you would prefer it your way."

Abigail grabbed Greymore's shirt and tugged him off to the house. She laced her arm with his and ignored the startled protest behind them. She kept her pace leisurely and her voice loud enough for the rest of the party to make out.

"Shall we go back?" Abigail flashed a toothy grin at Greymore. "There are…um…things we need to…discuss."

Greymore returned her smile. After a few steps, rustling and cursing sounded behind them.

Delia spoke dryly behind them, "Hugh, she's joking. You of all people should appreciate that."

"But—" Travers began.

"But nothing, for God's sake. Go take matters into your own

hands."

Carrington laughed, and she clarified, "I didn't mean it that way, but if it works."

Only muffled words remained from the distance.

Greymore gave her arm a squeeze and released her. "I did mean what I said. It would be a marriage based on mutual respect, but it would keep you out of jail."

"I know, but I don't want to regret marriage. I mean no offense, but it would be like a cage to both of us without love. We owe it to ourselves to find the right matches."

"I agree with you but not at the expense of your life. Let me know if you change your mind. I can live with whatever you decide." He paused as though to consider his next words. "I think you would be happy with Hugh."

She tripped on her feet and froze into place. "What?"

He stopped beside her. "He would make you a good husband but only when you're ready."

"I thought you hated him."

"I've never hated him even if he insists on consistently misunderstanding me. We're much alike, though our motivations are different. He reminds me of a younger version of William and me."

They walked toward the house again as she tried to unravel what he had just said. Had she misheard him? She knew Greymore had no romantic interest in her, but she wouldn't dream of him setting her up with someone, especially not Mr. Travers.

"You mean you want Mr. Travers to court me?"

"Why else would I choose the song you played on the harpsichord? Do you think it's any coincidence I've shown you more interest in his presence? His feelings were already there. I just needed to bring them to the surface."

Her frown scrunched up her face. "For the last time, what was the song about? If it was some bawdy French song, I'll die from embarrassment."

Greymore chuckled. "So no one has told you? How interesting."

"Greymore." Her tone held a warning.

"It's a song about unrequited love."

"That isn't so bad. Why hasn't anyone told me?"

His expression grew serious. "The opening is about desire and passionate love. It ends in the man's broken heart and subsequent death."

Her face fell. "How horrible."

He continued in his solemn tone. "It's a fate I believe Hugh feels is his own and one with which you have some experience."

Back in New York, she thought she would fade out of her life like so much ash carried off in the wind. Nigel had taken away a part of her, whether it was love or not. The pain of betrayal and rejection had left a bitter feeling in her chest that was softening still. She couldn't bear the heartbreak again; it would kill her.

She shook her head. "That's not the same."

"Maybe not for you, but Hugh is a different matter. Whether he realizes his love or not is up for speculation."

"Mr. Travers isn't in love with me." She forced every bit of conviction from her breast into her words. "I know his ideas, and they're not the kind that come from the heart."

Greymore gave a short laugh. "Some things can be connected in surprising ways." They had come upon the house and paused outside the door.

She didn't believe a word of it. Mr. Travers thought of her as just another woman, made more enticing as forbidden fruit. This argument with Greymore was pointless, especially since the group behind them had caught up.

They piled into the house together to find Constable North waiting for them. His lopsided wig seemed to hint at his troubled thoughts. He nodded to each of them in turn and addressed Abigail. His glazed blue eyes considered her above the purple crescents hollowed into his cheeks.

"I regret we'll need to leave in the morning, Miss Riverton." His voice was hesitant. "I hope that's enough time for you to be ready."

She shrank away from him. "Why so soon?"

"I've dragged this out as long as I can, but I don't take threats like Miss Archibald's lightly. She's written to her family, and they'll be here in a matter of days. It's better to get this over with before they've gathered their forces."

A solid pit lodged in her throat, and she swallowed it down. "I understand. What do I need?"

He stood silent for a moment. Each second stacked the weight of dread on her chest at his next words. What sort of fate awaited her in the morning?

"Just bring your person and maybe anything that can still your mind on the journey. Don't bring anything of value, or you may never see it again."

She fought the bile forced from her stomach and nodded.

In her haze, she did not notice her progress to her room. At one point, Delia joined her, a silent guardian. At the back of her mind, she heard the voices behind her, but they were foreign, senseless. The shock helped her keep her composure, and she applauded herself for not losing her dignity.

When they stepped into her room, Delia hugged her for a long while. Abigail wanted to pull away, to flee her friend's embrace before she fell apart, but Delia only squeezed her tighter. At last she sank into her friend's shoulder and sighed, letting the motherly gesture soothe her.

Eventually Delia released her and stood back, holding her shoulders. "We can get you out of this. You could flee to France or wherever else you might want to go. Carrington could arrange it."

"I can't allow that. The burden would fall on you, and then we'd all be unhappy." She retreated out of Delia's reach.

"This won't make me happy either. I'm so sorry. This was supposed to be an escape, and now an escape is what you need." Delia's emerald eyes shone with unshed tears. "Do you want me to poison them all? I would do it."

Abigail gave her a small smile. "That isn't necessary. I'm sure things will turn out all right in the end." She wished she believed her own words, but it was what her friend needed to hear.

"Is there anything I can get you? I'm sending Carrington along with you. I wouldn't be surprised if Hugh and Greymore follow as well. I expect Lynette and Mrs. Eddings will stay by my side."

She closed her eyes in a tight line. "They don't have to do that."

"Why not? Miss Archibald has already planned to follow you in a separate carriage. I don't think she trusts Constable North. It can't hurt to have a friendly face nearby. I'm afraid there won't be many of them."

"What has become of Mr. Graham?" She settled herself on the edge of the bed.

Delia frowned and sat down next to her. "He wants to bury his wife in her hometown in Devon. To his credit, he seems remorseful at her passing. Perhaps he'll find in her death what he missed while she was alive."

"What's that?"

"Hmm? Oh, forgiveness."

From what Abigail knew of Mr. Graham, she doubted he was a forgiving man. "I didn't know Mrs. Graham well, but she seemed kind. I can't imagine the pain she was in to end her own life."

"Yes, I wish I hadn't left her alone. I feel I'm to blame. She had nothing but misery since she arrived, though I'm sure Greymore cheered her for a time."

A dry laugh escaped Abigail, and she shifted her weight on the bed. "I imagine you're right, but he's probably blaming himself as well."

"A sad business, suicide. Everyone and nobody takes responsibility, and all answers are buried in the grave."

"What of the killer?" Her gaze flashed to Delia's thoughtful frown. "Could they be preoccupied with me while the killer gets away?"

"Nobody will escape. There are so few of us, and we know where everyone will be. Anyway, most of the guests have too much to lose to flee."

Abigail sucked in a quick breath. "What if Mrs. Graham was the killer? Maybe the guilt was too much for her."

"An interesting idea, but I don't know how she could've killed Sir Peter unless Greymore didn't notice her leave. It's something to consider though." Delia clicked her tongue. "That reminds me, I overheard Carrington discussing the letter opener with Hugh. Nobody recognizes it. One of the guests must have brought it, and I doubt you had such an ostentatious thing."

Abigail smirked. "Overheard through spying?"

"What do you take me for?" Delia's frown deepened. "Of course it was from spying. There's no way I'll let Carrington keep me out of this. I suspect he knows I'm listening, but for some reason, that's preferable to him than telling me outright."

"Dee, I'll miss you."

Delia brushed away a stray tear. "Don't you dare. You'll be back before you know it, and we can read awful novels until we're declared silly females."

"We're already silly females." After all, Abigail had a habit of mooning over men she could never have. Maybe the novels had made her dim-witted. Her invented romances and adventures left her hollow next to the reality.

"True, but nobody has threatened me with the asylum yet."

Abigail choked on a laugh. "You sound rather disappointed."

"Nonsense." Delia gave a short wave. "Will you be coming to dinner? I could have food sent up." Her friend groaned and held her back as she rose from bed.

"I better avoid Miss Archibald, so I suppose I'll eat in my room."

Delia stood over her, hand on her hip. "I'll deal with Miss Archibald. I want your company before this charade starts. You have friends here wanting to dine with you. Also, I imagine whatever they feed people in jail will be unpleasant."

"I suspect you're right." Abigail's shoulders rose and fell with her sigh. "How did it come to this?"

"I don't know, Abs." Delia opened the door. "I wish we could live in our books. In the real world, some of the best people receive the worst treatment."

CHAPTER SIXTEEN

A SENSE OF foreboding choked the air at dinner. Delia fulfilled her promise, and the emotional leech, Miss Archibald, was absent. Constable North and Mrs. Eddings had also elected to take dinner in their rooms, allowing their private goodbyes. Yet the dinner that would normally be an amicable experience fell flat in anticipation of tomorrow.

Abigail knew she should cherish every bite of the meal and every taste of freedom, but she pushed the food around on her plate. Greymore sat next to her and encouraged her to try this dish and that drink. She followed his guidance mechanically, tasting only dust. The others picked up on her mood, resulting in a somber affair.

Except Mr. Travers.

He was irritable and unreasonable with everyone who tried to talk to him. They ignored his attacks, having no energy to do otherwise. His fidgeting and restless leg under the table tugged at Abigail's nerves. After the third time of asking him to stop bouncing his knee, Abigail snapped.

"Must you persist? You're shaking my chair." She inched her chair further toward Greymore's side.

"How can you be so calm?" He stopped his movement with sudden restraint, frozen in his agitated state.

She closed her eyes. "I'm not. My insides are eating their way out of me."

"As are mine." Delia spoke softly from Travers's other side. Lynette nodded in agreement.

"I can't just sit here and do nothing." Mr. Travers rose to his feet.

Carrington sighed and set his fork down as his brother abandoned the room.

"Can't he wait until I've finished my meal?"

"You could just leave him to his own devices," Delia said, waving toward the door.

He favored his wife with raised brows. "In this mood? Yes, that'll go over well."

"We'll save you dessert." Lynette gestured to the selection of ices with a spoon.

He gave her a tired smile.

"What do you plan to do? Tie him down? I'd like to see it."

"How do you suppose I do that?"

"I could help you." Greymore grinned from ear to ear.

Carrington's head cocked, and he considered Greymore. "That isn't the worst idea. I'd welcome the company, at least. He's going to be difficult."

"You're putting that mildly." Greymore stood with Carrington and grabbed a few precious bites before he left the table.

Abigail ignored the proceedings. There was nothing they could do.

Not long after they left, Lynette rushed after them. Delia and Abigail gazed off after her sudden departure.

"Do you think maybe we should go?" Delia's lips pulled back, and she sucked in a breath through her teeth.

"Goodness, why?"

Delia shrugged. "Never mind. I'm sure they'll work it out."

"I'm glad you're here with me. I don't think I could face tonight by myself. I don't know what I'll do tomorrow without even Alma."

"Always." Delia's grin reached her eyes, but to Abigail, it

seemed forced. "Now, don't you worry about tomorrow. You have hours yet, and there isn't any need to give it any more of your time. If you like, I could stay with you tonight."

She thought of Delia's deafening snores keeping her awake on the last comfortable rest she may have in a while. She shook her head. "I'll probably just keep you up with my tossing, and that can't be good for the baby."

"All right, but I'm sure Lynette would stay with you."

Abigail glared at her.

Delia's lip twitched. "Yes, I know what you mean. She's good company at times, but she kicks in her sleep, and I swear she's more talkative unconscious than awake."

As though she was summoned by their words, the door crashed open against the wall and Lynette rushed in. Her eyes frantically darted between them as she caught her breath. "Abs, you won't believe it." She paused as though working to regain her speech. "You just won't believe it."

Abigail's skin grew chilled. "What is it?" Her voice stuttered as she struggled with her speech.

"You're free to go, at least for now."

The words were clear but the meaning foreign. Nothing could have prepared Abigail for this revelation. She sat motionless, not daring to move in case she might wake from this dream. Free? Had the constable come to his senses? Had they found the killer?

"What?" Delia asked while Abigail sat mute. "How?"

"I'm afraid you won't like it. Hugh's responsible for your salvation."

"I don't see how things could be any worse. What did he do?" Delia shot her sister with an impatient look.

"Carrington and Greymore tried to get him to change his mind, but they were too late. Constable North had already seen him, and everything was decided." Lynette dragged out her explanation as she did when she had news.

Delia slapped her hand on the table. "What did he do, damn

you?"

"He confessed."

Abigail's stomach dropped, and she observed the other women as though from outside her body. The world tilted as she tried to register the words. "Confessed what?"

"To everything." Lynette pronounced each syllable. "He said he killed Mr. Archibald and poisoned Sir Peter. North already declared Mrs. Graham's death a suicide or he would've confessed to that too."

Abigail's mouth went dry. As much as she wanted to remain free, she wouldn't have Mr. Travers suffer in her place.

"The idiot." Delia's lips puckered in a sour expression. "How'd he explain the murder weapon in Abigail's room?"

"He said he put it there for lack of a better place, not dreaming anyone would suspect her or discover it." Lynette spoke matter-of-factly as if the explanation was perfectly reasonable, though it made little sense.

Aside from the séance, what reason could he have for being in her room? Unless, of course, she invited him in under other circumstances, and he could prove their involvement after his trip to her door.

Abigail rested her forehead on her hand. "And North believed him?"

"I doubt it, but he doesn't think you're guilty either. At this point, he would take the confession of Starlight. He wants to be done with it all."

Delia raised her chin. "The magistrate won't believe it."

"Are you sure? They can't ignore a confession." Lynette chewed at her lower lip. "We could argue he's lying to protect another."

Delia shook her head, and her gaze fell on Abigail, who had sunk in on herself. "It would be better if we found the true killer."

"What if he's telling the truth? What if he's the killer? He must've waited until the last possible moment to confess in hopes they would clear Abigail."

"I don't believe it." Delia glowered at her sister.

"You have to admit he has motive."

"I'd like to think my brother-in-law's more resourceful than using a letter opener to kill someone."

"He didn't kill them." Abigail's voice was a breath of sound.

"What was that?" Delia leaned toward her.

Abigail hardened her voice with false confidence. "He didn't kill them. I heard him moving around the room all night. I'm sure he didn't leave the room. I would've heard it."

Lynette tapped her fingers against her crossed arm. "You could've dozed off." Abigail suppressed the urge to shake Lynette for her disloyalty.

"I suppose you're right, but I don't believe he did it." Abigail paused as the implications of his confession took hold of her. "Damn. Why would he confess?"

Lynette and Delia exchanged looks, brows raised.

Ignoring them, Abigail let out a puff of air and threw up her hands. "I can't let him do this." She bolted up from her seat and flew out the door.

She rushed to Carrington's study, where she was sure the mess had started. Carrington and Greymore looked up from their drinking only long enough to tell her Mr. Travers had gone to his room. She had a vague memory of where his new room was located, as far away from her room as he could manage. She directed her search there. The upstairs was quiet, everyone in their respective sullen moods.

She reached the area in the hall where he resided and looked around at the few doors. A faint shuffling came from behind one, and she hesitated before knocking. She said a silent prayer that it wasn't Miss Archibald's room.

To her relief, Mr. Travers cracked the door open, surprise was evident in his wide eyes.

She studied his weary face and wondered if she had made a mistake. "Can I talk to you?"

"Now?" He sounded as surprised as he looked.

"When else? Before or after they hang you?"

"They aren't going to hang me. Well, they probably will actually." He rubbed the back of his neck. "This isn't a good place. Do you want to meet in the library?"

She rolled her eyes. "For God's sake, you could die and you're worried about what's proper?"

"You're the one who'll have to worry about that. I'm more afraid of my sister-in-law than I am of death. You know she'll make me wish I were dead."

"Do shut up." She pushed her way past him. His room was a mess of strewn clothes and leather upholstery. It reminded her of Carrington's study but with more clutter. She wondered if a maid was ever allowed in here.

He shut the door behind her, and she spun to face him. He had dressed down for the comfort of his room, wearing only light trousers and a loose linen shirt. She suspected by his disheveled nature that he had thrown the shirt on to answer the door. She wished he had left it off.

He leaned back against the door. "You shouldn't be in here."

She furrowed her brow, unable to make him out. "How's this different from you coming to my room?"

"That was another time." He breathed out a slow puff of air. "Don't let me ruin your future."

"Are you mad? What could you possibly be thinking? I was ready to face whatever fate I had. You've so much more ahead of you. I won't allow you to take my place."

"It's already done."

"Absolutely not." Abigail stepped closer to him. "Come downstairs with me, and we can explain to Mr. North that you've come to your senses." She tugged on his hand.

He shook his head and pulled back on her until she stilled.

"Please don't do this." Tears threatened at the corners of her eyes.

"My mind's made up."

"Damn you." Her restraint fell as did the stream of tears.

He brought his other hand to her face and wiped them away, but new tears replaced them. He cupped her cheek with his hand to study her face. Defeat shadowed his tired eyes.

"I can't stand the thought of you in jail, even for a minute. I don't care what happens to me as long as you're safe." He ran his thumb over her cheek, and she pressed into his palm.

"We could escape. If we leave now, we can get a head start before anyone realizes we're gone." Her words lacked enthusiasm.

His hand dropped. "I can't do that to you. It wouldn't be right to our families either. You'd never see them again. It would break your heart."

"And this won't?"

He stepped away from her and gestured to the door. "You should go before anyone realizes you're here." He cleared his throat and looked away.

"It's probably too late for that. If Carrington and Greymore didn't already tell someone where I was going, then the servants who overheard probably will."

His mouth fell wide. "My brother and that ass told you where to find me?"

"They didn't seem too concerned they were sending me to your bedroom. Of course, if you still prefer I leave, then I guess I better go." She moved to the door, but he stopped her with a hand as she passed.

She gazed down at his hand. "Mr. Travers, if you don't mind, I'll be on my way."

He pulled her against his chest, and she squeaked in surprise.

He grinned at her as if he would devour her. His body heat blazed through his thin shirt. His smoky-sweet scent clung to the fabric, and she loosened her muscles against him.

"Oh, did you change your mind? I thought I'd have to look elsewhere." She peered at him through her lashes.

A growl-like sound escaped the back of his throat.

"You disagree? I thought it was the only logical alternative."

"If anyone touches you other than me, I'll have their head." He spoke through his teeth.

"Must you insist—"

He plunged into a rough, needy kiss, cutting off her thoughts. He pulled her hips flush against his, and his arousal peaked through their clothes. The kiss grew heated, sending ripples of urgency through her. She moaned into his mouth, which quickened his attentions.

He bent to kiss her neck, and his hands wandered to her breasts. Shock waves sent shivers dancing over her skin to pool between her legs. He tugged at the top of her gown, and she took a step back, allowing him the room to remove her clothes. Her limbs trembled as he did so deftly and with impressive speed. He eyed her chemise as though planning his next attack, but instead, she advanced on him and ran her hands up under his shirt. Her fingers brushed over his lean torso. A groan escaped his throat, and he lifted his shirt off for her.

Abigail smiled at the sight of his strong, healthy chest sprinkled with a dusting of hair. His breathing quickened as she studied him.

"My," she said.

He grunted and backed her up to his bed. It was as if she was penned in by a hungry wolf. She giggled as he lifted her and spread her over the mattress.

He leaned to get on the bed, but she stopped him with a raised foot. She pointed at his trousers. "Those have to go."

His gaze dropped to his legs, and he chuckled while undressing them. She got a flash of sculpted thighs and his excited manhood before he returned to the bed. His warm form crawled over her, and he pulled the chemise up as he went. He yanked the garment out from under her and over her head. Only her stockings remained.

He dropped to the side of her and watched her from where he propped his head up on his elbow. His eyes wandered over her body, and his appreciative gaze sent a tingling thrill through her.

His hand caressed her side to the top of her stocking, and he bent to untie the garter. With slow, deliberate motions, he tugged the stocking off and moved to the other. Her legs tickled under his administrations, and she squirmed beneath his hands.

His nude form next to her on the bed enthralled her, and she held her breath at every new movement. His long limbs took up much of the bed. Where she was small and rounded, he was tall and lean. He would cover her from head to toe. The thought made her thirst for his touch.

He removed the other stocking and kissed the arch of her foot. She inhaled a sharp breath and tried to pull away. Instead of releasing her, he worked his way up her leg with his tongue. His eyes shone with heat as he watched her reaction. He made it to her inner thigh, when she stayed him.

"I want you." She pulled at his hand.

"In good time. Let me savor this." He rubbed her thigh. "Please?"

She settled back in answer.

He spread apart her thighs, and she tensed under his hands. Their eyes met, and she nodded at his unspoken question. His hand trailed over her most sensitive parts, and she moaned, spreading her legs further. He grinned up at her and ducked between her legs.

She focused with rounded eyes on the top of his head until he licked, when she bucked at his touch and laid a hand on his hair. His warm breath heightened the sensation aroused by his tongue. The give and take of wet and dry heat. Blood pulsed through her body as in a wild race. His touch was velvet and magic, torture and death.

"Oh God. My heart will kill me."

He ignored her outburst and continued his attentions. The motions of his tongue muddled her brain, and she arched back into the bed. Her legs quivered around him, and her fingers threaded through his hair. She lifted her hips shamelessly, giving him everything. Her body tightened and broke apart in explosive relief.

She whimpered as he rose from his position between her legs and crawled up to her breasts. He stroked his thumb over her hard nipple and took the other in his mouth. Licking and sucking, nipping and caressing. The wild heat consuming her nearly set her ablaze. She embraced the inferno and gave in to the madness.

She twisted beneath him. "Hugh, please." If he wasn't inside her now, she would burst into flames.

He raised a brow in a mock question.

"Please, I need you."

He yielded to her demands and brought his lips to hers, and she raised her hips in invitation. His actions were slow as if he waited for her to change her mind. His gaze bored into hers as he settled between her legs.

A low moan swept from her throat when he filled her. The anticipated sensation nearly sent her over the edge.

Senseless, she let him guide their movements, and they developed a rhythm. Her eyes rolled back into her head, and all she knew was him. He held her close, the texture of his skin against her breasts a union of its own. Her every nerve craved more of him, and she thought she could melt into him.

His thrusts intensified, and he gritted his teeth as if he held on. He reached behind her with both hands, kneading her buttocks apart. The action plunged him deeper, and she clawed at his shoulders to ground herself to him, yet she floated along with him, euphoria just on the edge of her grasp.

Her feral urge sent him out of control, and he thrust with abandon. His breaths came in pants, and at the corner of her mind, she knew he was near release. She met him with each plunge. His jaw clenched with one last valiant effort to hold back.

She ground into him, and with his release, his moan filled the room. The force brought her to her own peak, and she clamped down on him as she shivered in his embrace. A brilliant light filled her, and for a moment, she lived among the stars.

He collapsed onto her, panting. His eyes were closed as he

gave her a chaste kiss. They merely existed, a tangled mess of limbs and sex. They stayed joined, neither one of them wanting this space in time to end.

She ran her fingers over his back lovingly as he nudged her face. "Mm, Hugh?"

"Yes?" He spoke into her neck.

"Can we do that again?"

He laughed, the sound vibrating through her body. "Give me a minute."

He napped for a while by her side, spooning her to him. When he woke, he took her again. The night continued in periods of lovemaking and rest. Exploring each other, discovering new pleasures. She basked in his attention and reciprocated when he would allow. They talked little but never about their future trouble.

At dawn, they dozed in each other's arms, cherishing the last moments of their time together. Abigail fluttered her eyes open and yawned. She combed her fingers through Hugh's chest hair, waking him. He kissed her hair lightly and closed his eyes again. A corner of her lips turned up, and she ran her hand down his belly until he caught her fingers with his.

He gazed at her through slit eyes. "I appreciate your enthusiasm, madam, but I must insist I rest."

She pouted. "Then rest. I'll do all the work."

He closed his eyes again and dropped her hand. "Carry on, then."

Abigail had just wrapped her fingers around his shaft when the door was flung open. She jerked the covers up to hide herself. Hugh's eyes flashed, and he frowned at his brother in the doorway.

"Can't you knock?" Hugh's voice was low and dangerous.

Carrington looked away. "I'm sorry. I didn't know she was here."

"I fail to believe you. What do you want?"

"There has been a disturbing development while you were,

er, enjoying yourselves." Carrington seemed preoccupied with his nails.

Hugh narrowed his eyes at his brother. "So you did know she was here."

Carrington let out a long sigh. "Honestly, Hugh, everyone in the house knows. I don't think anyone got any sleep. Which is probably one of the reasons for this new problem."

Abigail didn't know if she should be ashamed or curious. The burn crawling up her skin decided for her.

"What is it?" Hugh asked. "Can't you see I'm a dying man?"

Carrington snickered and gazed over at him, but at once forced his eyes away. "I wouldn't say you're dying. Constable North had a chat with Miss Archibald and now refuses to take you in. Miss Archibald won't budge in her position on Miss Riverton's guilt. It seems he'll take her to Truro after all."

CHAPTER SEVENTEEN

HER BLOOD TURNED to ice.

She stared dumbly at Carrington and waited for his words to untangle. Hugh wrapped his arms around her and brought her crashing back to his room. Her concern had gone from her own life to his. Yet no matter who took the blame, Miss Archibald had won. Abigail could never be with Hugh.

Last night had been a taste of happiness, but she'd known it wouldn't last. Even without the accusations, Hugh deserved better than a ruined American. Nigel had left a stain like a brand, declaring her mistakes for the world to see.

Already her family had suffered for her actions, having lost business in the wake of her troubles. Her brothers assured her it didn't matter, but their chances of finding suitable wives had dwindled.

Maybe she did deserve to hang.

"In any case, you're both needed below." Carrington shut the door behind him, leaving them to get dressed.

"Hugh, what will I do?" she asked.

"Let me think of something. There's still a chance the magistrate will declare it a weak case."

"I don't understand any of this." She peered into his face, hoping for some small bit of comfort there.

"I know." He wrestled his trousers on.

A light tapping sounded at the door, and Hugh cocked his head at it. "For once, somebody knocks." He threw on his shirt and cracked the door.

"Excuse me, sir. Lord Carrington sent me to dress Miss Riverton." Alma's voice filtered through the crack.

Hugh opened the door wider and nodded her in.

Alma carried fresh clothes with her as well as essential toiletries. The heat rushed to Abigail's face as Alma witnessed her bedraggled state. They waited as Hugh hurried with the rest of his clothes. He bent down and pecked her lips before leaving them. His affectionate display made her stomach flutter in front of Alma.

Abigail cleared her throat and swung her legs off the bed. Alma came to her, offering clean water and towels. Abigail wanted to get downstairs as soon as possible, and Alma helped her hurry through the routine.

"What you must think of me," Abigail said in a quiet voice.

Alma gave her a small smile. "I've never thought better of you."

She craned her head toward her maid. "How so?"

"I admire that you're going after what you want and in the face of terrible odds. None of us believe you're a murderer. Hopefully the right people can be persuaded."

"Thank you, Alma. That means a lot to me." If only Alma were the magistrate. Abigail couldn't imagine how to convince an Englishman not to hang her.

Alma finished Abigail's hair, putting it into a simple twist. She inspected her mistress and gave her an encouraging nod.

"I must warn you. I heard on my way up here the rest of the Archibald family is nearby. The elder brother has just arrived." Alma calmed her voice into a gentle lull, and the bad news almost sounded like a compliment.

"Why didn't Carrington warn us?"

Alma shrugged. "I suspect it was for the same reason I waited to tell you, to avoid worrying you."

"At least you had the decency to let me prepare for it. Hugh went down there without any warning."

"Hugh?" Alma gave her a puzzled frown.

"Mr. Travers." Abigail's blush returned.

Alma straightened her face and made no comment on Abigail's slip. "Ah, well, do be careful down there."

Abigail nodded and glanced around the room at her strewn clothes.

"Don't worry about it. I'll find your things. Now off with you." Alma shooed her out the door.

Abigail exited Hugh's room like a thief, taking care not to be noticed and dashing down the hall in silent steps. When she reached the stairs, arguing echoed from below. She slowed her pace, postponing the inevitable. Outside the drawing room, she inhaled deeply and rounded her shoulders.

"It would be an entertaining conversation if it weren't so serious."

Abigail jumped and almost collided with Lynette behind her. "Why aren't you in there?"

Lynette twisted up her lips. "I tried. They threw me out."

"Do you want to accompany me?" It couldn't hurt to have another friend in the room even if it was Lynette.

"I suppose if the yelling isn't directed toward me this time, then it can't hurt." She linked arms with Abigail.

Abigail frowned at her and opened the door.

Hugh stared down at a man she didn't recognize, presumably Miss Archibald's other brother.

"There she is." Miss Archibald pointed toward them. "Alexander, that's the woman who's responsible for killing poor Adam."

Mr. Archibald examined her with hazel eyes as one would a horse. He was almost as tall as Hugh but with broad shoulders, hinting at an athletic build. She would say he was handsome if it weren't for the circumstances. She had no desire to find out which man was the better fighter.

Lynette urged her forward to meet him.

Carrington placed himself beside them. "Mr. Archibald, may I present Miss Riverton?"

Hugh moved to cut him off, but Carrington stilled him with a glare.

"Miss Riverton." Mr. Archibald nodded in lieu of a bow. "So you're the American who's causing such a stir. Tell me, did you fancy my brother?"

Abigail hesitated and weighed her response. It was no use lying. She shook her head.

He dropped his gaze. "Yes, I didn't think so. Few people got along with Adam. Honestly, I'm surprised he wasn't killed sooner."

"Alex, how can you say such things?" Miss Archibald's face paled as she turned her outrage on her older brother.

He spared a glance for his sister. "Alice, you're the only one that was really friendly with him. I loved him because he was my brother, but he was a real ass."

Miss Archibald narrowed her eyes at him.

"Are you certain it's Miss Riverton you want to accuse? I'm sure most of the household including the servants had a reason to kill him."

"I'm quite sure. She had the murder weapon in her bedroom, and she has this ridiculous notion he attacked her. Imagine, our brother attacking that girl. She's obviously beneath his notice." Miss Archibald regarded Abigail with a sharp stare and a sour twist to her lips.

Hugh clenched his fists at his sides. "On the contrary, Adam was beneath Miss Riverton's notice."

"I see now. Hugh," Mr. Archibald said, "I'm sorry you're in the middle of this, but we have to have justice for our family."

"We're your family too."

"True, but it's between choosing my siblings and my cousins. I'm sure my father will choose the former. That is, unless you have another suspect?" Mr. Archibald scanned the occupants of the room.

There was no answer.

He nodded. "I thought not. We'll await my parents' arrival."

Constable North groaned.

Carrington eyed the man. "I see no reason Constable North need stay. If she comes peacefully, he can return to his other duties."

Mr. Archibald pouted. "I'd rather he accompany Miss Riverton, but we can hire a local deputy to fulfill his duties for him. I understand Mr. North has been detained for a while."

"And paid well for it," Carrington said, his voice like a whip.

Mr. Archibald squinted at Mr. North, perhaps to see what he was worth. "Then he can afford to hire another deputy to help him catch up with his duties."

Mr. North's face darkened at the suggestion.

"Now then, what's this about Adam attacking Miss Riverton?"

Carrington motioned for everyone to sit down. He recounted the events, since he seemed to be the only one who could calmly speak. He went on to explain the other murders in a cursory fashion. Mr. Archibald's face transformed from stone cold to openmouthed and surprised. He occasionally glanced at his sister to confirm while he listened to the account. When Carrington was through with his speech, the room fell quiet.

Mrs. Eddings broke the silence. "When can we expect your parents, Alexander?"

"Not long, Aunt Evelyn." Mr. Archibald rubbed at his eyes. "They weren't far behind me. I think maybe tomorrow or the next day, depending on how long they decide to stop."

"Maybe your father can talk some sense into Alice. I fail to see how a sweet girl like Miss Riverton can overpower a man like Adam. If my Hugh hadn't intervened, she wouldn't have had a chance. And with a letter opener?" Mrs. Eddings snorted. "Miss Riverton has a perfectly good dagger in her room."

Abigail caught Mrs. Eddings's gaze and gave her a sad smile.

If only the Archibalds had such sense.

Miss Archibald fixed her icy stare on the older woman.

Mr. Archibald faced Carrington. "I'd like to see this letter opener. That is, if you don't mind."

Carrington gave him a curt nod. "Of course. Perhaps you can identify if it was your brother's. We've never seen it."

"You've always been the intelligent sibling, Alexander." Mrs. Eddings's cool voice held a bite.

Abigail hid her laugh behind her hand.

"That's enough, Grandmamma." Carrington's stern tone carried across the room.

Mr. Archibald ignored them. "Is this everyone here?" He gestured over the room with his hand.

"Not quite. There's also Mr. Graham, who left to bury his wife."

Mr. Archibald glared at his cousin. "I assume he'll soon join us?"

Carrington stiffened his posture. "I sent my driver with him just to be sure. We couldn't fault the man for wanting to bury her. I was hesitant to even suggest he return, but I don't believe Miss Riverton is our killer, and I don't want to take the chance the real killer goes free."

"Really? Who do you believe the killer is, cousin?"

Carrington sighed, and his face seemed to slacken. "I have no idea."

"Then you can't fault our insistence we accuse the only suspect. Alice insists there is much to implicate Miss Riverton."

Carrington tightened his lips but nodded in agreement.

A dead weight coiled around Abigail's insides. How could Carrington agree she may be the killer? He had just said he didn't believe she'd done it. If the Archibalds got their way, she was doomed for being a victim. Mr. Adam Archibald would kill her as surely as he had nearly done that night. It was a clean break for the real murderer without their having to raise the blade to her throat.

"No," Abigail burst out, and all eyes went to her.

Mr. Archibald blinked at her as if she was a child interrupting. "No what?"

"No, this isn't right. Just because I'm the most obvious conclusion doesn't mean I'm necessarily the only conclusion. Excuse me, sir, but you're letting assumptions get in the way of judgment. If you'll examine the facts, the proven facts and not your speculations, then you'll see I'm not the ideal suspect. I understand presuming I'm the killer is the simplest route, and you must look into the possibility, but to call me guilty without witnesses and only the murder weapon in my room as proof? What do I have to gain from killing any of them?"

"My dear, what are you talking about? We don't need to know why you murdered him to know you did it. You must read too many novels." Mr. Archibald turned back to the men.

Her hands closed into fists, and her anger rose like steam just before a boil. *My dear?* So her argument wasn't worth considering because of her reading choices and her sex?

Hugh widened the space between them. "That's putting it mildly. Half the time, I don't know what she's saying." Hugh gave her a mocking smile. "We could all do without novels. They give women such silly ideas."

An iron weight slammed into her chest. Was this the same man with whom she had shared a bed? He must be joking. "Of course I read other things."

"This is the first I've heard of it. I suppose etiquette books count. One can't argue with the value of self-improvement." His dry voice grated at her nerves.

She gawked at him, not sure whether she should cry or scream. She doubted her own hearing. It was one thing when he teased, but she could see from his haughty expression he meant every word.

Miss Archibald laughed, a bark-like sound that echoed off the walls. "In her defense, Miss Riverton wasn't taught any better. However did you survive over there, Mr. Travers?"

"With patience and perseverance. The battle wasn't just fought on the field but also in the ballroom." He favored Miss Archibald with a small smile.

"Indeed. What a trying experience."

An itch crawled over Abigail's skin like she was dirty, violated. She couldn't summon the words to offer a retort. It left her naked to their criticism. She expected these comments from Miss Archibald but from Mr. Travers? Hadn't she come to know him? He was the snobbish bore she had always thought him, and all it had taken was a conversation with the Archibalds to bring him out.

A well of regret filled inside her. It was happening again. All the pretty words and passionate kisses faded like shadows on a moonless night.

"I have to applaud her efforts. You almost don't notice her background." Mr. Archibald's gaze examined every inch of her inferior breeding.

Abigail held herself firm under his criticism. At least she wouldn't be known as a coward.

"What does her background have to do with anything?" Greymore interrupted their conversation in a low voice. Abigail could have hugged him. The viscount was the only one who would defend her.

Mr. Travers squared his shoulders. "Everything, my lord."

Abigail fought the panic clenching her chest. She focused on slowing her breathing, but all she could think of was Hugh's hands on her and his promising kisses. She hadn't realized how strong her feelings were until they were torn out from her chest. What had she expected? His reputation spoke for itself. How could she be so blind?

She could be carrying his child.

Her hurried breaths caught in her throat. No other thought could be more unwelcome at that moment.

He spoke to Miss Archibald in hushed tones, and she tittered behind her hand and cast Abigail sidelong glances.

Lynette leaned into her ear. "You mustn't take him too seriously. He means well."

"How? Everyone has abandoned me."

"It isn't that. We know where to pick our battles. If we're to defend you, let it be when you need it the most. It won't do to insult the Archibalds any further. I'm sure Mr. Travers will pay for this in private."

Abigail frowned at her explanation. "Then why would Greymore?"

"He's the only one at liberty to do so. They aren't family to him, and he doesn't care if he appears rude."

Loud laughter stole her attention from Lynette. Miss Archibald smiled coyly at Mr. Travers as he spoke in a hushed voice. She gave him little slaps when he must have said something especially wicked.

"I want to vomit," Lynette said loud enough for them to hear. Abigail had to agree but for different reasons.

Abigail leaned into her friend. "Netty, I can't handle much more of this."

"Oh dear, do you want to leave?"

"Yes, please." Abigail averted her eyes from the man with whom she had spent a passionate night but who had betrayed her for a laugh.

Lynette hooked a guiding arm around her. Delia watched them with sullen eyes but stayed where she was.

"Leaving so soon, Miss Riverton?" Miss Archibald's sharp voice filled the room. Abigail wanted to punch her and not in the friendly way she had with her own brothers but the full impact of her fist in the she-devil's face.

Abigail cast her gaze over the gathered party. "I'm not well. Please excuse me."

"How unfortunate. England must be such a drain on you. Especially with the nights you've been keeping."

Abigail's muscles hardened, and a burning rush overtook her ears. If she would hang anyway, this woman would go with her.

She lunged toward Miss Archibald, but Lynette caught her before her nails tasted the awful woman's face.

Mr. Archibald chuckled. "You've snared a little wildcat, Hugh."

Mr. Travers wore his mischievous smile. "You've no idea."

Lynette dragged Abigail out the door.

"I'm perfectly capable of leading myself out," she said when they made it to the hall.

"Abs, you were putting yourself in a worse situation than you're already in. Miss Archibald would have loved for you to attack her in front of everyone. Nobody would've been able to defend your temper." Lynette urged her on to her room.

"Aren't you coming with me?" An emptiness settled inside her at the prospect of being left with her own thoughts.

Lynette shook her head. "Something isn't right, and I want to know what. The smart thing to do would be to stay in your room and rest until something happens. There's no need to put yourself into a mess for no reason."

"Is that what you'd do?"

"Of course not. I'd launch my own investigation. Once I'd proven my innocence, I'd focus on destroying Miss Archibald. Maybe that sly Mr. Archibald as well. However, that's not what I think you should do."

Abigail studied her. "If you're trying to keep me in my room, you're going about it the wrong way."

Lynette shrugged. "Might I add, everyone appears to be busy at the moment." She gave Abigail a final push and shut her out of the drawing room.

Chapter Eighteen

Maybe Abigail had overreacted. Everything must be some misunderstanding on her part. Miss Archibald was Hugh's cousin, after all. He couldn't just dismiss the woman; it would cause a rift in the family and put Abigail in greater danger without the influence of the Travers family. She knew they hadn't abandoned her, but they tread softly now.

Or maybe she lied to herself. She couldn't help but wonder if all men acted like this. Were they all like Nigel? She didn't want to believe Delia's husband, her brothers, or her father were duplicitous, but she'd never been in a position to judge their behavior. Would Mr. Travers abandon her now he had gotten what he'd wanted?

Whatever the case, she wouldn't let him tear her down. Nigel had been good for one thing: she had learned to guard against the pain. She would let this roll off her skin like the water off the cliff face outside her window. Nothing he could do would break her. She wouldn't give him the opportunity.

It had been one night. It wasn't like she was in love with him. She had believed he would hang for saving her. In the light of day, it was a rash decision. She only hoped she wasn't going to pay for it during the trial or otherwise. Miss Archibald would find a way to twist Abigail's illicit affair with him to suit her needs, but Miss Archibald wouldn't get away with this.

Abigail needed something, anything to cast doubt on Miss Archibald's character. She went in search of Alma, finding her prematurely arranging Abigail's dinner attire.

"I know I can trust you to be discreet." Abigail waited until Alma nodded in agreement. "I need to know where Miss Archibald's room is."

"I can show you easy enough." Alma frowned. "I hope you aren't getting yourself into trouble."

"Not if I don't get caught."

Alma tsked at her. "You could send me. I'm trained to be invisible."

"I appreciate the offer, but I don't even know what I'm looking for. It would be better if I did the searching."

"Then I'll accompany you."

She opened her mouth to refuse but stopped. She couldn't deny the advantages of having two people search the room. They could be out in half the time. Abigail agreed, and she followed Alma down the hall to the end. Her maid twisted the knob, but of course, it was locked.

"What now?" Abigail asked.

"I'll be right back. Don't start without me."

"There's little chance of that."

Alma gave her a level look and hurried back toward the stairs. Abigail busied herself picking at her nails and glancing nervously around the hallway. In five minutes or more likely two hours, Alma returned with Felix. He easily outpaced Alma, remaining silent and catlike. A master spy by all accounts.

"Why is he here?" Abigail asked.

Felix gathered trouble the same way some children collected wildflowers, and more problems were the last thing she needed.

"I asked to borrow his keys, but he wouldn't give them without an explanation. He insisted on coming along."

Sure enough, Felix brought out a large key ring and flipped through the keys until he found the one he wanted. This explained how he spied on everyone so well. No doors were locked to his prying eyes.

Abigail leaned into her maid. "Won't he tattle on us to Carrington and Delia?"

Felix smirked at her. "Only if it suits me."

"Why did you agree to help? Isn't it a betrayal?"

"Hardly. Who do you think gave me the keys? I haven't had much chance to search this room though. Plus, I was bored." He turned the key with a click and opened the door. He waved them inside.

She could have done without the red. At least this time, the bed was a sunny yellow instead of the deep scarlet she found elsewhere. The other furniture consisted of a neat-looking trunk, a dressing table, a tall wardrobe, and a feminine writing desk near a small window overlooking the front of the house.

Felix eased the door shut and went straight to the trunk. She chose the desk, and Alma searched the wardrobe.

"Haven't you gone through this room before?" she asked over her shoulder to Felix.

"Yes, a few days ago, but I only got through half this trunk before she returned. This is the best opportunity I've had so far."

"What about Mr. North?" Abigail doubted their search would yield anything, but she was out of options.

"He did too, but the man's irresponsible, and investigating isn't even his job. I think Lord Carrington was just looking for an impartial party to look into the murders. What little good that did, since it only brought suspicion on you. I was amazed Mr. North even found the letter opener." Felix's voice was muffled as he rustled through the stashed-away clothes.

She read and put aside papers as she went. "I'm amazed you didn't find the letter opener."

"I'm shocked you thought I'd search your room," Felix said in a low tone.

She peered over to him. "Did you search my room?"

Felix met her gaze with furrowed brows. "Of course."

Abigail rolled her eyes and went back to searching the desk.

"Then why didn't you find it?"

"Give me some credit. It was the day before Mr. Archibald was killed, and I missed my chance a second time by searching other rooms first."

"A pity."

They fell silent in their respective tasks. Miss Archibald's friends and family concerned themselves with fashion, status, and the marriage market. So far, Abigail hadn't found anything of interest. It was mostly Miss Archibald catching up with different families and people Abigail had never heard of.

"Hmm..." Felix broke the silence.

"What?" Alma asked.

He studied something in his hand. "She has a men's pocket watch in here. I don't know the coat of arms on it."

Alma and Abigail joined him and examined the elaborate design. It was an ornate gold watch with a delicate leaf pattern along the border. The back was adorned with a shield and cross flanked by jumping fish on each side. The motto, *Ex veritate fortitudo*, was engraved across the bottom. Felix snorted when he read it aloud. Abigail and Alma exchanged glances.

"'Strength of the truth' or 'Strength from truth.' A message of encouragement from the timepiece." He returned to the trunk.

Abigail gawked at him as if seeing him for the first time. "How do you know Latin?" He was a boy. No, a young man of hidden talents that Delia had hinted at from time to time, but Latin? Felix had been a street urchin and then a servant of the Wolcott family.

He didn't bother to look up from his work. "I studied under a great tutor of renowned knowledge."

"Delia said her cook was your teacher."

"Yes."

She rested a palm on her hip. "Why would a female servant need Latin?"

He sighed. "She wasn't always a servant."

"That doesn't explain it. I didn't even bother to learn Latin."

Her tutors had been some of the best in New York. Delia had envied Abigail's education.

Felix glared up at her. "I imagine she makes use of it. She's a papist."

"Fair enough."

She puzzled over the watch in her mind as she returned to her search. The origins were a mystery. Felix assured her the Archibalds didn't use anything of the like. He reasoned it could be from one of the other branches of the family, but there was no reason for Miss Archibald to have it. The watch was stored away like a memento to be brought out or forgotten as need be. It was important enough for her to carry it along or Miss Archibald had acquired it on her travels.

Abigail's hand fell on a slip of paper that caught her eye. The letter was from Mrs. Archibald and dated from two weeks ago. Miss Archibald's mother asked her to cease her improper relationship. The letter went on to lecture her on duty to family and how she'd disgraced them. Abigail couldn't find mention of the name of the man, but she got the impression from the letter that Miss Archibald had resided at Briarwyck at the time of the writing and the man had also been in residence.

She could rule out Carrington, Mr. Travers, and Greymore. Carrington was a devoted husband who hated Miss Archibald. Mr. Travers had been out of the country, and it pained Abigail to think he would've joined the list of possibilities. Greymore would have improved the Archibald family but not through money. He'd made it clear he was opposed to Miss Archibald.

That left Sir Peter and Mr. Graham. Of course, it was possible the affair had involved a servant or neighbor, but that seemed unlikely for Miss Archibald. Abigail wouldn't rule it out though. She tucked the letter away, back in the desk, and sought another page, when footsteps thudded in the hallway outside the room.

They glanced at one another and bolted frantically for hiding places. Alma and Abigail scrambled under the bed while Felix shut himself into the wardrobe. Felix had just closed the wardrobe door when Miss Archibald entered, accompanied by her brother.

Miss Archibald sat at her dressing table, and a grunt barked from her throat when her brother hoisted himself on the bed. "Must you? You're still dirty from your journey."

"It's nothing your bed hasn't already seen."

Abigail slapped a hand over her mouth to hold in her laugh.

"That's low, even for you. What did you want to discuss? Make it quick. You need a bath before anyone will eat near you."

The bed rocked as Mr. Archibald adjusted himself. "I'm under the impression you have designs on Hugh. I thought I'd find you heartbroken after your disappointment and Adam's death. What's going on?"

"I'm lost without Adam, but I don't have the luxury of mourning right now. As much as I loved him, I'd be happily married in Gretna Green by now if it weren't for him." Her forlorn sigh almost made Abigail pity her. "Instead, I have to settle for Hugh."

Abigail clenched her teeth on a retort.

"I'm not so sure Hugh will marry you."

Abigail let out a silent cheer from under the bed. She hoped Miss Archibald would be miserable for the rest of her life.

Miss Archibald snickered. "Just wait until I get him into my bed. He'll do the honorable thing."

"I really don't want to know the details, but I thought you had already slept with him."

"Sadly, no."

Abigail muffled her exhaled breath. She had thought along the same lines as Mr. Archibald. Alma clenched Abigail's hand, reminding her to keep quiet.

"Then Miss Riverton has succeeded where you have failed. Interesting."

Abigail squeezed her eyes shut as if to silence the conversation. He'd been here a matter of hours and somehow he already knew about it?

"Don't remind me of that little slut." Miss Archibald's voice dripped with disgust. "It's bad enough I'll have to share a man with her. Thankfully, we'll be rid of her."

"You still haven't answered my question."

"Alex, your question was too vague."

"No, it wasn't. You're dodging the subject." Abigail applauded his efforts for digging deeper, but did he have to dangle his foot so close to her head?

Miss Archibald faced her brother. "Haven't you already guessed? I need to get married to avoid scandal."

Mr. Archibald groaned, and the bed moved as he jostled around. "Oh, Alice, you aren't?"

"I'm afraid so."

Sneaking into Miss Archibald's room had proven more informative than Abigail could have ever guessed.

"How will you convince Hugh it's his?"

"I don't have to convince him if we're already married. His side of the family has a history of long marriages. I doubt he'll break the tradition."

If Abigail weren't out to prove her innocence, she would throttle the woman until she no longer remembered her own name.

"If that's the case, aren't you concerned he'll marry Miss Riverton?"

Abigail's heart slammed in her chest. The prospect seemed impossible, and yet Mr. Archibald must believe otherwise. Mr. Travers, marry her?

"You must be joking. She's obviously a diversion, too far beneath him to be a prospective bride. I'm sure he'll help with any brats she has by him."

Doubt reclaimed any hope Abigail had gained.

"You forget William married a girl not unlike Miss Riverton."

"Are you going to help me or not?"

A brief silence fell over the room. "I suppose I have to. I don't see any other way out of your problem. That is, unless we put you away somewhere, but there are bound to be whispers."

"Good. Now get out."

The weight shifted on the bed, and shoes thumped on the floor.

"I pity Hugh being trapped as your husband," Mr. Archibald said. Abigail shared his opinion. It would be a joyless marriage based on a lie.

"It's for the good of the family, remember? None of you will let me forget that."

Her gaze followed Mr. Archibald's shoes to the door. He turned back as he was leaving. "One more thing. Did Adam know about your condition?"

"If he had, this would've worked out differently."

"Yes, I believe you're right." He shut the door behind him.

Miss Archibald turned in her seat and sighed at her appearance in the mirror. Abigail held her breath and kept stiff as a corpse to avoid discovery in the reflection. A drop of sweat trickled down her neck. She held back a shiver and the urge to rub at her skin. The discomfort grew until stillness sent needles into her limbs.

Miss Archibald diligently preened.

Abigail allowed herself a quick breath when Miss Archibald stood and faced away from the mirror. Abigail's relief was short-lived when the woman walked toward the wardrobe.

Abigail tightened her grip on Alma's hand. Felix was still small for his age but not invisible. The wardrobe would be a tight fit, offering little concealment.

Miss Archibald stopped midstride and angled her head toward the door as if she heard something. For a second, Abigail thought they had given themselves away, and she willed herself invisible. Then a light knock relieved her fear.

Miss Archibald didn't move from her place in front of the wardrobe and faced the door as if it might make the visitor go away. "Who is it?"

A familiar male voice filtered through the wood. "It's me."

"Hugh?" Miss Archibald strode to the door and opened it a crack. "Did you need something?"

"There's a little time before dinner, and I thought maybe you'd like to go riding while you have a chance."

"How thoughtful. Let me change, and I can meet you at the stables. Unless you would like to come in?"

Abigail's mouth fell open, and her stomach churned.

The pause suffocated Abigail under the bed. She clamped her teeth together. If Miss Archibald got her way, they would be directly on top of Abigail and Alma. She didn't think she could prevent herself from running screaming from the room. For once, she wished she were the killer and she could be done with Miss Archibald. Then again, what was stopping her? She imagined plunging her dagger into Miss Archibald's pretty stomach.

Abigail blinked. What was happening to her?

"I'll see you at the stables," Mr. Travers said.

The door clicked shut.

It was a clear refusal but not as final as Abigail had hoped. Miss Archibald grabbed some garments set aside in anticipation of the occasion, and Abigail avoided watching her dress, with thoughts of warning Mr. Travers. As angry as she was with him, she wouldn't wish Miss Archibald on anyone.

Against her better judgment, her gaze caught Miss Archibald donning a riding habit. The garment was different from the ones Abigail was familiar with. It was cut low in a French style. So low, in fact, Abigail wondered how she would keep from popping out of the top while riding, which was exactly the point. The woman didn't mess around.

Abigail had shared a bed with Mr. Travers less than half a day ago, and already he would ogle someone else. She fought between giving him more credit and thinking him already lost to Miss Archibald.

She knew she shouldn't trouble herself. They had said no promises, made no declarations. What did she care if he took Miss Archibald to bed? Yet the twinge in her chest refused to budge.

After witnessing Miss Archibald's choice of attire, Abigail didn't think anything could surprise her. The woman resorted to rouge on her cheeks and lips. If Travers fell for Miss Archibald's tricks, he deserved it for his stupidity. Abigail would like to think the man she'd spent the night with wasn't that easy. She had her pride to protect, after all.

Miss Archibald gave one last look in the mirror and marched from the room. Abigail took an extended breath and crawled out from under the bed. Alma followed her and went to the wardrobe to let Felix know it was safe. Abigail returned to the desk to finish what she'd started.

"Shouldn't we leave?" Alma hesitated in front of the wardrobe.

"I finished with the trunk earlier and looked around the wardrobe the best I could in the dark. How's the desk coming?" Felix watched as Abigail worked.

Abigail kept her attention on her reading. "I've read most of the letters, but I could use help if you want to be out of here soon."

"Alma, you finish with the wardrobe while we read the rest of the papers."

They set to work but found nothing else of interest. Unfortunately, Miss Archibald had no outgoing letters, which would doubtless prove enlightening.

She filled them in on the contents of the letter from Mrs. Archibald as they left, and concluded on their way down the hall, "She must've been seeing either Mr. Graham or Sir Peter."

"Or both." Felix grinned at their wide-eyed looks.

"Perhaps you can find out?" If Delia and Carrington trusted him, Abigail respected their judgment. "It might have something to do with Sir Peter's death."

"I'll do my best, but it won't make a difference until Mr. Graham returns."

Abigail nodded. "When do you think that will be?"

"Well, his room has already been prepared again. I imagine

he'll arrive around the same time as Mr. and Mrs. Archibald." Felix met her eyes. "Don't get your hopes up too high, Miss Riverton. I've been spending sleepless nights searching for the killer with Lord Carrington and Mr. Travers. So far we've found nothing. The only witness is dead."

"You have? I'm truly grateful to you and Carrington for trying." She avoided the heartache that accompanied Mr. Hugh Travers's name.

Felix stared at her through slit eyes. "Mr. Travers is dedicated to solving the murders. Last night was the only time I have seen him rest since you were accused, and I doubt he got much sleep."

She swallowed at his open scrutiny. "I hadn't realized. I appreciate his efforts as well." If he cared so much, why had he abandoned her for Miss Archibald? She needed his guidance now more than ever.

They stopped at the top of the stairs, where Felix would leave them.

He studied Abigail's face and nodded. "A word of advice: be patient before making any rash decisions." He skipped down the stairs without further explanation of his cryptic remark, and they watched him disappear soundlessly to the floor below.

CHAPTER NINETEEN

ALMA LEFT AFTER helping Abigail straighten her appearance, and Abigail regretted her absence like a lost child's. She couldn't dwell alone right now. Her mind flew naturally to Delia, and she set off to locate her. Her friend's room wasn't far, and it didn't take long for her brisk pace to put her outside the door.

"Abigail, wait," came Mr. Travers's voice.

She hesitated and wondered how undignified it would look if she bolted down the hall or locked herself in Delia's room. She needed to untangle her emotions before she lashed out at him for deserting her in favor of Miss Archibald. After all, he had spent sleepless nights on the investigation.

She settled her hand on the knob, hoping Mr. Travers would be her imagination. She'd thought she would be safe, since he was supposed to be riding.

"Please?"

She refused to face him. It seemed easier to keep herself together without allowing his warm gaze to pierce the battered shield she had raised after Nigel. "I came to speak with Delia."

"She's downstairs."

Trust him to know that. She groaned inwardly and turned from the door to face the way she had come, dodging his gaze.

He stepped closer. "What I said earlier, I didn't mean it."

"Then why did you say it?"

His public shunning had echoed Nigel's. This time, she'd been trapped in range of the barbed words. Briarwyck shrank as she tried to distance herself.

He rubbed the back of his neck. "We can't make our relationship any worse with the Archibalds."

She huffed. "That's farfetched. Nobody else seemed to think they needed to insult me to keep good relations with them."

He shifted in place. "I know, but I'm in a unique situation."

"What situation?" She snorted. "The best way to get into Miss Archibald's bed?"

His eyes flashed toward hers, and anger sparked between them. "That isn't fair."

"It's true." She hardened her jaw. "She plans to sleep with you and guilt you into marrying her."

Travers nodded. "I know."

"How could you know?" Her face blanched as she hurried on. "Did you know she's pregnant?"

"I suspected as much. She shows the same signs Delia has described to me in graphic detail."

"Then why are you letting her?" Her question was a sputtered mess of words. Why had she tormented herself to speak with him at all?

"I can't tell you right now."

She folded her arms over her chest. "Can't or won't?"

"Both." He kept her gaze just as they had stared into each other's eyes in bed. The act conflicted with the sudden clench of her heart.

"Then I've nothing more to say to you." She pushed past him on the way to her room.

"Can I visit you tonight?" His words put her at a dead stop.

She rounded on him. "Did you not hear me? No. I'm not your plaything by night and whipping boy by day. I realize now I'm an embarrassment to you, and you can't acknowledge me in front of others. Whatever your reasons are, if you can't trust me with them, then I can't trust you."

She took off down the hall as fast as her skirts would carry her, fleeing from the words she had spoken. Her heart filled with dread at his presumed response. If he offered her insults, it would cut her deeply, but a plea for forgiveness would be equally unwelcome. She might lower her defenses, or worse yet, forgive him. In the end, her fears were for naught. He didn't follow or call after her. All that came was dead silence, the most deafening sound of all.

Safe in her room, she lingered in the view from her window. She gazed down at the ebb and flow of the water. The day was cloudy, and the water was murky. She wondered that the sky did not open up and burst forth with her grief. The time between sun and storm was a curious feeling. An empty one of promises forgotten.

Her gaze wandered over the horizon listlessly. She had hoped the window would give some kind of comfort or promise of life. She wasn't so lost that she preferred death, but it was an acceptable outcome if her current path led there. Her primary regret was the form her death would take.

If she was lucky, her neck would break, sending her into unconsciousness and death instantly. More likely she would feel every tick of the clock and every last morsel of air until the merciless rope squeezed out her life. She had witnessed a hanging where the convicted man had kicked and gasped for air for twenty minutes before he'd surrendered to his fate. When they'd brought him down, his face and eyes had been etched with river works of veins, and blood had stained the front of his trousers. Adding to this indignity, they had placed him in chains to hang on display and rot away in the wind. Her memory of the corpse festering in the sun week after week was chiseled deeply into her mind, and the thought of the smell could erase her appetite for days.

With this grim picture in mind, she realized she had just thrown away one of her most stalwart defenders. She could beg prostrate in front of the magistrate and plea her good name all she wanted, but to have the good word and witness of a credible gentleman would more likely sway the judgment to leniency. She could only hope her behavior had not lost her more than one voice.

The relief she had expected from setting Hugh free was absent. She had made her decision to walk this path alone, and she would stand by it even if it made the last of her days miserable. At least Hugh was spared the burden of helping her. He could find happiness without her dragging him down like a stone. She took solace in this even as she dreaded the empty days without him.

Abigail confined herself to her room and took dinner alone with her thoughts. Her meal was followed by a brief visit from Delia, who came to cheer her. Instead, her friend made no impression on Abigail and Delia left in her own contracted depression. The others seemed to avoid or forget her, probably focusing on entertaining the new arrivals. Alma offered the only comfort in Abigail's otherwise bleak world.

Her maid didn't try to empathize with her or downplay her feelings. Nothing so obvious and provoking. Instead, Alma sat with her in silence for intervals and performed small actions that had an overall calming impact. She didn't coddle her or jump to attention at a sad sigh, but she made herself ready for when Abigail would need her. In short, she let Abigail feel.

The cries of seabirds outside her window roused Abigail the following day. Exhausted from her overwrought emotions, she rose late and missed the usual breakfast time. Alma mended beside her in a red damask chair she must have brought in while Abigail had slept. Her maid glanced up as Abigail stirred and offered to find her a late breakfast. She declined and took only tea. She would prefer to regain her senses before she attempted food. When Alma returned, she brought news.

In Abigail's absence, Mr. Graham had returned this morning, tired and grim. Alma said he seemed unconcerned and distant to the events unfolding at Briarwyck. Mr. and Miss Archibald had not wasted any time in helping Constable North hire a pair of deputies, whom Alma described as local men with a great need of money.

The elder Mr. and Mrs. Archibald had sent word they were delayed on the road. Mrs. Archibald had taken a fall from the carriage, and they didn't know when or if they would arrive. Mr. Archibald urged his son to proceed in his absence. As far as Abigail was concerned, this would seal her guilt. Although she sensed the younger Mr. Archibald could be reasonable, Miss Archibald had a powerful influence over his decisions.

Abigail was on her second cup of tea when Delia made an appearance. Her friend wore dark circles under her eyes, but Delia dismissed her concerns and handed Abigail two bottles of dubious-looking liquids with tiny floating particles.

Abigail's lip turned up as she examined them. "What are these?"

"First, I want you to sit down." They sat together on the foot of the bed, and Alma left them in privacy.

"I made you some extracts, but I wasn't sure which one you'd prefer to take. I can't guarantee they'll be effective, but your chance of success will increase with them. That one"—Delia pointed to the bottle with the dark-brown seal—"can be used to…um…stop an unwanted pregnancy."

Abigail's eyes flickered wide, and she set the offending bottle down between two fingers as if it burned her. "It won't matter if I'm pregnant when I hang."

Delia nodded. "That's what the other is for. The herbs should increase your chances of pregnancy so you can plead your belly and save yourself from hanging."

Abigail stared at it with a curious frown. "Wouldn't it have been better if I'd used it before?"

"Yes, but that doesn't mean it won't work now. You could also, well, try again."

Abigail shook her head. "I don't think Mr. Travers would be up to the task now."

"You'd be surprised. I'm sure I could find volunteers too.

That is, if you're desperate enough." Delia smiled brightly.

Abigail groaned. "I wouldn't show signs for several months anyway. Do you think we can drag this out that long?"

"We're trying to gain as much time as we can to figure out who the real killer is. It can't hurt to have a backup plan in place."

"I'll consider it." Abigail let out a long sigh. Had her fate come down to this?

"Good. Now, are you coming down to dinner later?"

"I don't think it would be wise. Has anyone discovered who Miss Archibald is in love with?"

Her friend's brows rose.

"Yes, Dee. I know Felix reports back to you."

Delia's mouth twisted up. "Not as far as I know. It should be made clear now if it's Mr. Graham. I'll let you know what we find."

Abigail stood to locate her teacup again and looked back as Delia watched her. "What is it?"

"It isn't my place to say."

"I'll always respect your opinion." She forced a smile. "What is it?"

Delia cast her eyes down at her lap and played with the stitching of her skirts. She hesitated, a loaded pause. "Abs, I love you. You know that."

Abigail's smile never faltered as she nodded.

Delia swallowed. "Hugh's my brother, by law and by design."

Abigail turned her back and wandered to her place at the window. She'd known this would come; what had she expected after her argument with Mr. Travers? Still, she wished her friend would leave matters well enough alone.

Delia stayed seated and rambled on tentatively. "He hasn't been the same since he returned. At first, he was full of life and getting on Carrington's nerves with his positive airs. Then he became the opposite, a broody recluse. I think I saw one day of happiness. He turned into a man possessed, not sleeping or eating enough to be of any use to anyone. If he were a woman, he would be called hysterical."

Abigail folded her arms. "Maybe he'd benefit from an exorcism."

"Look, you're being stupid." Delia blurted out her words.

"I'm not his nursemaid." She continued to stare out the window, appearing unconcerned on the outside but quaking underneath.

"Why are you being so defensive?"

Abigail pivoted on her heel. "I don't have to explain my actions to anyone. I don't have the luxury of it. My mind is already full to the brim of visions of what will happen to me. This may sound selfish, but I only have so much time before some Englishmen will decide whether to hang me from a gibbet."

Delia refused to back down under Abigail's cynical outlook. "I'm sorry, but you'll be better off if you don't face this alone."

"I have you."

Delia closed her eyes, and her voice lowered. "That's not the same, and you know it."

"What would you have me do? I can't trust him not to hurt me after he turned his back on me in front of the Archibalds. His help's welcome, but even if we accepted each other, we would be ripped apart after my trial. I can't do that to him." She lost hold of the pain she kept inside, and it quivered in her voice. She turned back to the window to hide her face.

"At least talk to him. He views things differently than you think. You must care about him enough to give him the chance."

"That's not the point."

"Fine, but remember you're only lying to yourself." Delia's voice thrust knives at Abigail's back. "Hugh will suffer whether you shut him out or not. At least you could endure the suffering together. If I were him, I would prefer to spend the time I had left with you. Can you at least consider that?"

Abigail dropped her arms to her sides and turned to face her dearest friend. "I'll try, but I think you're wrong. As your brother-in-law, he's obligated to help me. He doesn't want me, and even if he did, I can't bear to hurt him."

"What are you talking about? It's true he did me a favor escorting you, but that doesn't extend into the investigation."

"It isn't just that." She bit her tongue and pushed the past aside. "I don't think I can handle more heartbreak now or ever."

"I know it's difficult, but I'm sure this time will be different." The concern in Delia's green gaze nearly sent her into sobs.

Abigail shook her head in a rapid burst. "You can't know that."

"True, but I have a feeling."

"I don't know if that's good enough. Can you leave me alone for now? I want to rest. I need to think, but my mind's too exhausted to get anywhere."

Delia got to her feet and hugged Abigail. They stood together for a moment, lost in the comfort of each other's arms. Delia pulled back to read Abigail's face. Satisfied, her friend nodded to her and made her exit. Abigail grew empty at the loss of her friend's company, but it was for the best if she would remain on good terms with her.

She settled back into bed without much trouble. Alma hadn't returned, and she hoped her maid was eating her own meal. She still didn't have any interest in food herself, but she couldn't deny her maid needed to care for her own needs for a change.

Abigail had forgotten to shut the curtains, but instead of getting up, she became fixated on the growing light. She wished she had gone riding. The deep-green grass would fly past as she took Soot out at breakneck speed until they were both breathless and sweaty. The Archibalds probably wouldn't allow her even that little freedom, and she didn't blame them. Of course, she had considered packing a bag and escaping on horseback. She could join a wandering caravan or find a ship back to the colonies. It wouldn't be too hard, really. They hadn't placed a guard on her. For once, she knew she was only dreaming.

Abigail rolled over, blocking the light from her vision. She wasn't the same awestruck girl from a couple months ago. Her rose-colored veil had been ripped from her eyes, and her naivety and joy had blown away with it. England was no better than New York, full of self-serving, immoral hypocrites. If her time at Briarwyck was any indication, she would prefer the open attacks of New York to the backstabbing of England.

She admitted she missed Hugh, and she would forgive anything he asked of her. It wasn't long before she realized she wanted him in her life, but to what purpose? Facing her punishment and grieving a doomed relationship was not the way she pictured her life ending. What kind of person would she be to make him suffer along with her? She'd experienced a few moments of happiness with him, and it would have to be enough. In time, he would forget her and find someone else, preferably not Miss Archibald.

The mere thought of Hugh with another woman made the pit of Abigail's stomach lodge in her throat. She wanted to sob out the injustice of it all. Delia wasn't wrong about her feelings, but Abigail refused to torture herself further about what she could never have. If she was found guilty and she was somehow spared from hanging, there was no happiness for a condemned criminal, transported or in jail. She didn't dare hope she would be proven innocent, but in such an outcome, she would have to return to her parents in New York.

Her parents. She had forgotten to write them. Every time she made the decision to put ink to paper, the words escaped her. Someone would have to tell them what had become of her, but it would be better if it came from her. She didn't know how she would tell them her trip had turned so wrong.

Dear Mother,

Thank you for allowing me to visit Cornwall. By the way, I've been accused of murder and I will probably never return.

P.S. You know the thing I said I would never do again? Guess what, I might be pregnant and your grandchild will die with me.

She laughed bitterly to the empty room.

After many a morbid thought, she dozed off into a light, dreamless sleep. A viselike pain in her head woke her. She fumbled for her now cold tea in the darkened room. She wet her mouth and then took deep gulps. It was some time after dinner. Her stomach gave a rumbling protest at her neglect. She grunted and lifted the covers from her heavy body.

She gasped at the shock to her head when she sat up. She needed to eat something to be rid of the pain, but Alma was likely in bed by now. The kitchen was her only option for nourishment. In any case, she was grateful she had slept through dinner, since her stomach might have changed her mind about joining the rest of the household. Her meal could occur in relative peace now. Of course, she might run into a late-night servant, but they were unlikely to her or accuse her of crimes she hadn't committed.

She was familiar enough with the room that she was able to rustle around to light a candle. She wrapped a sky-blue silk robe over her nightdress and slipped on thin kidskin slippers. If she encountered anyone of importance, she didn't care what they thought of her disheveled state. It couldn't be worse than being suspected of murder.

Never did she regret an outfit more than the one she'd chosen to wear that night.

CHAPTER TWENTY

ABIGAIL CREPT INTO the hallway, candle first. She stopped outside her door and listened for what may lie hidden in the shadows. She thought she heard the faint tapping of feet along the marble, but her imagination was playing tricks on her again. Briarwyck was a house full of ghosts and secrets but not in the way she had first believed. Any malevolent forces were due to the all-too-human inhabitants and not by supernatural design.

She hastened her steps anyway, not taking her chances with her fear of spirits, logical or not. She tripped on her skirts in her hurry down the stairs. Thankfully, she righted herself before toppling to the bottom, but a rush of air snuffed out the candle.

She sighed and waited for her vision to adjust. Sconces scattered along the wall, too high to light her candle by, but she could make out the stairs well enough to continue her descent. She would have to find another flame in the kitchen.

Her journey slowed without the benefit of a clear path, and it was some time before she reached the kitchen entrance. By then, she jumped at each creak and groan of the house.

Her attention caught on a fresh loaf of bread from dinner. Indeed, her distraction was such that she had forgotten her fears and did not hear the person close behind her until her headache exploded in a metallic clang. She lost consciousness without seeing the face of her attacker.

Abigail came to at the jostling of a carriage beneath her. She yelped at the intense pain radiating through the back of her head and neck and then cried out again at the shock wave from her yelp. She moved to hold her head, but her wrists were tied behind her. Her body lay across a velvety carriage seat, and her legs dangled awkwardly. She shifted to rest her head on the soft cushion but only managed to bump her head against the carriage wall. A whimper escaped her parched lips.

"None of that now," came a gruff male voice in a Cornish accent.

She attempted to glimpse the speaker across from her, but she lacked the strength to raise her head without the support of her arms. She licked at her lips. "Who are you?"

For answer, the man grunted.

"All right, can I have something to drink?"

"That's not up to me." The man's voice grated at her nerves. It was soft enough she struggled to hear but loud enough to make her head throb.

She rubbed her dry tongue over the top of her mouth, hoping to dislodge the stiff cotton taste. "Then who's it up to?"

He grunted again. If she weren't tied up, she would throttle him.

"Where are you taking me?"

He nudged her with a booted foot. "Stop talking. It's not my job to answer to you."

She took a quick inhale. "Then what is your job? Who do you answer to?"

"Nice try." A dry chuckle echoed in her head. "I'm only here to watch you."

"I'm your prisoner?"

"I said stop talking." He slammed his fist into her stomach. Abigail recoiled into herself. The sudden pain startled her into the requested silence. Too afraid to cry, she squeezed her eyes shut against the desire.

Instead, she concentrated on her breathing and gaining control of her emotions. If she went into a panic, she wouldn't be any help to herself. The carriage was unlit, and she had no way of knowing where they were. She hadn't been unconscious for long, since it was still dark. The sliver of moonlight offered little comfort.

Her mind refused to focus with the pain from each bump of the road. Bindings cut through the skin on her wrists. Her pulse drummed from there and up her arms. She tugged at the restraints, earning her another knock to the head.

When she came to again, the faint light of dawn peeked through the carriage curtains. The woozy sensation in her head had moved to encompass her stomach.

The carriage lurched, and the movement forced her to throw up on the floor. What was left of the contents of her stomach was soon gone, and she dry heaved until the pain in her head burned up her skin. After the forceful purging ended, she whimpered and panted against the carriage wall. Her body trembled into the fine upholstery.

"You're disgusting," her captor said.

If only she had the foresight to vomit on him.

She didn't dare answer for fear of being knocked back into unconsciousness and losing more time. The man pounded on the roof of the carriage, and the sound jolted through her. Abruptly, the carriage stopped and dislodged her from the seat to land next to her vomit. The sour smell forced a gag from her throat.

A breeze wisped over her heated skin as the carriage door opened. Then another unfamiliar voice spoke with a similar but deeper Cornish accent. "What do you want?"

"She vomited all over." The first man must have a delicate constitution. If she didn't value her hide, she would laugh in his face.

"So? Deal with it."

"I'm not riding back here with that. Let me drive."

It really was a shame she hadn't vomited on him.

"No, you drive like an idiot." The second man's driving

couldn't be much better. He seemed to hit every hole and bump in the road.

The first man grunted. "I'm not being paid enough for this."

"Hush." The second man turned as the sound of hoofbeats neared.

"Why are you stopped?" a third voice asked from outside.

The second man appealed to the third person, who spoke as though they were the leader. "Charlie is afraid of a little vomit."

"'Tisn't a little, Martin." The first man, Charlie, grumbled out his words.

"Hush, both of you. We haven't the time. We need to get to the coast by night or we'll never make it back to Briarwyck in time." As the third voice grew closer, Abigail recognized the feminine tone with a lurch to her stomach.

Charlie held his ground. "She's as sick as a drunk, ma'am."

"For God's sake, I'll ride along. Come take my horse. I'll have no more delays from either of you."

The weight of the carriage tilted as Charlie climbed out and shut the door. Muffled voices came from outside, but she couldn't make out the words. She rested her cheek on the seat and cherished the still, silent carriage. It didn't last for long. The carriage door slammed open and destroyed whatever relief she had achieved.

Someone made a sound of disgust from the back of their throat, and a second later, a saddle blanket covered the mess. The carriage rocked to the side once more, and her fellow passenger, Miss Archibald, took the seat opposite her. "You look a fright."

Abigail lifted her head to glare at the woman. Miss Archibald wore her more sensible riding habit of the two, and she showed no signs she had ridden for hours beside them. Miss Archibald stared back at her but lost the battle and glanced away. Abigail settled her head back on the seat.

A fearful curiosity settled over Abigail, and she couldn't keep from opening her mouth. "What are you going to do with me?"

Miss Archibald trained her gaze out the window, but she

couldn't have seen much of anything in the dawn light. "You'll see soon enough."

"Why are you doing this?" Abigail's voice sounded pathetic even to her own ears.

"You already know the answer to that."

Abigail stared up at the hateful woman, a puzzled frown wrinkling her brow. "No, I don't."

"Do I have to explain everything to you? You're stupider than I thought." The disgust in Miss Archibald's voice tightened Abigail's throat.

"Do you truly hate me that much?"

"Hate you? I won't expend the energy to hate you. No, Miss Riverton, you're an inconvenience to me. An insect pecking at my life that needs to be smashed. In a way, you've also had your uses, but I wonder if I should've done away with you from the start and saved myself the trouble."

All this for one man? England was full of men who could prevent Miss Archibald from ruin.

"Hugh will never love you."

"What does marriage have to do with love?" Miss Archibald laughed to herself, a joyless sound in the darkened carriage. "As soon as he sees you ran away from him, I'll have no trouble bending him to my will. Of course, his pining over you will be depressing at first, but I've no doubt he'll soon recover. After all, he'll have his heir to comfort him."

"His heir? He isn't that stupid."

"Of course not. I'm sure he'll claim the child when he's born. It would be quite an embarrassment to his family if he didn't."

"You won't get away with this," Abigail said under her breath, almost to herself.

Miss Archibald burst into wild laughter. "Oh dear, how rich. I have no doubt I already have."

"What of your brother? Surely he doesn't approve of your kidnapping me?"

Miss Archibald sobered. "No, he wouldn't."

"He'll at least notice your absence."

She looked out the window as though bored. "Alexander's busy having a long sleep."

Abigail gasped. "He's dead?"

"Heavens, no. The tea I brewed him should put him out for a while. I made our excuses through my maid. We're quite contagious to the rest of the household, you know." Miss Archibald gave Abigail a mocking grin.

"What of my absence? Alma and Delia will notice me missing."

"I count on it. That's why you left a note behind telling everyone goodbye. Your words were quite touching. I was nearly moved to tears reading your account of your hopeless plight and longing for death. A tragic tale for such a young woman."

"Then we aren't going to Truro?" The last shred of her hope rested on the sympathy of the magistrate.

"You know, that was the original plan, but it's too expected. I decided you would like a little sightseeing instead. I hear North Devon is beautiful this time of year."

"Why?" By all means, Miss Archibald could have pushed her off the cliff back at Briarwyck and been done with the mess. It seemed ridiculous for Miss Archibald to put herself at risk to drive across the countryside.

"Hmm? Oh, I don't know. I figured your body would be harder to find there. I do love the North Devon coast. It's where I met my love."

"Mr. Graham?"

Miss Archibald started and narrowed her eyes at Abigail. "No, not him. Though it was at his estate we met."

"Sir Peter, then?"

Miss Archibald nodded. "I suppose you aren't completely stupid if you worked out that much."

"Why would you kill him, then?"

A strangled sound came from Miss Archibald's throat. "I take that back. You're miserably stupid. I'd never hurt Peter."

Abigail opened her mouth to ask more, but Miss Archibald stopped her with a hard stare. "I grow tired of your whiny voice. Shut up or I'll call Charlie. I promise he won't be gentle."

Abigail hadn't gotten a good look at Charlie. His shoulders and chest were broad, and the smell of old cheese wafted off his sweaty body. She didn't want to take the chance he might beat her again or worse. Now she understood Miss Archibald must have ordered him to hold back, and he was capable of far worse abuse. So she kept her nagging questions to herself.

Abigail let the carriage toss her about as they traveled along. The rocking motion took hold of her, and she dozed in and out of consciousness. With her head injured, she struggled against falling asleep, but she couldn't keep her heavy lids from closing.

The mumbling beside her brought her out of sleep from time to time, and she was awake enough to wonder if the woman was insane. She caught snippets of sentences when her head allowed her to concentrate. The first time this happened, her eyes snapped open at the realization. Miss Archibald spoke to her dead brother, Adam. At least, Miss Archibald seemed aware Adam was dead, but it was still unsettling.

In times of consciousness, Abigail wondered if it was good or bad Miss Archibald showed signs of being unhinged. Abigail had considered reasoning with her, but now she doubted it would do any good. On the other hand, she could take advantage of the weakness and make her escape.

Miss Archibald had lost the person closest to her, her twin brother. Alexander had described them as friends, and Abigail suspected they hadn't often been apart aside from his time at school. She didn't have any experience to compare it to, but she imagined the death was much like losing a limb or part of one's heart. Miss Archibald was accustomed to his constant presence, and she must still notice him like a lingering ache. Really, it was no wonder she spoke to his ghost.

"I'd let you have her, dear," Miss Archibald rambled at the window. "I don't see why you had to ruin things for me. Mother and Father would accept him eventually."

Abigail raised her head from the seat. "Your brother killed Sir Peter?"

Miss Archibald flickered her gaze to Abigail, but her unfocused eyes appeared to see through her. "A cowardly act. Poison is a woman's weapon. I'm ashamed to call him brother."

Abigail blinked at her and scrunched her eyebrows. "Why did you kill Adam?"

Miss Archibald threw her head back and laughed. Her eyes cleared with her laughter. "He ruined everything. I would've been happy with Peter. I couldn't stand the sight of Adam even if it was for the sake of the family. Miles thought it was for the best."

"Mr. Graham? Why would he want your brother dead?"

"Adam chose the wrong man to blackmail. Miles was going to leave his wife anyway, but Adam threatened him with ruin. Miles had to stop him from revealing his affair with him. He was only too happy to assist me. Then his fool wife found out, and we had to kill her too."

What was wrong with these people? No wonder the Travers brothers had failed to discover the identity of the killer, since most of the guests were guilty. Her head still throbbed, and she struggled to grasp all the information.

Abigail squeezed her eyes shut. "You mean Mr. Graham and your brother?"

"Yes, Miss Riverton. My brother would sleep with anyone with two legs, especially at the right price. Don't flatter yourself that you were the only one he desired. Mr. Graham, however, wasn't used to sex with men, but I understand it was an epiphany. I'll never know how Adam convinced him the first time. Alcohol, I imagine."

"I don't understand. He was still your brother." Abigail narrowed her gaze at Miss Archibald as though to steal a glance beyond the shadows of her face.

"Making his betrayal even worse. How could my dearest

friend and closest companion kill the man I loved? I relished every time the blade ran through Adam's flesh. You see, when Adam poisoned Peter, he also killed himself."

"You're insane."

"I assure you, I'm aware of what I'm doing. Now, then. I'll enjoy watching you die. You're my last obstacle to freedom."

Abigail's stomach crept into her throat as she pictured Miss Archibald plunging the letter opener into her brother. "You couldn't possibly be happy after all this."

"I never claimed to be happy. I'm afraid any possibility of happiness died with Peter on the day I met you. This curse you brought on Briarwyck dies with you." That was it? Miss Archibald would blame her for a coincidence of timing?

Abigail steadied her words and chose each one with caution. "You think I'm somehow responsible for your ill fortune?"

"I know you're responsible. If it weren't for you, we wouldn't have delayed our trip to Gretna Green, and Peter would be alive. The news came just as we were readying to leave, and I was forced to await your arrival. Delia insisted I meet you, and I couldn't afford to upset the Travers family. It seemed a harmless wait of a few hours at the time. If Peter hadn't died, Adam would still be here."

"You're forgetting Mrs. Graham and the footman."

"No, I'm not. Mrs. Graham was unstable, and the footman was expendable. What do I care of them?"

Mrs. Graham was the unstable one? "That's needlessly cruel."

Miss Archibald shrugged. "You're talking to the woman who will end your life. What exactly do you expect of me?"

"I don't suppose you'll drop me off at the nearest port? I'll promise to return to New York and never come back here." It wasn't a difficult promise to make. She'd had enough of England.

"I'm afraid not. It would be better if Hugh never discovers you alive. You have to disappear. That means your body, and I don't trust you to move to some desolate heathen nation."

"You can't be content with hanging me for your crimes?"

Miss Archibald scowled at her. "You can blame Alexander for that. He's too observant for his own good. Imagine, when he found out about Adam, he insisted I come clean or he'd do it for me. My own brother."

"Yes, your own brother. Fancy that."

Without warning, Miss Archibald struck Abigail across the face. She fell back against the carriage wall and slammed her head in the process. She stayed there, mouth opening and closing but no sound coming out. Liquid trickled down her neck, and the earth rocked contrary to the carriage's movement. She closed her eyes to avoid retching again.

"Remember the pain you've caused when it's time. Maybe then you'll have the decency to die gracefully. Of course, if you decide to be a nuisance, I can always have Charlie and Martin make it slow. It might even be worth being late for."

"Why don't you just kill me now?" She wasn't sure if she had spoken or not until Miss Archibald answered.

"I thought you were enjoying our little conversation? No matter. Tell me, what would be the fun in killing you now when I can have the pleasure of watching you kill yourself? Sounds poetic, doesn't it?"

Chapter Twenty-One

Miss Archibald's words struck Abigail dumb. A blurry cloud settled over her vision, urging her to keep her lids shut. She had no way to tell if the bleeding on her head had stopped, but she no longer noticed the blood's movement. Whether that meant the wound had clotted or she had lost feeling, she didn't know.

She blinked open her eyes when the carriage slowed. Light shone through the windows, slashing across her vision. Miss Archibald's enthusiasm at the early-morning scenery did nothing to comfort Abigail. The carriage continued on at a crawl, the ride a symphony of bumps and craters. The vehicle rambled to a halt, and Miss Archibald peered out the windows on both sides before poking her head out the door.

"This isn't it. Why are we stopping?"

"It's as far as the road is passable, ma'am," Martin said from somewhere outside.

"Fine. Call Charlie and have him grab the girl. I'll take Lady."

Miss Archibald disappeared out the door, and Abigail used the opportunity to steady her back against the wall. Her arms presented an unfortunate obstacle, but she managed a defensive position to await Charlie. He didn't disappoint.

When Charlie opened the door, she had a split second of action before he was on her. He reached for her, and a well-placed kick to his forearm sent him back out of range. He howled with rage and rubbed his elbow. His eyes narrowed on her, and he tried again. This time, she pushed out with both feet and slammed into his groin. He toppled back into the door and sucked air through his teeth.

"You'll pay for that, bitch." Charlie yelled something unintelligible outside, and Martin came up from behind him.

"What's the trouble?" Martin asked. His irritation was plain even to Abigail's muffled hearing.

"The bitch keeps kicking me."

Martin snorted. "You need to be gentle like. Treat her like a skittish mare, and when she least suspects it, throw the harness over her."

"Harness? You fool, why don't you get her out if you think it's that easy."

"Move over. I'll show you how it's done."

Did Martin think she didn't understand English? Abigail readied herself to fight, hoping she proved up to the status of kicking like a mare. The men switched places, and Martin advanced on her, slow and deliberate. He feigned right, and she kicked prematurely, her foot landing on air. The mistake cost her time. Martin grabbed her nightgown by the collar and dragged her from the carriage.

"Dumbest mare I ever saw." Martin chuckled as he dropped her to the muddy ground. The frequent rains had transformed what had used to be a road into a swampy pathway. Miss Archibald sat primly atop her horse and peered down at them.

"Lead on, Martin."

"Yes, ma'am." He jerked Abigail to her feet and pushed her forward.

Abigail stumbled and lost a slipper as the mud sucked it into the earth. Her robe had fallen open at some point, and she grasped at it. Miss Archibald laughed at her efforts and motioned to Charlie in a quiet command.

Abigail backed away from Charlie's hands, but she didn't see

Martin come from behind. He ripped off the robe and tossed it aside, removing what remained of her decency. She stood in her thin nightgown and slumped inward against their prying eyes. Miss Archibald motioned her forward, but Abigail hesitated to put her back to them. Charlie stepped toward her, and she pivoted around, sliding forward through the mud.

The salty air of the ocean engulfed her as she shambled in a more or less straight path. They fell into a pattern. Miss Archibald watched their progress from behind and then walked her horse to catch up with them. The madwoman's eyes never seemed to leave Abigail, who made the steady climb in front.

Abigail struggled to keep her footing as the mud pulled her down the incline. She often slipped to her knees but managed to regain her feet before Charlie caught up. After a few more sliding steps, the earth claimed her other slipper.

Once, she considered switching direction and running for her life with everything she had. Between the two men and Miss Archibald on horseback, it was a futile hope.

They must have walked for miles, when the land dropped away in a sharp cliff. Abigail stopped too close to the edge and peered down hundreds of feet below to the waves. She backed up to slam into a wall of solid brute, Charlie. He cut her hands free, and she dropped to her knees on the semisolid earth. She crawled away, her hands and arms screaming in protest, but Martin cut off her path. Half rising, she tipped backward onto her bottom and stared up at them.

Miss Archibald dismounted. "I thought we would untie you, just in case your body is found. Now, do you know what they call this place?"

Abigail shook her head and regretted the world-spinning motion at once.

"Of course not. You wouldn't know up from down if someone didn't tell you." Miss Archibald towered over her. "These are the Hangman cliffs. An appropriate place for you to die. Don't you agree? You see, Miss Riverton, I'm giving you to the hangman after all. Who says I don't have a sense of humor?" She gave a short, throaty laugh. "Just look at this view. It was here Peter declared his love for me. I should've known it was a bad omen to speak of romance in such a place. Well, here we are." She shrugged and pulled out a dagger from behind her back.

"I thought you were going to make me jump?" Abigail crawled back to the edge.

"Oh, I will." Miss Archibald played with the blade, resting the point against her middle finger. "First, I want to have some fun with you. You remember this dagger? Hugh's little gift to you."

Abigail shook her head, this time with less dizziness. "Delia gave me that."

"Oh, bother. I was hoping it was from Hugh. It would be like he's stabbing you. Still, it'll cut you all the same." Miss Archibald raised the blade and leaned toward Abigail.

The three of them cornered her, and her only escape was the long fall behind her. Her mind raced over her options. A fraction of a second passed in a slow-motion moment of panic. Her mind slammed to a stop, and she pushed herself back, off the precipice.

Her body tumbled a few feet from the cliff edge. Her limbs skimmed over the broken rocks and plant life. Her death wouldn't be the sharp drop she'd hoped for, but a slow agony played out all the way down.

Mind overwhelmed, her body acted of its own accord to save itself.

Her hands scrambled to find purchase. They met with only debris and weak plant stems. She kicked to slow her fall along the cliff face, but she didn't feel the cuts and bruises raining across her body through the anticipation of hitting the water.

Another moment of dead air sent her stomach and heart into her throat.

She covered her head with her arms to shield herself from the broken path. Moments stretched before her, and she found more of the cliffside's undergrowth. Pain shot through her leg as she landed at an odd angle, and she smacked her elbow on a jagged rock.

The earth fell away again.

She hit a thicker patch of bushes, which absorbed most of the impact of her fall. This time, her hands caught on a tree limb, and she clung to it with every inch of strength. Once she stilled her shaking limbs, she ventured to look down.

She had rolled down the cliff for a matter of seconds, but her downward journey had been swift. If she had hit her head, she wouldn't have survived. If she had jumped or been pushed, nothing would have slowed her fall. Instead, she had tumbled down to less than twenty feet above the crashing waves. She thanked whatever force of nature had guided her down the cliff.

She peered up to the top and hoped the others hadn't seen her. All she could make out was the long, dizzying path she had taken over the rocks. Seeing what she had been through made her aware of her injuries. Her whole body was a mass of bruises, and blood trickled down her leg and arm. The arm holding her in place shook from the strain. Worst of all, her leg pulsed, a useless weight dragging her down. It wasn't over yet. She would have to jump down into the water soon.

She'd never learned to swim.

Abigail watched the waves below her, anticipating her moment. She waited until one of the larger waves neared. Then, taking a deep breath, she kicked off the cliff to plunge into the water.

The chill hit her first, sending a violent shiver through her. The salt ignited tiny burns along the cuts covering her skin. She attempted to paddle her arms, but instead, she fought the water to regain the surface. It was a losing battle. The murky liquid filled her nose and mouth.

Her body sank, and the world darkened.

Splashing disturbed the water near her. Somewhere across her consciousness, she wondered if it was a fish coming to make a meal of her. A hand closed over her arm and was joined by a supporting arm. She was dimly aware of being pulled to the surface. The man behind her hefted her over the edge of a small boat.

Abigail coughed over the edge of the boat, water and phlegm rushing out of her. The man slapped at her back and pulled her soundly into the boat. She dropped back onto the wood and stared up at the sky while taking great, heaving breaths.

"It was foolish walking so close to the drop like that." The man took up the oars at the edge of her vision.

She glared at him, and her restless mind brimmed with anger.

His shabby, waterlogged clothes didn't match the aristocratic face of the man who stared back at her with startling hazel eyes. His hair was clipped short as though he wore wigs, but he had the strong arms and athletic build of a fisherman.

"I didn't fall."

"Then it was foolish to jump off the cliff."

She inhaled a deep breath and coughed out another round of water. "I couldn't very well help it at the time. It was either that or be stabbed."

He stopped rowing and studied her expression. Then, smiling down at her, he threw her a blanket. Abigail looked down at her soaked-through transparent nightgown and covered herself gratefully.

She cleared her throat. "Thank you for saving me. I would've surely drowned."

He nodded, unconcerned. He acted as though he rescued women from cliff falls every day. "I saw you fall while I was fishing and thought I was retrieving a body."

"In any case, I appreciate knowing someone would have found me."

"We get quite a few jumpers here." He sighed and shook his head. "Sours the fishing experience."

She dropped into silence. Was he joking?

She blinked at him, studying his face as though it would unravel the key to his humor. "How thoughtful of you to retrieve them. I'm sure they wouldn't want to spoil your appetite."

A broad grin lit his charming features. This man wasn't what he seemed. His accent wasn't quite English or American. She was sure he was from an upper-class family, which was unusual. He rowed like he knew where he was going, but all she saw was the cliff face.

"Who are you?" Her tone was cautious.

"I'm Maxwell Rycroft, or I am today, anyway." He lowered his head in a bow. "And you are?"

She saw no reason to lie to him; he had saved her life. "Miss Abigail Riverton."

"Do you have any friends around here, Miss Abigail Riverton?" He spoke as though she was a package needing delivery. "You're an American, right?"

"Yes. I've been visiting my friend, Lady Carrington."

He stopped rowing again. "Viscount Carrington's wife?"

"Is there another?"

"Hmm." The ideas worked like cogs over his features.

She spoke in a rush before his thoughts could take a wrong turn. "I'm sure I can offer you a reward for rescuing me. You don't have to kidnap me to get money. My family's wealthy, and I'm prepared to pay you if you take me back to Briarwyck."

He chuckled and continued their progress. "You take the fun out of it."

"No, I'm taking the hassle out of it and probably saving your life."

He tilted his head quizzically. "How so?"

She eyed him with a cool stare. "Lord and Lady Carrington are good friends of mine, along with Viscount Greymore and Mr. Travers. You'd have an army after you." At least, she hoped Hugh cared enough to fight for her. Now that she had dodged fate and gained the knowledge for her freedom, she would take every opportunity she had with him. If that meant only mutual tolerance, so be it.

"Really? Point taken. I'm surprised by you. Greymore and Hugh? I didn't think anyone but Carrington could be friends with both of them, though he is blood, so I guess he doesn't count."

"You know them, then?"

"Of course." He turned up the side of his lips.

"Then you'll take me to them?"

"Yes, but first I need to get some things from the cave yonder." He pointed to the area they rowed toward, which she had failed to see.

They pulled up to the coast at the entrance of the cave. Rycroft jumped to shore and guided her from the boat. She shivered as if drenched to the bone and clutched the blanket. When the sand met her feet, her leg gave out, and she collapsed to the ground. A lance of pain burned through the skin, and she gurgled on a gasp, her mouth agape.

He hastened to help her rise, but she pushed him away when he attempted to examine her injury. He shrugged at her refusal and continued on into the shadowed cave, gesturing for her to follow. She hopped after him in the sliding sand and somehow managed not to make a fool of herself. Every hair of weight on her toes intensified the pain.

Wooden crates were stacked up along one wall. He turned the opposite way, where a mismatch of household items and fishing gear rested. He dug through a pile of garments, and his hand stopped on a light-yellow pattern with green flowers. He tossed it to her.

"That might fit you, but I don't have any shoes." He left her there as he went to the back of the cave.

Her gaze lingered where he disappeared. She didn't think she would get any more privacy than now, but she couldn't take off her nightgown here. Instead, she put the dress on over it and used the dainty nightgown as a shift, which wasn't far from the truth. She half leaned and half sat against the crates to keep the weight off her leg. Her elbow allowed little movement, but she managed through gritted teeth. The gown fit snugly: the fabric was tight against her breasts, and her hips were more pronounced than usual.

He reappeared wearing a fitted black coat and trousers with a white linen shirt, red silk waistcoat, and tall black boots. She stared wide-eyed at his transformation and had the foolish notion of being underdressed for the cave.

"You forgot your wig." A smile creased her lips.

"Indeed. It's a nuisance in the wind, and I left it at home." He threw a bag over his shoulder. "Shall we go?"

"Yes, please."

They pushed off from the shore and caught the current, which glided them along. He dug into his bag and brought up a bottle of brandy, which he handed to her.

"I'm afraid I have no cups." He threw his head back and laughed when she upended the bottle and gulped it down.

She leaned back into the boat in contentment. "That was wonderful, thank you." It had been a shame not to savor the excellent brandy, but the drink had slid down her throat.

He smiled at her, the look familiar and not, next to his brilliant hazel eyes. "I haven't seen a woman so satisfied in…well, forever."

She studied his features, sure she had seen them somewhere. "Who are you really?"

"I told you." His smile didn't falter.

She raised a brow. "Is that your real name?"

"The one I was born with."

She decided he spoke the truth, or all the truth he would provide her. "Where are we going?"

"I thought it would be safer to go to my house first." He nodded at a point in the distance. "I'll send word to Lord Carrington that you're there. Someone needs to assess your injuries before you travel."

"You don't live in the cave?"

He chuckled. "No, not usually. Tell me, who's trying to kill you?"

"Miss Alice Archibald." The name left a foul taste in her mouth.

"I didn't know she had it in her. What on earth did you do?"

Abigail hesitated but saw no need to hold back, so she told him what happened at Briarwyck. She skipped over parts involving Hugh and other embarrassing details. Rycroft sat in silence and rowed, listening to her while keeping his eye on their destination.

When she finished, he glanced at her briefly. "Are you sure you want to go back there? I could find a ship for you to New York."

"Quite sure." She needed to see if she could make things right with Hugh, no matter the outcome.

His upturned brows showed his regard for her sanity. "I have to agree with you. My demanding a ransom for you would've been a grave error. I wouldn't be surprised to take up a paper and see Miss Archibald and her companions had been brutally beaten and killed."

"That is, if anyone realizes their guilt. Miss Archibald had everything figured out and would have probably gotten away with it if I had died."

His smile returned. "True, but you didn't die."

They both became lost in their own thoughts as Rycroft rowed them along. Abigail continued to wonder about the man but kept her questions to herself. They were aimed toward a beach opposite the cave, and a horse grazed on the grass nearby. The horse relieved one of her worries. She was still without shoes, and hopping to his house would have taken an eternity.

When they reached the shore, Rycroft whistled to the dark-brown stallion, and Abigail's eyes widened when the great beast galloped over. The white blaze on its face became a streak of motion. Rycroft lifted her into the saddle and leaped up behind her.

"You're in luck today. I don't usually ride with a saddle." Rycroft urged the horse into a gallop. The horse's movement didn't hurt as much as she expected. A dull ache through her head and limbs accompanied the horse's hoofbeats, but it was preferable to the agony of walking.

She peered back at him with a lopsided frown. "Mr. Rycroft, I no longer know if you're embellishing the truth or outright lying to me."

"Oh, a little bit of both, to be sure."

Abigail faced forward. He could have left her to die or murdered her by now. Of course he would want money, but there was no guarantee he would free her when he got paid. She wanted to believe she had been saved for the better and not just to be thrown back into the fire, so to speak.

Chapter Twenty-Two

Rycroft House was light and new against the fading daylight. It reminded her of the houses in New York. Abigail hated it on sight. A country house that was out to prove something to its visitors. If Briarwyck was a mysterious but pestering aunt, Rycroft House was the haughty, pretentious mother-in-law. It boasted three stories of chalky-colored stone and lofty windows to welcome in the sunlight.

For such a large estate, there were few servants. Rycroft ordered his skeleton staff to feed her and make her comfortable while he sent a letter to Briarwyck and called for a doctor. He returned when she was on her third bowl of soup, the warm broth working over her cold, worn bones. The local doctor followed him in—Dr. Pascoe, a young man who kept his distance from Rycroft and trembled when he spoke.

Rycroft discreetly left the room while the doctor looked her over as she ate in the dining room. It was an odd sort of arrangement Rycroft said he preferred while he decided what to do with her. The doctor spent much of his time examining her leg and the back of her head, which proved to be the most serious. He wrapped her leg and washed the dried blood from her wounds.

When Rycroft returned, Pascoe handed him a nasty-looking vial filled with bits of floating matter and spoke to him as though Abigail weren't in the room.

"She needs to take a drop of this with tea three times a day. I suggest she rest at least until tomorrow. Any upset to her head could send her into fits of vomiting and convulsions. Watch for fever. She has a bad cut on her elbow and scalp." Pascoe cowered next to Rycroft, who handed him an atrocious sum of money.

"Good man." Rycroft patted the doctor's shoulder.

Pascoe flinched away at his touch, and Rycroft gave him a toothy grin. The doctor scurried out the door, not looking back. Abigail stared after him, brows raised as Rycroft settled into the seat across from her.

"It seems you'll be my guest tonight. I thought as much and took the liberty of informing Briarwyck of my intentions to bring you around tomorrow if you're recovered then. I'll have my housekeeper ready a room for you." He gestured to a footman, or at least who she thought was a footman. He wasn't dressed in livery, but his clothes were finer than Rycroft's and complemented the darkest skin she had ever seen.

Rycroft ladled his own soup and poured them both port.

Abigail sipped at her offered glass. "Why was the doctor afraid of you?"

"Pascoe? I don't know. He's a new doctor in the district. I'd wager he's heard rumors about me and he's taken them to heart."

"What rumors?"

"Oh, the usual." He waved his glass in the air. "I've been away for weeks, so I can't be sure what they're blathering about now. Probably something about me being a lawless vagabond or a treacherous scoundrel. Those seem to be the favorites. I'm partial to the rumors about my lecherous affairs, always so creative."

She coughed on her port. "Then they aren't true?"

"Some of them are likely true, but by the time I hear them, they're embellished to the point I come off as the area demon."

"Doesn't it bother you?"

His smile lit his face from ear to ear. "No, it hides the truth quite conveniently."

"If there's truth to the rumors, what is it?"

"Guess." He gazed at her over his soup. She didn't realize her hand shook until she dropped her glass. It clattered to the table intact, spilling the last of her drink. Before she could move, he had wiped up the mess and refilled her glass. She took a deep breath and sipped her port.

"Miss Riverton, there's truth to every rumor. Don't believe everything you hear, but don't dismiss the information outright." His eyes sparked with merriment.

"Can I trust I'll be safe here?"

"Yes, I've no plans to harm you, and it's unlikely Miss Archibald will find you here. If by some chance she comes looking for you, she won't be admitted." He swirled the liquid in his glass. "Don't misunderstand me though. Just because I'm not an immediate threat to you doesn't mean you should trust me."

"I'll keep that in mind." She stared down at her glass of port and questioned its contents.

"Do that." He nodded. He gazed over her shoulder and acknowledged an elderly woman who entered. "I see your room is prepared. I trust you'd like to bathe and rest. It's already late, and I'd like to set out for Briarwyck before Rycroft House is under siege."

She swallowed the rest of her port and followed the housekeeper, Mrs. Johns, out of the room. The old woman set a slow pace, which Abigail appreciated as she limped along. She doubted the woman could move any faster, but with Abigail's injuries, she didn't care for the reason.

Without Mrs. Johns, Abigail would be lost in the darkened halls. The housekeeper carried one of the only lights, and the house was an imposing labyrinth of halls and doors. Abigail tried to keep her bearings, but she soon lost track of the pattern of the lavish green carpet and the generic landscape paintings.

Mrs. Johns turned the knob of a nondescript door, which opened into a room lit by a single oil lamp. Abigail expected the scent of loosened dust from a recently cleaned long-neglected room. Instead, the air was fresh as though cared for by well-disciplined servants. She hadn't seen a speck of dust or a misplaced item since entering the house. The memory of the frightened face of Dr. Pascoe hovered over her thoughts. Could the servants be afraid of Rycroft?

Her room was accented in creams and soft yellows with a view overlooking the front of the house. She peered around as Mrs. Johns ordered a bath, but there wasn't much to take her notice. A bed larger than her bed at Briarwyck took up most of the room. An oak armoire and small cream dressing table completed the furnishings. Steam wafted from the adjoining room, where a bathtub awaited.

Abigail settled herself at the dressing table. Her face was purple with bruises in contrast to her pale skin, and her dark hair was a muddy, tangled mess. She inhaled, a deep rise and fall of her chest, and readied the wide-toothed comb set out for her.

She wished her life were as easy to sort out.

This was a strange house inhabited by a strange man, and she wanted to avoid any unnecessary interactions. For once, she nourished none of her hazardous curiosity.

The events that followed her arrival in England had rid her of any desire to entertain her past romantic notions of danger and mystery. More specifically, her kidnapping had left her with a stunned shock, and she barricaded herself in the room.

If Mr. Rycroft was involved in something nefarious in the house, she had no intention of finding out and wanted no part of it. She would rest the best she could while waiting for their trip to Briarwyck, but until then, she would hazard no more adventures.

She settled into the unfamiliar bed, in her borrowed nightgown. Her throat tightened, and the urge to cry crept to her eyes. She longed to see Hugh's wicked smile and to forget her troubles in his protective embrace. A sharp pain pinched her chest at the thought of how they had parted. He must think she hated him, giving her up for dead and forgotten. She hoped it wasn't too late already.

Regardless of Rycroft's reassurances, Abigail wasn't certain she would see Hugh again. Rycroft was a wild card, an unknown factor in a chaotic world. Against her better judgment, she believed he meant to take her back to Briarwyck unharmed. Yet she had a nagging suspicion he would take advantage of the situation, gaining profit at her misfortune. In that she didn't trust him and worried what trouble he would cause her and her friends.

Abigail slept little. The strange environment and her anxiety refused to allow her adequate rest. Instead, she stared at the ceiling and dozed. When the dawn light blazed through the window, she dressed. The gown from yesterday had been cleaned and fit better with proper undergarments, but her elbow made it difficult to put on. They were unable to find her properly fitting shoes, so she went without instead of injuring herself further.

She managed to comb out her hair, but the soreness in her scalp prevented her from styling it in any way. In the end, she resembled an undone tavern wench who had been painted with a rowdy patron's fists. At least she would no longer seem a threat to Miss Archibald. Her own mother probably wouldn't recognize her strange appearance, and if Hugh didn't believe her dead now, he would when he saw her.

Mrs. Johns led her to the breakfast room at her crawling pace. When they entered, Rycroft was nose-deep in a newspaper.

"Any news?" She sat across from him at a circular table of polished wood. He settled the paper down and poured her tea.

"This paper is days old. Not much to report." He handed off her cup.

"I suppose we're a ways from sources of information." She served herself some eggs and kippers, gritting her teeth as her elbow shook.

He caught her gaze through his lashes. "That's right. Nobody hears the screams."

She spit out her tea and coughed. Her face heated at her private thoughts being repeated to her. They weren't her exact thoughts, but they had an uncanny similarity to her fears since she had arrived. She resolved to trust him to keep her safe on this journey and refused to let her imagination lead her as it had in the past.

"I'm sorry, that was in bad taste. I assumed you hadn't decided to trust me yet and thought to make a joke of it. I promise the house doesn't have a dungeon of wailing victims longing for death." He poured her more tea. "In fact, the only screaming that goes on is from me falling off Hermes."

She forced a wry smile. "Right."

"In any case, it seems you're well enough to travel. If you're not opposed to riding on horseback, then we can leave whenever you're ready. I've left my carriage and most of my horses in London, but we can borrow a second horse for you."

"Are you trying to be rid of me?" A nervous laugh bubbled in her throat.

"No, I simply would rather it be over with."

"I was joking. I'm just as eager to be off. Who knows what Miss Archibald has done in my absence?" She attempted to focus on her food, but the heaviness in her head made her stomach uneasy. "What's your relationship like with the Travers family?"

"There isn't one. We prefer it that way. They're too high and mighty to associate with me."

She blinked at him. "How so?"

He let out a long breath as if he was annoyed with her line of questioning. "To be blunt, Miss Riverton, I'm the third son of an untitled family from new money."

She frowned at him. "That doesn't seem to bother them with Delia and me."

"I also have some…dealings they don't approve of."

"I see." She had no idea what he was talking about.

"Do you? Well, I'll have the horses readied, and we can be off." He left without waiting for her response.

After Abigail ate all her stomach could manage, she steadied herself to her feet and hopped out to the front of the house, where Rycroft waited. When he lifted her into the saddle of her nag, she noticed he wore a sword with the familiar crest from the pocket watch in Miss Archibald's room.

"Is that your sword?"

He glanced down at it. "Of course. Wouldn't want to be robbed by highwaymen."

She recalled Hugh's angry frown on the cusp of her mind, and she swallowed back her shame. If only she could turn back time and not behave like a childish fool. Highwaymen were nothing to be excited about.

"I thought that was the Rockwell coat of arms."

"So it is." He studied it as if seeing it for the first time. "I won it at a poker game."

"You said you don't associate with men like the Traverses. Sir Peter would certainly count as one of them. Which is it?"

"Yes." He mounted his horse.

When she opened her mouth to reply, he urged his horse forward and called back, "Try to keep up."

She sat still a moment, mouth hanging half-open. At last, she recovered and followed after him. The nag, Mist, was unfit for bursts of speed. She was a speckled, gray mare who had seen better days. Abigail missed Soot and looked at Rycroft's Hermes with envy. At least Mist didn't jostle her injuries. Her horse fell further and further behind until Rycroft turned Hermes to watch her impatiently.

"Is something amiss? A Mist?" He laughed at his own joke.

"You're going too fast for the poor dear."

He nodded and slowed his pace. The horses continued on, Hermes racing forward while Mist struggled to follow. Mist fell back again, this time refusing to urge on. Abigail came to a crawl, and Hermes joined them.

Abigail sighed. "I don't think she's going to make it."

"We're more than halfway there." His lips twisted down as he watched the sweating nag.

"It seemed much further by carriage."

"By carriage, it is. Come, let's leave her at the next house we see. I'm sure they could use a nag."

"Won't her owners miss her?"

"Oh, I'm sure they will but not until tomorrow at the earliest." He had the wide grin she associated with trouble.

"Tomorrow?"

"They're away from home," he said offhandedly.

She squinted. "How did you borrow her?"

He favored her with an odd twist of his lips followed by a sweet smile. He trotted Hermes forward without answering.

"Do they even know she's gone?" She trailed after him.

"Hell if I know." His words were so low she scarcely made them out over the hoofbeats.

"I'm riding a stolen horse?" Her near shout made Mist lower her ears.

He waved back at her. "I had every intention of returning her."

"Now you don't?"

He tilted his head to the side as he seemed to consider the idea. "Does seem a bit inconvenient."

"You could hang for this."

He snorted, sounding not unlike the horse in question. "Relax, Mr. North will barely notice."

Her gaze pierced into the back of his head. "You stole this horse from a constable? Are you mad?" What had she gotten herself into with this man?

"I forgot he'd taken up the job. No matter." He shrugged.

"You forgot? What else have you done?" If she had a shoe, she would throw it at him.

"We both know you don't want the answer to that. Come along. I see a farmhouse."

As expected, the family was more than happy to take the nag, but they had no horse with which to replace her. Abigail and Rycroft would have to share Hermes to Briarwyck. Fortunately, it was no longer a great distance away.

They spoke little. Abigail was wary of the thief who road behind her, and she suspected he was tired of her questions.

The changing scenery flew past as Hermes's hooves pounded over the ground. It seemed like a homecoming after a long trip away, but the thought was out of place. Briarwyck was not her home, but it housed many of the people she was safest with, which outweighed the danger behind its walls.

She chanced a look back at him. "Rycroft? What's the likelihood your message didn't reach Briarwyck and Miss Archibald is happily sipping tea inside?"

"Quite remote. My messenger is dependable, and I gave him a detailed description of her crimes. I'm actually surprised we haven't run into any of your friends on the way." His tone was amused, and she wondered what he wasn't telling her.

"Would they trust your correspondence?"

"Not in normal circumstances. They might even think I'm in league with Miss Archibald, but it's in their best interest to believe otherwise."

"Why would they believe that?"

"Past dealings. Bad blood. Take your pick of the reasons. I'm sure they'll give us plenty when we arrive." His voice grew bored again.

"I think they'll be reasonable. You did save my life and bring me back to Briarwyck."

He snorted. "I'm not so sure. Don't be surprised at their violent reactions when they see me. Hugh will likely run me through, but William might be dealt with."

She peered back at him a moment. "Because of me?"

"Even without you. Hugh and I have never been on the best of terms. You said you were involved with him?"

She hadn't, but he must have assumed as much during her retelling of the events. It could account for his careful behavior around her, all jokes aside. She wondered at his asking now of all times but shrugged it off to curiosity.

She hesitated, unsure at the answer herself. "Yes, though I

don't know his thoughts on it at present."

"We'll soon see by how he reacts to your sharing a horse with me."

"Does he hate you that much?"

"Let's just say there's a rivalry that isn't settled." He skirted her questions, but she wouldn't be persuaded to drop the inquiry.

She scrunched up her nose. "Similar to Hugh and Greymore? I assure you, they're on better terms now. I think they'll prove good friends in time."

"No. This is beyond that."

She shook her head and found it strangely clear for the first time in many hours. Her mass of loose hair tossed from side to side. "I won't hear of it."

His sigh sent a breath of air tingling over her sore scalp. "I'm afraid you may have no choice. He's determined against me. Why would you want to sacrifice your relationship with him for a stranger?"

"It isn't a sacrifice. As much as I wish he did, I'm not sure he has feelings for me anyway. Besides, you seem to be growing on me." She smiled to herself.

"Madam, that may be your undoing."

Chapter Twenty-Three

Rycroft pointed out Briarwyck as they approached. Riders sped toward them in their path, and Rycroft slowed his horse to await their arrival. As they neared, she spotted Ember and Coffee, naming them for Rycroft. He grunted and watched the men advance with a wary eye. His hand rested on his sword.

When Hugh and Greymore were within better range, Rycroft drew his sword and laid it across Abigail's neck. She pushed back from the blade, pinning herself to his chest.

"What are you doing?" She wiggled a fraction in his grasp. "There's no need for this."

His breath tickled her ear. "I'm not so sure of that. Just go along with it and nothing will happen to them."

"To them? What about me?"

"You have nothing to worry about." His confident tone was not reassuring.

"Your blade biting into my skin tells me otherwise."

Hugh pointed a pistol skyward, and Greymore had his own sword out. They stopped within ten paces of Hermes.

"Let her go, Rycroft!" Hugh's shout made Hermes flinch, and the movement squeezed Abigail's throat.

"I intend to. Did you bring what I asked?"

"That depends, did you do that to her?" Hugh hoisted his pistol as though he readied to aim.

"No, but would you believe me?"

Greymore shook his head beside Hugh. "Miss Riverton, did Mr. Rycroft hurt you?"

Abigail gulped with some hope it would give her distance from the blade. "No, he saved my life."

Hugh studied her a moment, perhaps wondering if her words were forced. "Then why do you hold her hostage, Rycroft?"

"A matter of my own safety. I remember the last time I was with you, Hugh. I'd rather not have a repeat performance!" Rycroft's shout echoed through Abigail's head.

Hugh stiffened in his saddle. "You ass, you broke my winning streak. What did you think I was going to do?"

"Perhaps if you'd been a good fellow about it and stayed quiet, I would have split the earnings with you."

Hugh cocked his head and stared Rycroft down. "Would you have?"

"Of course not. It isn't my fault you're terrible at cards."

"A winning streak." Hugh bit out his words.

Rycroft chuckled to himself, the rumble vibrated through Abigail's back. "Even a monkey can win occasionally."

Hugh leaned forward in his saddle as though he had forgotten a sword was raised to her throat. "How did you even do it?"

"If I told you, I wouldn't be able to play another card game again. Nobody would play with me."

Greymore rubbed a hand across his face. "Would you two shut up? Mr. Rycroft, hand over Miss Riverton and Hugh will give you the purse."

"I'm not giving him anything until he releases Abigail." Hugh's reply was laced with acid.

Abigail sighed but caught herself midexhale as she recalled the sword. "Is this really necessary? Rycroft, I can give you the money if you take me to the house."

Rycroft spoke into her ear. "It isn't money, sweet."

"Then what is it?"

"A family heirloom, something they should never have had."

Rycroft raised his voice enough for the other men to hear across the distance.

She closed her eyes. All this for a thing? "Hugh, give Rycroft the damned purse."

"He's wrong. It's a Travers family heirloom. He's been trying to buy it off Mother for years. I don't know why he wants it so badly." Hugh seemed to believe what he said.

"Which is it?" Abigail's gaze flew to Greymore.

"Both." Rycroft shifted behind her, and the sword sawed a breath away from her skin. "It was my mother's by right."

Hugh spit to the side. "Your mother was no more a Travers than you are."

Rycroft brought the sword against her skin, drawing a small drop of blood. She cried out from the paper-thin cut. Hugh paled and aimed his pistol toward them.

"No, she was no Travers, though it was her wish. She was promised the necklace upon my birth and thought of nothing else for the rest of her days. It was the closest thing to joining the family as she could get."

"It wasn't Father's to give. My mother is the matron of the family, and it was hers to do with as she pleases. By right, it passes to Lady Carrington."

"Tell me, why did you bring it?"

"Miss Riverton is dearer to us, to me, than a necklace," said the man aiming a pistol at her.

"If that's so, hand it over."

Hugh shook his head. "Set her down first."

"I'm not going to do that. She's injured her leg." Rycroft's explanation seemed reasonable enough to her ears, but she wondered if he would have pushed her off Hermes by now if they were alone.

Hugh's eyes narrowed on Abigail. He studied her face and moved his gaze down her body as he assessed her condition more closely. "Where are her own clothes? Her shoes?"

"This is far more than she was wearing when I found her

wading in the Channel." Rycroft's voice held unshed laughter. "It was fortunate I had any clothes for her. Would you prefer her to ride practically naked against me?"

"I'd prefer you didn't touch her at all. Clothes or otherwise. If I find out you harmed her in any way, I'll butcher you and use your head as a footstool."

Rycroft laughed under his breath and whispered to Abigail, "I believe we have our answer. Still think this is unnecessary?" She said nothing. His attention turned to Hugh. "Then give me the bag and you can have her back."

Hugh walked his horse forward.

Rycroft stopped him with a hand. "I want Greymore to bring the bag. He isn't stupid enough to get Miss Riverton killed. I'll lower her off the horse after he gives me the bag."

"I would never let her come to harm," Hugh said in a firm tone.

"You're pointing a pistol in her general direction." Rycroft let out a long breath, and she sympathized with his impatience. "You know, I actually believe you, but I'm going to ignore that, since you insulted my mother."

"Your mother was a whore." Hugh's affront lanced through Abigail. Was he trying to get her killed?

"Whores are paid. Give me the necklace, and we can make good on that. Put some truth to your words."

Greymore sucked in a breath. "This has become tedious. Both of you dismount and trade on the ground. Nobody will be running away from anyone else."

Rycroft paused to consider. "A sensible idea, Greymore. What do you think, Miss Riverton?"

"You'll want Greymore off his horse as well. He's an excellent rider, and I wouldn't trust him to keep to the bargain." Abigail wanted this over without bloodshed, and from what she knew of Rycroft, tricking him would not end peacefully.

Hugh groaned and looked back to Greymore, who shrugged.

Rycroft shook with laughter. "You know, I change my mind.

I'll take Miss Riverton with me. Keep the damned necklace."

"Like hell." Hugh's horse pawed the ground as if sensing his master's anger. "If you take her, I'll make you regret it with your every breath."

"My brother, so cranky. Are you sure Miss Riverton wouldn't prefer me?" Rycroft's voice betrayed his smile.

Hugh analyzed Abigail's face. "No, I'm not sure, but I know she wouldn't like to have her decisions made for her. All I'm asking is for her safe return to Briarwyck, where her family entrusted her to William's care."

"An honorable man. Now, you heard Miss Riverton, both of you dismount and drop your weapons."

Greymore did so at once, and Hugh reluctantly followed his lead. Rycroft motioned for them to step forward, then stopped them with a hand.

"Miss Riverton," he whispered in her ear, "when I let you down, stay there. Do you understand?"

She gave a short nod, and he inched her off the horse. She cried out when her foot hit the earth and sent a bolt through her leg. Her body dropped to the ground. Hugh moved to help her, but she shook her head at him. A moment later, Rycroft stood behind her.

Hugh widened his stance. "Drop your sword."

To her amazement, Rycroft threw his sword to the side. She gazed at the weapon, calculating her chances.

"The bag?" Rycroft beckoned Hugh forward.

They advanced on each other, and Rycroft took the red velvet bag from Hugh's hand.

Abigail saw her opportunity and grabbed Rycroft's sword. She waited for him to step back. When he was in range and distracted as he inspected the contents of the bag, she grasped the sword by the blade and swung the handle at the back of Rycroft's head.

He sank to his knees and moaned, clutching his head. He tucked the bag into his pocket and glared at her. "Why did you do that?"

She frowned. "You cut my neck."

"I saved your life."

"I'm tired of being a pawn."

He grunted. "Fair enough." He rose to his feet and offered her a hand. She took it without hesitation, and he pulled her to her feet. She winced at the shot of pain through her leg and leaned into him for support.

Hugh's gaze danced between them. The pain in his expression clutched at her chest. She gave him a weak smile in answer to his unspoken question, and he rushed forward to embrace her. He scooped her up and leaned into her face, kissing her lightly. It was as if she'd floated into her dreams and every possibility rested below her fingertips. This was a dream she never wanted to wake from.

"Hugh?" she asked.

A grin tugged at his lips as he carried her to Coffee. "Hmm…?"

"Invite Mr. Rycroft to dinner," she said loudly enough for everyone to hear.

A crease formed in the center of his brows. "What?"

She favored him with her widest smile. "Please? He did save my life, and he's been good enough to escort me here."

His gaze flicked away. "We don't usually allow him at Briarwyck."

"I don't usually get saved from drowning."

"I gave him the necklace." His voice was stern, but she could see his resolve waning.

"You get an inheritance." She snapped out her words and then softened her voice. "Please, I won't ask anything else of you."

Greymore grunted. "Never believe a woman when she says that."

"Shut up, Greymore." Abigail smiled back at him.

"Fine. I won't refuse you anything. What else would you like?

A mermaid?" He nudged her face with his. "A leprechaun?" He kissed the tip of her nose. "I could capture Nessy and you could keep her for a pet?"

She giggled and squirmed at his attentions in front of the others.

He turned his gaze to Rycroft. "My love says you're to come to dinner. I don't dare refuse her."

"Miss Riverton, what did you do to Hugh?" Rycroft asked through his laughter.

"Max, I almost lost her. I'd give anything to never lose her again. I have you to thank for her return. So if that means tolerating your presence, then by all means, come to dinner. Live with me. Whatever she wants."

Amusement shone in Greymore's eyes. "What about William?"

"He can handle Max for a meal," Hugh said. "Besides, he went with Mr. Archibald to track down Miss Archibald."

"Then you got my letter in time?" Rycroft's posture relaxed. "I sent my fastest rider."

"We were able to catch Mr. Graham and the so-called deputies since they were still in the house. They've taken up residence in jail." Hugh's smile waned. "Unfortunately, Miss Archibald overheard us and fled on Lady. I'm sure they have everything in hand. A lone woman on a tired horse can only go so far." He breathed in deep through his nose. "Let's go inside. And Max? Hide the necklace."

Hugh grabbed the horse's reins and pulled Coffee along as he carried Abigail. Rycroft and Greymore mounted their horses and rode in front of them. It wasn't long before Abigail and Hugh were left alone to follow.

Abigail favored him with a crooked smile. "It would be easier if we rode Coffee."

"That horse is spoiled. I won't share you with him."

She stifled a laugh. "Won't you get tired?"

"I don't care. I'm not missing another minute. I was a fool not to confide in you, and I almost lost you because I wasn't by your side." His admission sobered her.

"What were you hiding?"

"My dear, William and I suspected Miss Archibald after her brother died. Something about her reaction didn't sit well with us. Then there was the manner in which Mr. Adam Archibald died. The letter opener was dainty for the task, a silver blade with a mother-of-pearl handle. Mr. Archibald claimed he didn't recognize it, but we decided at once he was lying."

"Then how did the letter opener kill him?"

"It didn't. We believe he was poisoned first with the same poison he used to kill Sir Peter. The wounds to his back were made in an outburst of anger, but the cut to his throat was the final act upon his life. He might've survived the rest. I suspect Mr. Graham was the one to slit his throat, possibly with a second weapon we haven't recovered.

"Anyway, we needed to investigate our suspicions before accusing her. Since she was already pursuing me, had been for years, I watched her for more evidence." His gaze darkened. "If I'd warned you or kept you at my side, this would never have happened."

"Give yourself some credit. You couldn't always be there."

"I should've done something. I know she's a thoughtless, scheming woman who doesn't stop until she gets what she wants. She tears down anyone who gets in her way. Meaning you." He kissed her forehead.

"Why didn't you tell me?" She couldn't banish the tide of anger that tightened her jaw.

"We were afraid of giving anything away. We thought the competition would force her to act. Of course, we were right, but we had no idea she would become so violent. I'm deeply sorry you were harmed. If you don't wish to forgive me, I understand."

He stopped to meet her eyes, and her anger at his secrets melted in his warm brown gaze. "Know this: I'm desperately and irrevocably in love with you. If you'll have me, I want you to be with me forever as my wife."

"Hugh." A brilliant glow spread like dawn inside her until her head became weightless and her frown twitched into a wide grin. "You fool. Do you think I'd allow you to carry me like this in front of everyone if I weren't already yours?"

"You mean that?"

"Almost dying has a tendency to remind one of what's important. I couldn't bear the thought of Miss Archibald marrying you, destroying you. I wanted you for myself. I was going to die before I could tell you how I felt."

He raised an eyebrow and waited for her to go on.

She broke into easy laughter and held back the urge to kiss him until he believed her. "Hugh, I'm in love with you. I've been in love with you for so long I no longer remember what it's like without your name at the tip of my tongue or without you visiting my dreams. I don't know how or when it started, but I know I don't want it to ever end. Yes, I want to marry you."

A gasp burst from him, and his lips found hers. He kissed her soundly, lovingly. Then he rained soft pecks on her lips, playfully adoring her.

"Can I expect a new sister now?" Delia's light tone recalled Abigail to the moment. They hadn't heard her approach, and Abigail jumped in Hugh's arms. He grunted and readjusted her.

Abigail beamed at her friend. "I've always been your sister, Dee."

Hugh grinned like a fool, his gaze never leaving Abigail. "Now you can make it official."

"Good." Delia beamed at them. "I'm getting a bit tired of throwing you two together. You're both tough work, and I'm retiring from matchmaking. And Hugh, next time, don't make me walk out here. Forget the damned necklace. My feet are already sore enough."

Abigail's eyes widened. "You've been planning this the whole time?"

"Why do you think I had him escort you? One of your brothers would have done just as well. You're a good match, and I wanted you as a sister. Of course, Hugh needs to settle down. He drives Carrington mad."

"I'm glad to be of service to you," Hugh said in a dry voice. "We were just coming in."

"Why do I doubt that? Anyway, we appear to have a problem, and with my husband gone, you're going to have to deal with it."

Hugh's frown would send a lesser woman running but not Delia. "Can't you see I'm a busy man? I trust you're capable of handling whatever it is in William's absence."

Delia stared him down, her startling green eyes like daggers. "I don't think so, no. I don't have enough familiarity with the situation to make any kind of decision, and frankly, I'd rather not put the baby in danger."

"Can it wait?"

She lowered her brows. "That depends on how much of the house you'd like intact when Carrington returns."

Hugh looked skyward. "All right then, what is it?"

"It's about that man who brought Abigail to us. It's about Rycroft."

CHAPTER TWENTY-FOUR

"DON'T YOU DARE."

A crash resounded beyond the library door.

"It's mine, give it back."

Another crash jostled the door and sent a tremor through the floor to vibrate beneath their feet. Abigail, Hugh, and Delia hesitated in the hallway, frozen at the unknown chaos awaiting them.

"Never."

They exchanged glances, one daring another to go inside. Hugh sighed and cracked the door with slow caution. Through the gap, Abigail saw Lynette dodge behind a writing desk to avoid Rycroft, throwing anything available to dissuade him.

Hugh advanced inside the room and ducked when a glass rooster paperweight brushed past his head. He held his arms in front of him and placed himself between the warring parties.

"Lynette, what's the problem?" Hugh caught her with a warning stare as if he dared her to throw something else.

"This horrid man took the Travers family necklace. It was lucky I noticed he had it. He's a thief. It belongs to Delia." Lynette dangled the bag for him to see.

Hugh held Rycroft back from pouncing forward.

Rycroft scowled at her. "It's mine by right."

"No, it isn't." Lynette launched a copy of *The Iliad* at Rycroft.

He stepped aside just in time, and the book slammed against Hugh's shoulder. Hugh rubbed at the area, his face hardening in a deep frown. Lynette cracked a sheepish smile.

"Lynette, you're right to believe he's a thief." Hugh's lips pressed into a thin line. "However, as much as it pains me, the necklace is his now. Give it back to him and apologize."

Lynette's face froze. "No. This is Delia's."

Delia stepped up to stand beside Hugh. "I tend to agree the necklace belongs to Rycroft."

"What does Carrington say?" Lynette folded her arms.

"Leave that to me, but I believe when he returns, he'll agree with my assessment. The man saved Abigail's life, a jewel far more precious than the necklace."

"That doesn't explain who he is or what he wants with it." Lynette directed her frown at Rycroft.

Rycroft's expression hardened. "That's none of your concern."

Abigail squeezed Hugh's shoulder to get his attention. "You might as well tell her. She won't give up the necklace without an explanation. She's far too curious for that."

Hugh rubbed the back of his neck and raised his hand for silence. "Dear little sister, we don't discuss the circumstances, but it's an open secret. Maxwell Rycroft's the by-blow of my father. However, he's been recognized as the third son of Mr. Henry Rycroft. My…our father promised the necklace to his mother, but my mother refused to give it up, since he's illegitimate. As you know, it was recently passed on to William and Delia upon their wedding. We'll consider it payment for services rendered."

Lynette tilted her head, seeming to consider this. "It isn't right."

"I could always take Miss Riverton back with me. I like the idea of a rich wife." Rycroft arched a single brow.

"This time, I'm going to pretend I didn't hear that. I've been accused of being a jealous man, but no more. My she-cat would put up quite a fight. Try it." A wry grin tugged at the corner of

Hugh's mouth. "Lynette, now."

Lynette directed an openmouthed stare at Abigail. "You're marrying Hugh? Are you sure you want that burden?"

Hugh puffed out a breath of air and threw his arms out in exasperation.

Lynette swung the bag in circles. "I mean, he's not that bad. I guess he's a step up from Nigel, but you can do far better."

Hugh regarded Lynette with a sour expression. "You know, I'm right here."

"It would appear so." Abigail's voice held a somber note, but humor crinkled her eyes as she took Hugh's arm.

Hugh beamed at his future bride. "I'm fully aware she can do better."

"What did Mr. Riverton say?" Lynette tapped her lip, the bag swinging under her chin. "I think he'd have some objections."

"You're the nosiest woman. If you weren't Delia's sister, nobody would tolerate you. I'm sure you're aware I haven't spoken to Mr. Riverton, since we're on the other side of the Atlantic." Hugh's voice was coated with ice.

"And your father?" Lynette gave him a sweet smile. Abigail held back her laughter. Lynette must enjoy throwing doubts at Hugh.

"My father can hang himself if he doesn't approve."

Rycroft barked a short laugh. "I'd like to see that."

The library doors thudded open, and Mrs. Eddings came rushing into the room, a vision of swirling skirts and purpose. She planted herself in front of Abigail and grasped Abigail's hands in hers. The dear woman's gaze filled with tears. "Is it true? Are you going to be marrying my Hugh?"

Hugh spoke from Abigail's side. "Of course, Grandmamma."

"Hush." Mrs. Eddings waved Hugh away. "I was asking Miss Riverton. The girl has the right to her own mind."

Abigail lowered her gaze. "If you'll have me."

"Have you? My dear girl, I wouldn't dream of having anyone else." Mrs. Eddings turned to Hugh. "It's about time you made a sensible decision. I thought I'd be in my grave before this day came."

Hugh opened his mouth to reply, but she went on, "Don't you worry about your father. I'll see to him." Her gaze flew to Rycroft, and she lowered her brows. "What is he doing here?"

Lynette stepped forward, drawing Mrs. Eddings's attention. "Stealing family heirlooms."

"What?" Mrs. Eddings's eyes darted to the bag in Lynette's hand. "Then he finally helped himself to the Travers jewels?"

Hugh cleared his throat. "He isn't stealing the necklace. We're giving it to him."

"Why would you do such a thing? Have you consulted with William?" Mrs. Eddings's glare settled on Hugh.

"Consulted me about what?" Carrington emerged from the open library doors.

Hugh inhaled a long, preparative breath and explained the situation to his brother, leaving nothing out. Carrington watched Rycroft, a predator calculating the movement of its prey. Mrs. Eddings tried to interrupt a number of times, but Hugh held her off. When Hugh finished his account, Carrington congratulated the couple and slapped Hugh on the back. He offered Abigail a wide grin.

"What seems to be the problem, then?" Carrington requested his best brandy be brought around to celebrate the occasion.

Mrs. Eddings's frown pinched her face. "William, you can't just hand off the Travers jewels. It would break generations of tradition. Your mother and father would be most displeased with you."

Carrington sighed. "As far as I'm concerned, if Delia and Hugh want to pass the necklace on to Rycroft, I'm not going to stop them. We have enough family heirlooms as it is."

Mrs. Eddings sniffed. "You may not value family tradition, but to give the necklace to Rycroft is sacrilege."

"From what I've heard, he's earned it." A hint of a smile sparked in Carrington's eyes.

"We'll discuss this no further, Grandmamma." Hugh gestured to the bag. "Lynette, give Rycroft the necklace."

Lynette thrust out her lower lip but made no argument as she passed the bag into Rycroft's hands. He gave her a wicked grin and settled the bag into his greatcoat.

"Now, then, I hate to spoil the occasion but I have some news." Carrington took up a seat next to where Delia reclined. The rest of the party followed his lead and settled into a semicircle around him.

Abigail studied Carrington warily. "Is it about Miss Archibald?"

Hugh squeezed her hand from beside her, and the tight set of her shoulders relaxed a fraction.

Carrington noticed Hugh's gesture and passed around glasses of brandy. "The magistrates have ordered her arrest, and some of the constables are out searching for her in parties, but so far there's been no word. Mr. Archibald is consulting with his family, but there's nothing they can do. I assume they'll denounce her shortly."

"What of Mr. Graham? What happened to Charlie and Martin?" Abigail's voice tremored, and she grasped Hugh's hand tighter.

"Charlie and Martin will face the magistrates soon. Their best chance will be relocation, though I doubt they'll get it. You can rest easy, Miss Riverton. You'll never have to encounter them again." Carrington paused to sip his brandy. "Mr. Graham will most certainly hang. I'm afraid Miss Archibald will face other punishment once she makes her pregnancy known. Nothing is certain at this point."

"Can't we do something?" A chill ran through Abigail's veins. "I won't feel safe until Miss Archibald is captured. She'll want her revenge now she knows I survived."

Hugh lowered his gaze to meet hers. "You'll be safe here. I promise."

She took her hand from him. "I appreciate your optimism,

but you can't possibly be sure of that. The woman is a viper, and we've already suffered for underestimating her. I won't make that mistake again."

Greymore's comforting tone claimed her attention. "I think everyone will agree that we're here to ensure your well-being."

Abigail gazed around the room at their murmured agreements. She met Rycroft's eyes, and he gave her a short nod.

"I didn't pull you out of the water like some drowned cat in order to throw you to the hounds."

Carrington searched Rycroft's expression. "We're grateful for your assistance in Miss Riverton's rescue, but you aren't obligated to stay. However, I'd welcome another set of eyes."

"Throw in a game of cards and I'll be happy to assist you. Just keep that damned harpy away from me." Rycroft tilted his head toward Lynette.

"Done."

Hugh's face transformed into his devilish grin, but he said nothing to warn his brother about Rycroft's card playing. Lynette's furious glare encompassed everyone in the room, and she stormed out of the library without a word.

Abigail rose from the sofa, but her leg protested the sudden movement. "How can you be planning card games right now? Miss Archibald's free, a harm to anyone she encounters."

Hugh grasped her hand with both of his. "My dear, we can't know what you must be feeling right now. None of us have experienced anything quite like what you went through, but your worries are unnecessary. We can handle Miss Archibald."

"I think I'd like to rest now. If you'll excuse me." Abigail took her arm from Hugh and rubbed at her face. She hop-limped her way across the room, the lance of pain through her leg doing nothing for her dignity. Carrington rushed to her side and offered his support back to her room. He accepted much of her weight without comment.

When they reached the bottom of the stairs, Carrington stopped her. "My brother means well. He isn't used to being afraid. I didn't even know he possessed the emotion until you went missing." He paused, watching her. "When we received Rycroft's message, we had to retrieve him from hunting the parish for you. I insisted he rest for Coffee's sake, or he would've ridden to death to Rycroft House. I don't think he's slept or eaten anything for two days."

"What would you have me do? I can't ignore this feeling I have. It's as if there's some new horror waiting for me at every turn." She slumped against the handrail. The familiarity and comfort of her friends had not given her the reassurance she needed. On the contrary, the rest and calm were only giving her the liberty to think and feel what she hadn't been able to through the shock. Her nerves were electric, sending a deep ache through her bones. She had no chance of resting, but she couldn't sit in the suffocating environment of the library.

"For now, you should consider switching rooms. It would be ideal if you bunked with someone else for the time being. Maybe Lynette or my grandmother."

"She'll stay with me." Hugh walked briskly to join them.

"I'm not sure that's wise." Carrington shook his head. "Are you planning to elope? I don't think her parents will be too happy about that."

"It's a little late to turn back. Besides, it's unlikely we could get word to them anyway. Conditions are getting worse, and we don't even know if New York will last."

"What do you think, Miss Riverton?"

"Under the circumstances, I believe my family will understand. They won't be happy about my staying in England, but at least I won't be in the middle of a war. We have few agreeable choices in the matter." She hesitated, meeting Hugh's eyes. "I should warn you, Hugh. Many of my father's finances are tied to a positive outcome for England. If things go poorly, I'll bring little to a marriage."

The warmth of Hugh's smile rushed over her like the comfort of a winter hearth. "I don't care about that. Your safety is my only concern right now."

"Fine, but I expect you to have your banns read or take a trip to Gretna Green as soon as possible. I'll probably catch hell for this as it is. This conversation is making me uncomfortable." Carrington stepped back from them.

Hugh's lips tugged up on one side. "You could always blame Delia for this."

"What little good that would do me." Carrington gave his brother a half smile. "No, you're an adult, and I expect you remember both families are at stake here."

Hugh replaced Carrington to escort Abigail up the stairs. "Just think, William, you'll be a father. Imagine the headaches you'll have soon."

"At this rate, you won't be far behind." Carrington strode off before Hugh could respond.

Hugh stared after Carrington as though his thoughts could inflict pain on his brother's back. He escorted her without word up the stairs to his room. He left the door open as he made sure she was comfortable and sent a maid to find Alma. The laborious trek up the stairs relieved some of her restlessness, and she settled on top of his bed, fully clothed. The bed was a welcome retreat from the chaos and turmoil of the past week. The energy seeped out of her as her head sank into the down pillow.

Hugh occupied a chair near the window. She sensed him watching her, but when she turned to him, his gaze found the scene outside his window. Contrary to her wayward thoughts, his watchfulness soothed the sharp tightness in her muscles. Her uneasiness softened to a dull awareness at the back of her consciousness.

In the space between reality and dreams, she wondered at Alma's absence. Her borrowed dress left a nagging tightness she wished to relieve but was no longer bothered to fully perceive. She surrendered comfort to the times of wakefulness when her thoughts held the sharpest barb. She would rest now and take care of her conscious body on waking. It wasn't long before she fell into a deep sleep.

Through her dreams, she relived the nightmare journey to the Hangman cliffs and her struggle against the fall to her death. This time, she experienced it all with enhanced senses. Miss Archibald laughed with a deafening roar as Abigail thrashed about the carriage. Charlie's pungent smell invaded Abigail's nostrils and churned her stomach as he wrestled her to the endless precipice. She could see the murky, turbulent waves crash to claim her, scaling the cliffs with an unnatural appetite.

The insistent cuts and blows of her injuries rained upon her from Miss Archibald, Martin, and Charlie. The pain sent a buzz through her veins, rendering her dizzy and helpless on the muddy ground. A blow from Miss Archibald sent an overpowering metallic taste through her mouth and nostrils. Abigail spit and screamed through the nausea only to be hurtled from the cliff by a battering ram of arms.

This time, her fall was not slowed on the broken rocks and underbrush of the cliff face. She dropped off, unable to turn or measure the crushing speed to her death. The cliff's edge crawled away from her. Hugh stood at the precipice, screaming her name, unable to see where she fell. She cried out in answer as she spiraled down, and Hugh became a dot along her horizon as the cliff seemed to grow. The wind in her ears and hair growled as a whoosh of motion slapped her into stillness.

She startled back in Hugh's bed, warm arms holding her against a firm chest. Hugh had cradled her as she'd been tormented in her sleep. Her head rested on his tear-soaked shirt as he stroked her hair.

Abigail sobbed and held him closer. He made soothing noises between kisses to the top of her head. She eased into the sound of his heart, the intake and exhale of his breath. He was real and safe, an unwavering beacon in the storm. She inhaled his travel-infused scent. The wild residue of dust and horse hair mixed with his own spicy scent carried her thoughts on their future adventures.

He continued to run his hand along her hair as she uncoiled and drifted back to sleep. He didn't move to leave or otherwise disturb her rest, content to be there as she needed him.

This was what it was like to be cherished, to be protected and loved without condition or incentive. To give herself openly and absolutely. This was what it was like to be home.

Chapter Twenty-Five

Sometime in the night when the nightmares had abandoned her and the male presence beside her nudged at her senses, Abigail opened her eyes to Hugh's cocooning warmth. He moaned with her movement and shifted in his slumber. She ran her fingers along his chest, and his eyes snapped open.

"You should be sleeping." His voice was filled with tiredness and barely intelligible.

She brought her lips to his in response and tasted his bottom lip. He grunted and moved her away with his hands on her shoulders. His gaze met hers through the tension between them, his eyes sparked with heat as they took her in.

"I don't want to hurt you." His words were a whisper as though his voice would cause her pain.

"Leave that to me." She leaned in to kiss him, but he sat up and rested his back against the headboard. This time, her lips met his, the soft skin yielded to her, and he couldn't keep himself from returning the gesture. The aching behind their touch gasped in her chest. Swirls of desire heightened her pulse.

He stopped, their lips half-parted mid-devour. "I don't think I'll be able to control myself." His thumb skimmed over her chin.

"Then don't," she whispered into his mouth.

He cupped her head with a hand and deepened the kiss. Her low moan escaped into his mouth, and she pinned him to the headboard with her body. She straddled him under her dress, heedless to the upset the shift caused her leg. His desire prodded her through the fabric of his breeches.

He rubbed his hands along her back and tugged her dress down. A rip ran through the air when he succeeded and the dress loosened. He slid the offending material down, his focus feasting on her breasts like an offering. His lips caressed her nipple, teasing and sucking as he stroked the other.

Her low moan was pure wantonness, and she arched into his mouth. Her hips glided over him, and he inhaled a quick breath. He suckled her other breast, a sense of urgency in his movements. Her pooled desire rose to a rapid boil, and she reached between them, releasing him from the too-tight material.

He fell back as she grasped his length, pleased to distraction.

She began to stroke him, but he guided her hips forward. A shiver raced down her spine as he filled her. She threw her head back as she lost herself in the sensation.

He kneaded her hips as she rocked the length of him in and out. He thrust her thighs wider, demanding full entrance. She bit his shoulder to hold back the shout caught in her throat.

The pleasure built with each rocking motion, rippling through her like the turbulent sea. Their limbs entangled, their skin melded, and they climbed together beyond thought. Everything else fell away as touch became euphoria. Heat surrounded them, and the musky scent engulfed them.

Light filled behind her eyes, but she held back, not wanting to end the moment. He ground into her with circular thrusts.

She broke apart, allowing him to push her over her peak. His hot panting, breaths tickled at her neck as he kissed and nipped her skin. She cried out as she convulsed around him, clutching at his shoulders.

He captured her cry with his mouth and moaned into hers. He gripped her hips, latching her on as he pushed her onto her back.

His actions turned carnal, and he thrust with abandon. She

clasped her legs around his buttocks, claiming him. He shuddered into her, not stopping his thrusts as his release came in spasms.

His eyes searched hers as he gazed down at her from atop unsteady arms. A long sigh burst from his throat, and he dropped to her side. She crawled to rest across his heaving chest. He placed his arm around her, and his gaze flickered over her features.

"Are you all right?" A sheepish grin crept over his face.

"Hugh, from what I can tell, my leg didn't factor into our lovemaking. My headache has cleared since napping and was never a problem. You can rest easy you didn't hurt me. If you had, I only have myself to blame for that." Her faint headache tugged at her mind, and her leg felt as though a hot poker had been rammed through it. She wouldn't have missed their lovemaking if she were in a coma.

She pulled a blanket over them and closed her eyes. She needed a bath and a change of clothes, but while there was time before dawn, she would hoard the seconds she had with Hugh. He would be hers now as she was his, but time was an illusion that could snap back at any moment. She would take what she was offered and count every breath granted.

Abigail woke in a haze, her eyes blurred and heavy. Hugh snored softly, a light rumble through his chest beneath her head. She eased out of bed with delicate motions so as not to wake him. He needed the rest, and she wouldn't be the one to disturb him. She kissed his cheek with featherlight pressure and edged off the bed.

The remains of her gown had left imprints along her side, and she stifled a grunt as she stood. She glanced around the room to see if Alma had visited while they slept, but there was nothing. She considered changing into some of Hugh's clothes but thought better of it, since she would have to appear presentable before too long. Her maid was a diligent worker, and Abigail worried she had taken ill. More than likely she had left the couple in peace.

Clutching her torn dress in place, she spied out into the hall.

The area was sparsely lit by a few dim candle sconces along the walls. It was just enough light to guide her along to her own bedroom door. She advanced with a queer, shuffling hop-skip to avoid tripping and injuring herself further. She ran a hand along the wall as she went, not so much to guide her as to reassure her of its presence. No movement disturbed the stillness, no silhouettes in the shadows. By the time she reached the door, her confidence had grown.

Just as she grasped the knob, she remembered Carrington probably left the door locked. When the door came open, she berated herself; her worries were to no avail. The room was encased in darkness, only a faint glow from the window allowing her to avoid falling over herself. She stumbled along to the window and widened the curtains enough to find the candlestick she had long abandoned in her room.

The bed came into focus as her eyes adjusted, and her goal rested beside it, but the way forward was painted in shadows. She adopted the same shuffling steps and cursed herself for not being selfish and taking Hugh's candle.

She was a few paces from the bed when her foot caught something on the floor. Her bewilderment at the obstruction made her steps uneasy, and she teetered, dropping her dress. She clutched at the hem as it fell, an unnecessary reaction to protect her modesty. The awkward movements sent her falling forward, landing on the same mass she had tried to avoid.

Her heart jumped into her throat as she identified Alma in a coarse gown.

She held her hand to her maid's chest. The shallow rise and fall of life eased the tightness in Abigail's throat. She scrambled in the dark, assessing Alma's condition the best she could. Alma's hands and feet were bound with some sort of tight fabric, but whatever her injuries, she didn't seem to be getting up anytime soon.

Abigail shifted to regain her feet. Her mind jumped through the steps she needed to take for her maid. First, she needed more light and also Hugh to help Alma from the floor. Someone would have to go for a doctor, but at this hour? What if they were too late?

"Stay where you are."

The pounding pulse in Abigail's ears became a gallop as the unmistakable voice came from behind her. Her legs shook where she crouched, hovering over Alma. Her mind raced along her memory of the contents of the room, conjuring up any weapons or escape routes that would aid her.

"I said. Don't. Move." Miss Archibald pushed the familiar sharpness of a blade into the back of Abigail's neck.

Her kidnapper inched to light the candle Abigail had sought, but Abigail couldn't move, the chance to flee lost in her moment of shock. She blinked at the sudden light from the candle and steadied herself next to Alma protectively.

Miss Archibald's blonde hair was loose and falling free of a sloppy updo. Her riding habit was creased from wear, flaking dried mud along her skirts. Her red-laced stare held the full loathing and contempt of the woman behind it. Miss Archibald's ill regard hit like a physical blow.

Abigail took the weight of it, and she was sickened with the disgust of herself. She grew aware of her half-dressed position on the floor. An unclean discomfort raked over her skin.

Abigail gulped back her rising tide of dread. "Why did you come back?"

"My dear, I never left." Miss Archibald brandished the dagger she had taken from Abigail.

Abigail swallowed, an attempt to banish her fear. "But your horse...you rode away."

A short laugh shot from Miss Archibald. "I'm sure they'll find Lady happily grazing in some field or a farmer's stable. Do you know what's beautiful about poverty? People will do anything for bread. It didn't take me long to find someone willing to ride off with my horse."

"Why would you stay here? You could've escaped."

Miss Archibald's tightened lips matched the frost in her eyes. "That's questionable. I may be a murderer, but I'm no fool. It's only a matter of time before I'm captured. It's smart to admit when you've lost but even wiser to see how you may still win. Why waste my time fleeing when I can take you down with me?"

"Then you've been here this whole time with Alma?"

"I'm not one to beat servants, Miss Riverton, but your maid came in at the wrong time. As long as she remains unconscious, she'll live. You, however, won't be so fortunate." Miss Archibald clamped onto Abigail's hair with nails like claws.

Abigail cried out at the tearing pain lancing her sensitive scalp.

Her kidnapper pushed the dagger to her throat. "Be quiet or I'll change my mind about your maid. If that isn't reason enough for you, I'm not opposed to poisoning the household."

Miss Archibald sliced the skin at Abigail's throat, watching her openmouthed, silent gasp as the blood ran. The cut was shallow, a mere demonstration of power, but it stole the breath from Abigail's body.

Instead of shutting down, Abigail sprang into a frenzy. She kicked out at the other woman, clawing and snarling as they wrestled on the floor.

Her ruined dress limited her movements and made escape impossible.

She slammed her clenched fist into Miss Archibald's stomach, causing the woman to shield her belly with her free hand. Abigail crawled away and pushed herself to her feet, a jolt of pain to her leg teetered her in place. Miss Archibald caught Abigail's uninjured foot and yanked her back to cut the tender flesh of her calf.

Abigail tugged at her leg, teeth gritted against the pain, but Miss Archibald's grip was firm. Abigail dug her nails into the floor as Miss Archibald pulled her closer and rolled aside a moment before pointing the dagger at Abigail's chest, moving them further from Alma.

Miss Archibald dragged Abigail by the hair to kneel, and she held her head to protect her scalp from the strain. The small woman lifted Abigail to meet her blade, slicing open the skin at Abigail's collarbone.

Abigail whimpered and struggled at Miss Archibald's crazed strength.

A commotion erupted in the hall, and the door flew open. Lynette stepped into the room, accompanied by Carrington and Hugh. They stopped inside the door and took in the scene before them.

"Let her go, Alice." Hugh's tone was deceptively calm.

"Why would I do that?" Miss Archibald ran the dagger under Abigail's chin.

Hugh looked ready to spring. "You've nothing to gain by this."

Miss Archibald grinned down at Abigail. "Alas, I have nothing to lose."

Hugh advanced a step. "Let her go and you can go free. We won't chase you or have you arrested."

"Nice try, but my brother won't agree to that."

"He doesn't have to know." Hugh shook his head. "You can be free. Run off to France or the Americas. Just let Abigail go."

"You'd like that, wouldn't you? You'd send me off so you can be with your slut after all the trouble you've caused me? You don't get to be happy. You've lost the right." Her voice snapped with a bite.

"Trouble we've caused you?" Hugh took another step forward.

Miss Archibald carved at Abigail's skin, warding him off.

Abigail clamped her mouth shut over a pathetic yelp.

Hugh held out his palms. "Stop. What do you want?"

"Hmm…?" Miss Archibald's focus was trained on running the blade along Abigail's skin.

Hugh's face twisted in torment. "Is it me? Take me. I'll give you whatever you want: marriage, money, a father to your child.

Just don't harm her."

Abigail's eyes grew round, and she tried to get Hugh's attention. The blade barred the words from her lips. Her life wasn't worth the misery he suggested.

Her kidnapper's lazy gaze watched him. "I don't know, Hugh. I've grown tired of the idea. Plus, you'd think of her while we share a bed."

Hugh flinched. "What, then?"

"For a start, I'd like to finish skewering Miss Riverton. Then I'm going to make sure everyone believes you took me against my will and ruined me. You see, my poor female mind couldn't take the strain, and I turned on my tormentors."

"Nobody will believe that."

Miss Archibald tilted her head. "Are you so sure? A woman's mind is awfully suggestible. I don't know what has come over me. People will see Briarwyck as the house of scandal and murder it really is, and anyone who was present will fall with it."

Carrington's face was stone. "Never mind our reputations. Let Abigail go."

Miss Archibald's lips widened into a smile. "No."

Hugh's fists clenched at his sides. "There must be something you'd rather have."

"Yes, there is."

"What is it? Name it and it's yours." Hugh's promise rang hollow in Abigail's chest.

Her eyes threatened tears. Some problems couldn't be solved, even if he was determined to move heaven and earth.

"I want Sir Peter and my brother alive."

Hugh shook his head. "That's unreasonable. You should've thought of your brother's loss before killing him."

"I didn't kill him!" Miss Archibald's scream jolted Abigail back. "Your slut poisoned him against me. If she'd just let him have her, he would've left me alone." She let out a strangled sob. "It's this house. It's a disease festering into my life."

Silence fell over the room like a thick fog, each of them staring at Miss Archibald in horror as they came to realize what she was saying.

Abigail's cheeks streamed with tears, mirroring Miss Archibald's. The dagger shook feebly against Abigail's throat.

"I didn't want him to die." Miss Archibald dropped to a whisper. "He wasn't supposed to die. He didn't want to hurt me. It was this girl's doing. You see, he was rarely refused, but when it happened, he'd still get his way. He couldn't tolerate the disappointment."

"But he killed Sir Peter." Carrington seemed to feel around with his words.

She nodded and wiped away a tear. "I could stand that, and I went to tell him I forgave him, but then he attacked me. I had to erase what happened, and when Miles found me, he offered to help. Oh God."

Miss Archibald dropped her weapon and cupped her face with her hands.

Hugh rushed forward and pulled Abigail into his arms. Carrington bent over Alma, untying her and easing her unconscious form onto the bed.

Shouting echoed in the hall, and Mr. Archibald pushed his way past the others, Greymore and Rycroft with him. Mr. Archibald launched himself at his sister, jerking her arms back as she screamed. He slapped her hard across the face, silencing her with the blow and deafening everyone with the crack of his palm.

Mr. Archibald bound his sister's hands behind her back with the rope Greymore offered. He hoisted her to her feet and hauled her out of the room. When Miss Archibald caught sight of Rycroft, she shrieked again, to his amusement. Mr. Archibald rolled his eyes and pushed her past them into the hall.

"Wait." Lynette stopped Mr. Archibald's progress. "What about what she said?"

Miss Archibald stood mute as the witnesses related the new details she'd revealed to them.

Mr. Archibald shrugged when they finished. "It makes little

difference if it's true. She still killed my brother."

Lynette glared at him. "Surely there's more to consider now."

Mr. Archibald's face hardened. "All right, let me be more specific here. My sister has said a great many things, some of which are true and some which are not. What we know is she killed or helped kill at least three people and kidnapped Miss Riverton. What we don't know is why. Of course, we have the stories she told us, but none of us have any firsthand knowledge of the events. Nobody knew how intimate she was with Sir Peter, since he never spoke of her, though she's full of stories about him. We don't know if my brother actually killed him or attacked my sister, since she's the only witness. Mr. Graham has been forthcoming and admits he helped kill my brother, the footman, and his wife, but he has little knowledge about what happened with Alice."

"What reason does she have to lie?" Abigail couldn't help the growing discomfort spreading along her nerves.

"Only the reason she was born a liar and will die a liar. She's invented these little fairy tales since she was a child. She once accused my father of having his way with her shortly after she was denied a new dress. This was later followed by stories when she was taught by nuns at a convent. She claimed they beat her regularly and let the visiting priest abuse her. She's a troubled brat who couldn't stand not getting her way. So let me be clear: she's guilty of murder, and whatever reason she gives is unlikely to be true." Miss Archibald's head lowered as her brother led her off.

"That woman is evil." Lynette handed a shawl to Abigail to cover her shoulders.

"I wouldn't be too quick to judge this situation." Rycroft was uncharacteristically solemn. "There's more to this than Mr. Archibald knows. I think if we looked hard enough, we'd discover Miss Archibald's a tormented individual who's never been believed in her life. I'll bet her father originated the practice when he was accused, deflecting her claims. After that, nothing she said would be believed solely because she'd been caught lying before, and nobody would take her word over her father's. Now she probably lies out of habit, a way of dealing with the tragedy surrounding her life. I doubt she even knows what the truth is anymore."

"You speak from experience?" Lynette raised her brows.

He nodded. "I know the family well enough, and I've heard stories."

"I have as well," Carrington said. "I always thought they were rumors. The father seems agreeable enough, but it always unnerved me when he spoke to Miss Archibald. It was like he spoke to a subservient mistress, but I reasoned it was in my head."

Lynette stiffened. "Isn't there something we can do? Miss Archibald will pay for her crimes, but what of her family?"

Rycroft and Carrington both shook their heads, the identical gestures branding them as brothers.

"We have no way of proving anything." Carrington's solid frame grew languid.

"But they created that monster." Abigail spat out her words, her fists clenched at her sides. She huddled closer to Hugh.

"Oh yes." Rycroft's voice was hollow. "And men will continue to generate monsters until they realize those monsters strike back with claws of their own."

Chapter Twenty-Six

The next morning, Abigail stood on the front balcony, looking on as a carriage rambled away from Briarwyck. The road was plagued by ruts and dips left over from the passage of vehicles in the wet earth. Miss Archibald wouldn't have an easy journey, nor would she ever again.

The Archibald elders had at last arrived at Briarwyck to condemn their daughter and claim their deceased son. They made no apology for Alice and treated her as a stranger who'd murdered their beloved Adam. She wouldn't find sympathy with them. The Archibalds had lost two children when Adam had died.

Alexander was the one to ask forgiveness for Alice's murderous campaign. Like his parents, he didn't acknowledge Alice as a loved one led astray. He treated her with indifference, only finding it his duty to make amends with the Travers family.

Abigail sensed this wasn't new behavior on account of the murders, and in spite of herself, pity tugged at her breast for Alice. Abigail would like to think she had the unconditional love of her family even if it meant their locking her up for everyone's protection.

Hugh pressed against her back and wrapped his arms around her as he nuzzled her neck. Since Miss Archibald's breakdown, he refused to leave her side. They had spent much of yesterday and last night cocooned in each other's arms, exhausted from their ordeal. The longest they had been separated was when Hugh had gone to make arrangements for their wedding and jot off a note to his father.

Abigail had written a letter to her own family, hoping they would get it and forgive her for the hasty marriage. She knew in her heart they would understand the circumstances, even approve of the match, though her courses had arrived, and she didn't need to explain a pregnancy. Her family had met Hugh at some of their parties and reacted favorably to him. Her father had even had a lengthy discussion with him before Hugh had escorted her to Briarwyck, when he'd entrusted him with her safety. Later, months after the marriage, she would learn she was correct in her reasoning. Her parents had already considered the match privately and had had secret hopes for it. It seemed she and Hugh were the last ones to be made aware of the notion.

The wedding was set for three weeks, barely enough time to prepare but the latest Hugh would accept. Luckily, Abigail had the help of her friends to get everything settled. Delia and Mrs. Eddings would stay behind and help with planning. Lynette would go with her to London to find her wedding clothes.

Hugh wanted to go to London with her, but he had business on his own estate in Bath, and Carrington needed to go with him. Greymore and Alma agreed to escort the ladies to London, and Rycroft would ride with them as far as their paths joined on his mysterious errands. She only hoped that between her and Greymore, they could keep Lynette and Rycroft from killing each other.

"Is something the matter?" Hugh kissed her cheek.

"I can't help but wonder if all this would've happened if I'd stayed at home. Would everyone still be alive? Would Miss Archibald be free from her family and happily married to Sir Peter? Maybe Mrs. Graham would've escaped her marriage. I can't help but wonder if Miss Archibald was right about me. What if I brought a curse down on the Briarwyck estate?"

"Nonsense. They made their own choices, and you had nothing to do with influencing them except poor timing. Remember, my arrival would've disrupted things as well. Miss Archibald was looking for someone to blame for her own troubles and actions."

"How can you be so sure?"

Hugh turned her to meet his eyes, his hands grasping her shoulders. "My dear, you're the most wonderful, caring creature, and nobody sensible would blame you for any of this. The fact that with no fault of your own, it still weighs on your mind is proof enough you're a decent person."

She found only warmth in his features, no lies or accusations. His bottle-brown eyes grounded her as she lost herself in them. "Still, the guilt eats at me."

Hugh leaned in to kiss her forehead. "My little saint."

A small smile tugged at her lips. "You don't believe that."

He chuckled. "Certainly not in bed, but yes, you are. You can be my spark of sanity or insanity depending on your mood. I wouldn't have it any other way."

She sighed and rested her head against his chest. He rubbed his hand down her back and looked off with an absent expression.

"Hugh?"

"Hmm…?"

She stared up at him and allowed herself to drift away with him. "I'm sorry to be such trouble."

He laughed and kissed her hair. "You're my kind of trouble."

Her smile widened. "I try."

He raised a brow at her and showed her with his lips exactly the kind of trouble she was. Their kiss was caressing, a lost fragment in time as he worshipped her with his mouth. They savored each other with every breath and every touch, as they would with their lives.

EPILOGUE

SNOW CASCADED OFF Abigail's fur-lined coat as she attempted to dodge the well-aimed missile. She laughed in bursts as she stumbled out of range behind a snow-laden tree. Birds burst from the branches while the missiles continued to fly toward her.

"Samuel, I concede." Abigail panted out the words.

She peeked around the tree at her eldest child and ducked away from the volley. The crunch of snow signaled his advance, and she braced herself for the onslaught of snowballs, but they never came as the smiling face of Hugh rounded the tree.

"Breakfast is ready." He enveloped her in his arms and nuzzled her face. "You shouldn't let him get the best of you."

She pecked him on the lips. "He has too much energy. I can't keep up."

He chuckled. "Next time, allow me. You can sit with the baby."

"Don't I do enough sitting? I do love Charlotte, but I think I'm growing fat."

"Nonsense. You're as beautiful as the day I met you."

She beamed up at him and tugged him toward her. "You, my dear, are a flatterer, and flattery will get you everywhere." She stretched on tiptoes and brought her lips to his.

The kiss sent a shiver over her skin that had nothing to do with the Christmas Day chill. She probed his mouth with her tongue, and he groaned in appreciation, pulling her closer by her bottom.

"Trying for child number three?" Carrington laughed behind them.

Hugh shot his brother a sharp look as Abigail pulled away. "Must you always interrupt?"

Carrington coughed. "I wouldn't, but Samuel is asking for you, and I don't want to explain why he shouldn't try to ride the cat." His lips turned up. "Besides, Charlotte needs changing, and I have already met my limit today."

Abigail chuckled. "It happens when you have twins. Twins. I still don't believe it." She met Carrington's dark eyes. "Any word from Lynette?"

Carrington wiped a hand over his face and shook his head.

Abigail gave him a reassuring smile. "Not to worry, brother. You know how she is."

"Indeed, I only wish she would take part in Christmas for a change."

Hugh slapped his brother on the back. "She'll grow out of it, and hopefully she will spare us the presence of that no-good husband of hers."

Carrington's smile reached the graying hairs at his temples. "I wouldn't count on that, but at least we see her now and then. In any case, I wish Delia wouldn't worry so much. Her sister is quite capable of taking care of herself."

Abigail laced her arm through Carrington's and pulled Hugh to join them. "I agree, but there is no taming Lynette. She's almost as bad as her sister-in-law, but that's a whole other story. Let's eat. I'm famished."

"Maybe you've already started on child three." Carrington laughed.

Hugh cuffed his brother. Abigail blushed, and Hugh blinked at her. "You can't be serious. I'm just getting used to number two."

Carrington slapped his leg, allowing a full belly laugh to take over. "I'll see you both inside." He left them behind, a stunned Hugh staring after him.

"Is he correct? Are you pregnant again?"

"I wasn't sure. You know we've had a few false starts. I was going to tell you tonight when the babies had gone to sleep. Are you angry?"

He braced his hands on her shoulders and gazed into her eyes. "I will never be angry at another child." He paused. "It's just so soon."

She nodded. "I know."

He clapped his hands together, and almost on command, snow drifted down onto the couple. "I hope it's another girl. No, I hope it's two girls."

She chuckled. "Only two?"

"Only? My dear, I hope we have a whole nursery of girls."

She leaned into him and squeezed his arm. "I'm so glad you think so. One boy is quite enough trouble."

"Have you seen Charlotte? She's a beauty. She'll have every man in England after her."

"And in America."

He kissed the top of her head and led her away from the tree. "I'm glad you decided to stay with me."

She wrapped herself more firmly into his warmth. "Whyever would I leave? I have you and my wonderful but vexing children. I'm home wherever you are." She poked him in the chest. "Don't you forget it."

"Never." He beamed down at her. "Happy Christmas, my love."

"Happy Christmas."

About the Author

Mae Thorn enjoys being romanced and terrified – a combination not normally found in books so she writes them. Her favorite stories include kickass women and the men they fall for. She writes historical romance and fantasy.

When she isn't writing she battles for equal access for those with hearing loss, discovers hidden records as a volunteer archivist, geeks out about Legos, torments her feline minions, and watches bad movies.

Mae holds a Bachelor's degree in English from the University of Utah and a Master's degree in Library and Information Science from San Jose State University.

She lives near Salt Lake City, Utah with her cats; Church, Shadow Moon, and Sabrina.

Website:
Maethorn.com

Twitter:
Twitter.com/maethornwrites

Facebook:
Facebook.com/maethornwrites

Instagram:
Instagram.com/maethornwrites

Pinterest:
https://pin.it/15qQIQ6

www.ingramcontent.com/pod-product-compliance
Lightning Source LLC
Chambersburg PA
CBHW071742190726
48292CB00003B/846

* 9 7 8 1 9 5 8 0 9 8 1 5 8 *